FF

Corsair

Also by Dudley Pope

Corsair

A novel by
DUDLEY POPE

An Alison Press Book
Secker & Warburg · London

First published in England 1987 by
The Alison Press/Martin Secker & Warburg Limited
54 Poland Street, London W1V 3DF

Copyright © 1987 by Dudley Pope

British Library Cataloguing in Publication Data

Pope, Dudley
  Corsair: a novel.—(An Alison Press
  book).
  I. Title
  823'.914[F]   PR6066.05
  ISBN 0-436-37754-3

Photoset by Wilmaset, Birkenhead, Wirral
Printed in England by
Mackays of Chatham Ltd

For Frank and Ann McEwan

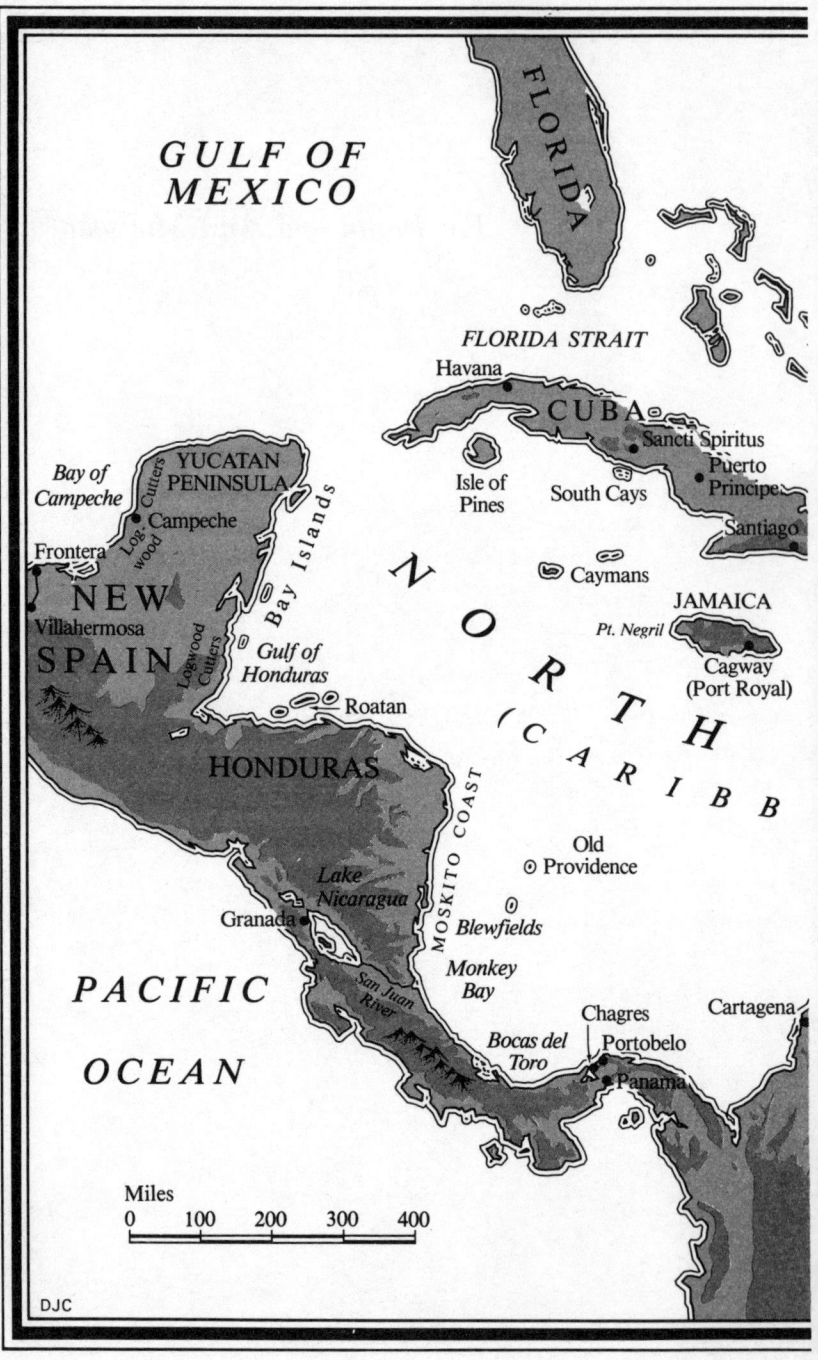

GULF OF
MEXICO

FLORIDA

FLORIDA STRAIT

Havana

CUBA

Sancti Spiritus
Puerto
Principe

Isle of
Pines

South Cays

Santiago

Bay of
Campeche

YUCATAN
PENINSULA

Campeche

Frontera

NEW

Villahermosa

SPAIN

Logwood Cutters

Bay Islands

Gulf of
Honduras

Caymans

JAMAICA

Pt. Negril

Cagway
(Port Royal)

NORTH

Roatan

HONDURAS

(CARIBB

MOSKITO COAST

Old
⊙ Providence

Lake
Nicaragua

Granada

Blewfields

Monkey
Bay

San Juan
River

Chagres

Cartagena

PACIFIC

Bocas del
Toro

Portobelo

Panama

OCEAN

Miles

0   100   200   300   400

DJC

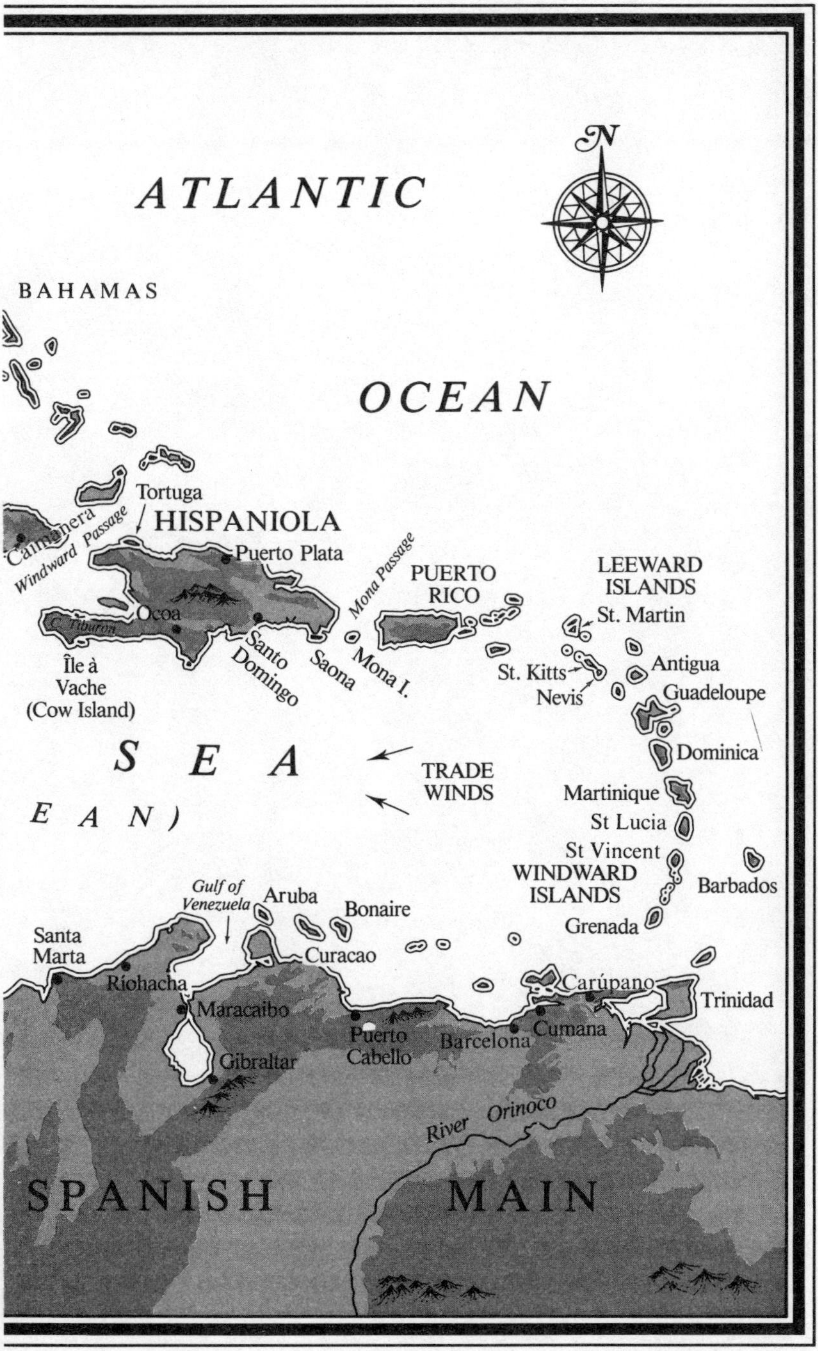

ATLANTIC

BAHAMAS

OCEAN

Tortuga

Cameñera

/HISPANIOLA

Windward Passage

Puerto Plata

Mona Passage

PUERTO
RICO

LEEWARD
ISLANDS

St. Martin

Ocoa

St. Kitts

Antigua

Santo
Domingo

Saona

Mona I.

Nevis

Guadeloupe

C. Tiburón

Île à
Vache
(Cow Island)

Dominica

S E A

TRADE
WINDS

Martinique

St Lucia

E A N)

St Vincent

WINDWARD
ISLANDS

Barbados

*Gulf of
Venezuela*

Aruba

Bonaire

Grenada

Santa
Marta

Curacao

Carúpano

Trinidad

Riohacha

Maracaibo

Puerto
Cabello

Barcelona

Cumana

Gibraltar

River Orinoco

SPANISH

MAIN

# Chapter One

"The brothels have to close: all of them. I don't care what happens to the women," the governor added hurriedly, as though trying to ward off arguments. "And the taverns. One to each street is quite enough: the rest must be shut down."

A round-faced and plump man with a normally jolly manner, whom Ned recognized as O'Leary, the ship chandler in Port Royal, said: "This is only the second meeting of Jamaica's legislative assembly. I'd have thought we'd be deciding about more important things than whorehouses and rumbullion shops."

"But these *are* important things," the governor objected crossly. He was a small man with a whining voice. His pointed face, urine-coloured beard with tobacco-stained moustache, tiny dark eyes and yellowed teeth made him look like a harassed ferret, and the skin of his face was pale, freckled like peppercorns sprinkled on cold pork rind.

He tapped the table with a claw-like hand. "Why, my wife can't walk along somewhere like Cannon Street without seeing these – these *women* – flaunting themselves at the windows of the establishments."

"Then she shouldn't be walking along Cannon Street," snapped Kinnock, Port Royal's pawnbroker. Kinnock had a narrow and mean-looking face from which protruded a sharp and heavily veined red nose, and long moustaches once blond but now greying and sagging from perspiration. Kinnock was a heavy drinker and perspired as a result, as though heated by a personal furnace. "This is a seaport," Kinnock added peevishly. "Seamen look for taverns and brothels. Where else are they going to spend their money?"

"I'm certainly not pandering to all this lechery," the governor said. Sir Harold Neil Luce was almost out of his depth: a recent Roundhead and only just able to change to being a Royalist in time as the King was restored to the throne, Luce had been lucky enough to badger the Privy Council into giving him the governorship of Jamaica without the Council knowing too much about the man or the island, or caring that he would have to be given a knighthood to go with the job.

"Steady on, Your Excellency," O'Leary persisted. "Jamaica depends on trade. That means ships, and ships mean seamen. No seamen means no ships and no trade."

"Shutting the brothels won't drive away ships," Luce said stubbornly. "Ships go where their owners say, not where seamen please. If there's a cargo in London for Port Royal, then that's where the ship goes."

O'Leary sighed and looked round at the other eleven councillors, as though trying to draw patience from them. "Your Excellency forgets the shipowners already have to pay more to get seamen to come here: the sickness and the Spaniards mean a seaman is reluctant to sign on in London, or Bristol, or Liverpool. But it isn't only the ships with cargoes that matter here: you'll drive away the rest of 'em, and that's what we have to worry about."

The governor looked puzzled, his lips drawn back to reveal his yellow teeth. "What do you mean, 'the rest of them'? I don't understand you, Mr O'Leary."

The chandler looked across the table at Ned and then sighed without trying to hide his exasperation. "Your Excellency, remember this: the Spaniards surround us – the Main, Cuba, Hispaniola, Puerto Rico. Very unwisely our King, while he was in exile in Spain and before he was restored to the English throne, promised to return Jamaica to the Dons. That you know.

"Fortunately, he hasn't taken any steps to do this yet, but the Spanish are prodding him: you know as well as I that the Prince de Ligne is in London for that very purpose.

2

"Quite apart from that, the Spaniards claim the whole of the Caribbee for themselves: every foreigner is a trespasser who risks the garrotte round his neck for being a heretic. Yet, one of the first things you did when you arrived here was to disband the Army and pay off the soldiers. So any minute the Dons might try to recapture Jamaica – and how many of the King's ships do you have to drive them off?"

"Ah, answer that!" Kinnock said sharply, knocking on the table with a thick gold ring he wore on the middle finger of his right hand. It was heavy enough to sound like a gavel.

"You know perfectly well I don't have any ships," a startled Sir Harold admitted. "Anyway, the Spanish haven't made a move yet."

"That's not to say they won't," O'Leary persisted. "Once they hear about you disbanding the Army and driving away our defence, they'll be here, never fear! You can't keep a dog away from a bone."

"What do you mean, 'driving away our defence'?" Luce demanded.

"I mean," O'Leary said deliberately, raising his voice and looking round for the approval of the other councillors, "that we have to look after the buccaneers. Drive them away and we are defenceless. The Dons could capture the island with one ship carrying a hundred men, a priest and a donkey."

"I fail to see what all this has to do with closing the brothels," Luce said pompously. "Really!"

O'Leary, his face growing red, pressed his hands flat down on the table, as though to prevent it rising in the air. "Your Excellency," he said, his voice tight with suppressed anger, "there are more than a thousand buccaneers and thirty or so of their ships using Port Royal as a base. They can get cordage, sailcloth and that sort of thing from my chandlery. They get fresh meat from the market and salt meat and boucan from shops. That means the ships can be kept in good order. It also means," he said emphatically, "that we have thirty ships and more than a thousand trained men to defend us against the Dons. Providing they stay here."

He pointed at Luce and asked: "What do a thousand men do when they are not working on board their ships? Go to church and pray? Pick bananas? Throw mangoes at the wild dogs? Perhaps it's

3

escaped Your Excellency's attention that we don't have a proper church, even if the buccaneers were given to praying, which they aren't. No, wenching and boozing is what they want to do o' an evening, and now Cromwell and his Puritans are dead and gone, who is to forbid them? Surely not the governor of Jamaica, who depends on them for his defence."

"No," Luce said stubbornly, his tiny eyes blinking like a dazzled ferret emerging from a rabbit warren into bright sunlight, "my mind is made up. Port Royal is not going to continue to be a city of sin and debauchery. It's an indication of what I mean that there are more than twenty brothels and, as you've just pointed out, no proper church."

"Twenty, eh?" O'Leary said sourly. "Well I'm damned, I never heard of anyone going round counting them. That's the advantage of being governor."

Ned coughed and the governor and councillors looked at him.

"I was just going to say that the brothel owners and tavern keepers have all built their own establishments and have to pay out money to run them. If Port Royal is to have a church, perhaps the governor could give instructions . . ."

"Where's the money to come from?" Luce demanded.

Ned coughed again and said nothing, but Sir Thomas Whetstone, sitting beside him, burst out wrathfully: "The Brethren of the Coast have supplied the present government with guns, gold, silver and gems worth scores of thousands of pounds. Pieces of eight have fallen like rain. Where has all *that* money gone?"

"Into the Treasury," Luce said sharply. "There are dozens of expenses the government must meet. Sometimes I think you don't understand."

"Your Excellency," Sir Thomas said, making no attempt to keep the sarcasm out of his voice, "long before you arrived out here Mr Yorke and I, along with the Brethren, were raiding Spanish possessions – like Portobelo, for example – to bring riches to this island. Why, the island's currency is founded on the very pieces of eight brought in by the Brethren. Its forts bristle with guns the Brethren brought over after the raids on Santiago and Portobelo. And the Treasury only recently received even more bullion from the Spanish galleon Mr Yorke and I captured at St Martin. Are you *sure* the Treasury can't afford a church?"

4

"We're not discussing the church," Sir Harold said evasively. "We're discussing the closing of the brothels."

"Ah yes," Whetstone said, "the sacred and the profane. Well, the choice is yours. Brothels, buccaneers and the island defended; or no brothels, no buccaneers, and no defence."

"I don't think the safety of Jamaica should depend on a lot of pirates hanging about brothels and taverns," the governor said stiffly.

"Pirates!" O'Leary said wrathfully. "I thought by now you could tell the difference. I find it alarming that the governor of this island in the second meeting of the legislative council can talk of 'pirates'. If you mean Mr Yorke's buccaneers – the Brethren of the Coast – then please refer to them as buccaneers. But if you really mean pirates, then remember that if you want them hunted down you have to ask the buccaneers to do it: you don't have a single ship of your own."

Ned looked up at the ceiling of the small room and said quietly: "If you don't intend to rely on the buccaneers lounging in brothels and taverns to defend the island against the Spanish, who had Your Excellency in mind?"

"The whole idea is absurd," Luce said. "The Spanish will never attack Jamaica."

"Why not?" Sir Thomas asked. "After all, they do own Cuba, Hispaniola, Puerto Rico, and all the Main. Apart from a few little islands up to the eastward that they can't be bothered with, they own everything else. Don't forget, they value Jamaica enough to get our King to agree to give it back!"

Luce looked patronizingly at Sir Thomas. "You can take my word for it: the Spanish will not come."

"Oh, most reassuring, most reassuring," Sir Thomas said. "You have been out here, Your Excellency, for fewer months than I have years, but I must admit that I'd never dare give such an assurance – and with so much authority, too. Most grateful," he said caustically.

"The Spanish won't come and we don't need brothels," Sir Harold repeated emphatically, banging the table as if to drive home the point.

"But supposing the Spanish *do* come?" persisted Kinnock.

Sir Thomas Whetstone gave a bitter laugh. "The first thing

5

they'd do is plan a church. And while the plans were being drawn they'd reopen the brothels. After all, they are men and fighting men need brothels and taverns."

"Why do they?" the governor demanded angrily. "Lewdness and lechery, venery and vileness." He lingered over each word as if savouring it. "They don't have them on the Main."

"Oh, don't they?" asked a startled Sir Thomas. "How do you know, Your Excellency, you who've never been to the Main? All I can say is that every Spanish town and city I've ever visited had its share of what looked remarkably like brothels to me. Shall I describe them?"

"There's no need," Luce said hurriedly. He looked around the table defiantly and said: "I shall be signing the decree closing the brothels at the end of this meeting."

Ned Yorke looked up and said: "Your Excellency, as Admiral of the Brethren of the Coast, I should warn you that what you have heard – that the Brethren base themselves here in Port Royal because it has all what I might call the amenities – is perfectly true. If you start removing those amenities they'll go elsewhere."

"Rubbish," the governor said curtly. "You must order them to stay, and anyway there's nowhere else for them to go."

Ned shook his head sadly. "Your Excellency has forgotten. I am the elected leader of the Brethren, and if we are raiding some Spanish town they will follow me, but the question of where they should base themselves would be put to the vote of all the Brethren. And there most certainly is somewhere else for them to go: Your Excellency forgets Tortuga. That's where they'd go. They know the island well, they like it, and once there they'll be too far from Port Royal for you to cry to them for help if the need arises."

Sir Harold shook his head. "My mind is made up. We will pass to the next business."

O'Leary stood up with a violence which hurled his chair backward so it fell with a crash.

He said angrily: "I've just heard that my business is to be ruined and it's only a matter of time before the Dons find out that the island is undefended. Then they'll be down on us like a wolf on the fold. There's nothing I can do to prevent it, but I don't have to sit here and vote for my own destruction."

"My dear fellow," the governor said ingratiatingly, "that's the wrong attitude. Just think, your wife will be able to walk through Port Royal without seeing all the lewdness and lechery . . ."

"She's never complained," O'Leary said abruptly. "She understands that's the price she pays for sleeping safely o' nights." With that he left the room.

Then Ned stood up and turned to Sir Thomas. "Well, I suppose that goes for us too. There's not much point in being present at a council meeting which does not interest itself in Jamaica's safety."

Sir Thomas stood and said, with a contemptuous wave towards the governor: "Seems as though the Puritans are back. I expect the next item on the agenda is to forbid laughing on Sundays. Then everyone will have to have their hair cut short. Roundhead style."

 # Chapter Two

As the two men left the building and walked across the sandy path to the jetty, sheltered from the scorching heat of the sun by a row of rustling palm trees, Ned said: "It's hopeless, we'll never get that fool to realize the Spaniards may be just waiting . . ."

Sir Thomas Whetstone sniffed. "When he goes on about brothels and sin, he sounds just like my late and unlamented uncle Oliver Cromwell. There's more sin than sunshine in the governor's life. His wife is shocked by seeing the whores in Cannon Street! What's that sour old bitch doing in Cannon Street anyway? It doesn't lead to anywhere she'd want to go."

"Don't tempt me to speculate," Ned said. "Perhaps she wants to build a chapel there and hold prayer meetings for the fallen women."

At that moment both men stopped walking: the sound of a cannon firing echoed across the anchorage, sending pelicans flapping off, unbelievably ungainly until they got into the air.

"Not shotted," Ned said. "It's a signal." He glanced across the anchorage and pointed. "Look, there's a ship coming in now. And another puff of smoke – she's firing a second gun. Come on, let's see what it's all about!"

They hurried down to the boat waiting at the jetty to take them back to their ships. They jumped in and Ned told the crew: "Row for where that ship's going to anchor."

By now the ship was turning as she tacked her way up the anchorage and Thomas said: "Looks like the *Perdrix*. I wonder what news Leclerc has got?"

"That Frenchman has enough experience not to rouse out the anchorage unless it's something urgent," Ned said.

Ten minutes later, while the *Perdrix*'s men were still paying out the anchor cable, Ned and Thomas climbed on board the French ship and were greeted by Jean-Pierre Leclerc, the ship's owner and master and one of the very early buccaneers, who had been with Ned and Thomas on all their raids. Leclerc was gross and unshaven; his ship was always filthy. But he was one of the shrewdest of the buccaneers.

"Riohacha!" Leclerc said excitedly. "I've just come from there. The Dons have got Gottlieb and Charles Coles. They've seized both their ships: I saw the *Dolphyn* and the *Argonauta* at anchor and flying the Spanish flags."

"What happened?" Ned asked.

"I don't know," Leclerc said. "I was passing the port when I saw both ships anchored off. I bore up to join them and was just about to anchor when one of my men spotted the Spanish flags. Then I realized there were no men on deck."

"What did you do?"

Leclerc slapped his hands together as though brushing off dust. "I hoist my sails again and get out quick: there was nothing I could do."

Ned scratched the back of his neck. "Gottlieb and Coles had about sixty men each. There's a fort at Riohacha, and that's about all apart from the little town. The Spaniards would keep prisoners in the fort."

"Yes," Whetstone agreed, "but what the deuce are the Spaniards doing?"

"Probably the mayor thinks he can ransom the men and he's emptied the ships of any trade goods and spirits they were carrying," Ned said. "Maybe a new mayor who wants to impress the governor of the province. He must have taken both ships by surprise."

"What'll we do?" Thomas asked, running his fingers through his thick curly beard.

"The Dons don't give us much choice," Ned said. "We go across with a dozen ships and sack the place, release Gottlieb and Coles and their men, retake their ships – and that's that. Make the mayor pay compensation if he looted the ships."

9

"And the governor here?"

"What about Sir Harold?"

"Are you going to ask him for commissions?"

"After the performance he's just given, do you think he'll issue commissions?" Ned asked sourly. "More likely he'll forbid us to do anything and say that Gottlieb and Coles must have done something to offend the Spaniards. I can just hear that sanctimonious voice . . ."

"No commissions makes us pirates."

"So it does," Ned said calmly. "With that bushy beard you'll make a good pirate if you scowl hard enough."

By now several boats from other buccaneer ships were converging on the *Perdrix*, roused out by the gunfire and anxious to hear the news. Ned wiped the perspiration from his forehead and sat down on the breech of a gun, realizing that soon there would be enough captains on board to have a meeting and give orders.

One of the first captains to clamber up the side of the *Perdrix* was a red-headed Englishman, Edward Brace, who owned and commanded the *Mercury*. Brace waved to Leclerc but walked across to Ned. He was a tall man with an angular face and very neatly dressed. His beard was well combed, softer in colour than his hair, which hung in curls.

"What's the matter – has he spotted the Spanish fleet coming?" Brace asked with a grin.

Ned shook his head and told Brace what little he knew. The Englishman grunted. "Going to Riohacha shouldn't take too long. By the way, I hear you and Sir Thomas went to the legislative council meeting this morning. Anything of interest?"

Ned gave a sour laugh. "The governor is shutting down all the brothels, and there's to be only one tavern in each street. Oh yes, and he assures us that the Spanish will never attack Jamaica."

Brace stared down at the deck. "People like him never learn, do they? Nothing new about the King's idea of returning Jamaica to the Dons, I suppose?"

"No, nor will there be until we get another frigate out from England with fresh despatches from the Committee for Foreign Plantations. In the meantime the governor contents himself with closing brothels."

"It's that wife of his, I expect," Brace said shrewdly. "Only seen her once but she has a mouth like an old leather purse with the drawstring pulled tight."

"You're right: he grumbled that his wife couldn't walk down Cannon Street without seeing the ladies of the town displaying their wares. Didn't say what her ladyship was doing in Cannon Street – it doesn't lead to the market. Couldn't have been buying mangoes or bananas, and the governor's lobsters come direct from the crawl at the fish market. Just being nosy, and getting shocked for her pains. Knowing old Maude, she probably offered her ladyship a berth in her establishment. The best offer she's ever had!"

Brace turned to Ned and said seriously: "He's dead set on closing the brothels?"

"He's signing the decree this afternoon."

"The men won't like it. And one tavern to a street – why, half a dozen to a street don't hold our men when they all go on shore. They won't stay here," Brace warned. "They're not monks."

"We told the governor," Ned said. "We warned him quite clearly."

"But he didn't listen?"

"Oh, he listened – and then assured us we were wrong, and told me I should order the buccaneers to stay."

"Well, that man's an asset," Brace said bitterly, "to the Dons. As soon as they know, they'll wait for us buccaneers to move to Tortuga and then arrive here with all the ships they can muster. Nothing to stop them, now the Army's been disbanded."

"We told him all this," Ned said. "He told us the Dons would never come. The man's a fool."

"That wig," Brace said. "Was he a Roundhead before the Restoration?" Brace knew how popular wigs had become among former Roundheads, disguising their cropped heads.

"You're not the only one to wonder if his hair is short under that wig, as if he used to be a Roundhead. The man's a puzzle. His attitude towards the Dons makes him sound like a Papist but with his wig and determination to close down the brothels, he seems a true Puritan."

"It's that wife," Brace muttered darkly. "Oh, hello Secco," he said to a black-haired and sallow-faced captain, who had just come

11

on board. Secco, a Spaniard with a neatly trimmed pointed beard, his hair held back by a red cloth band, said in good English: "You hear Leclerc? Poor Gottlieb and Coles, they'll be tortured."

Ned said: "It means going to Riohacha as quickly as possible. Will you come?"

"We watered yesterday, so all I need to do is send men on shore to buy a beeve, salt it down and then we can sail. One, two hours."

"I've just stowed more boucan and we watered yesterday," Brace said. "I can be under way in an hour."

Ned looked at the men now assembling on the *Perdrix*'s deck. Saxby had just come on board from the *Phoenix*, his lame leg making its distinctive thump. That made his own *Griffin*, Thomas's *Peleus*, Saxby with the *Phoenix*, Brace and the *Mercury*, Leclerc with the *Perdrix*, the two Portuguese with the unpronounceable names, two Dutchmen who had followed Saxby on board, Secco and one other Englishman. Eleven ships so far, and glancing over the side he saw five more boats approaching. That would mean sixteen ships. The rest of the buccaneer captains must be on shore, or late getting into their boats.

Sixteen would be enough. It was just a question of waiting for the five boats to get alongside, and then telling all the captains what he proposed. Not that it was a very complicated plan: he did not know enough to be able to give them details.

As he stood waiting, he noticed the smell of Leclerc's ship. The Frenchman was an odd fellow. Ned knew from previous visits that Leclerc's own cabin was scrupulously clean, but the rest of the ship looked like a back street: scraps of meat and bits of fruit and vegetable were lying rotting in the scuppers, which obviously were only cleaned when a heavy sea swept the deck.

Ned thought back to the legislative council meeting. A dozen councillors, the governor and the deputy governor, all crowded into that tiny office which used to belong to Major-General Heffer, the former acting governor and now Luce's deputy. A small room with one window: hardly suitable for Jamaica's legislative council – although, to be sure, if there were many more meetings like today's Luce would end up with only four or five members attending, the usual residue of sycophants.

Of course, Luce would always have two or three allies on the council: the optimists who wanted to trade with Spain, which they saw as a source of slaves. But trade with Spain was just a dream: there would only be smuggling, which had been going on for years and which Gottlieb and Coles were doing when they were – for reasons quite beyond Ned's comprehension – captured.

The whole affair of supplying the Dons with what they needed and their own merchants could not provide depended on trust. So few ships ever came from Spain now and the Spaniards living on the Main and on the Spanish islands were short of everything – pots and pans for cooking, thread and needles, cloth to sew, wine and olive oil, spades to dig with and rakes and hoes . . . All they had were the vegetables and fruit they could grow – and gold and silver from the mines. You could not eat gold and silver: the Dons were in the ironic position of having gold in their pockets but no pots to cook with and only threadbare shirts on their backs – except for what they bought from the smugglers.

Although trade with other countries was officially forbidden by the Spanish authorities, there was no way they could stop smuggling: with many hundreds of miles of open coastline, the smugglers of many nations brought their ships in at night and unloaded whatever the Spanish wanted and could pay for in gold, coin or specie. Most of the Spanish – mayors, commanders of garrisons, customs and excise officers – were involved in the illicit trade. For all the regulations that came from Spain, the fact was that people had to live, which meant that officials had to look the other way when the smugglers came. Look the other way and pocket bribes.

Which made it all the more puzzling that Gottlieb and Coles should suddenly be met with trouble in Riohacha. A new mayor? Had the Viceroy received new and strict orders from Spain? Was this the first hint of a new policy towards the smugglers? Even a straw in the wind that the Spanish planned an attack on Jamaica?

As soon as all sixteen captains were on board, Ned jumped up on to the breech of a gun and waved the men to gather round. They were, he reflected, a desperate-looking crowd. Some, like Brace and Secco, were dressed with fastidious tidiness, hair and beards neatly combed, jerkins and breeches clean, hose without holes, shoes polished. But the others: they looked as though they had all sat round in a circle, stripping and throwing their clothes in a tub, and when someone gave the word, reached into the tub and

13

donned what came to hand. One captain wore the old seaman's apron of a century ago; another's jerkin had more holes than material. Most of them wore scarves round their hair, to prevent it blowing in their faces and also to catch the perspiration before it went into their eyes.

Ned looked round at them. "You'll have heard Leclerc's news," he said. "The Dons have taken Coles and Gottlieb at Riohacha, and captured or massacred their crews. Both ships, the *Dolphyn* and *Argonauta*, are at anchor in Riohacha flying Spanish flags. That's all Leclerc knows: he saw the ships at anchor and very sensibly cleared out.

"I'm planning to rescue Coles and Gottlieb and their men. Apart from anything else we have to show the Dons they can't get away with this sort of thing. In the meantime, until we find out *why* the Dons have suddenly turned on smugglers, be warned.

"Now, who's coming to Riohacha with me? Hands up those not coming."

One of the two Portuguese held up his arm, explaining apologetically in halting English that all his running and most of his standing rigging was now down on the deck: the ship could not be ready for sea in under a couple of days.

"Very well," Ned said. "I make it fifteen of you are coming. I want you under way in a couple of hours. The weather seems set fair, and Riohacha is about 475 miles away to the south-east. All of you are familiar with it. With this wind we should take four days. So provisionally we meet five miles off Riohacha at midnight in five days' time. That gives a day to spare for calms. Then we go in with boats and attack the fort – that's where they'll be holding prisoners."

"Just muskets and pikes?" asked Brace.

"And swords and pistols," Ned said. "I'll be responsible for the petards. I don't know how many gates and doors the fort has, but better go through a door than have to climb over a wall. We don't want to have to carry scaling ladders in the boats. And remember – we have to rely on surprise. No talking and coughing as we approach. Muffled oars. Once we're all ashore, rendezvous at the fort."

The woman waiting for Ned on board the *Griffin* had fine ash-blonde hair, grey eyes flecked with gold, and was heavily

14

suntanned. Her nose was small, the cheekbones were high and her mouth was generous. She wore a cream-coloured smock and her skirt, of faded blue, was split and divided, like very long breeches.

"The guns – what is the trouble?" she asked Ned in a voice which had a distinct and very attractive French accent.

Ned wiped the perspiration from his brow and told her Leclerc's news. She nodded and said: "I saw all the boats going to the *Perdrix*: what have you decided to do?"

"We sail at once for Riohacha."

She nodded again: Aurelia had been Ned's mistress from the days when they had both fled from Barbados, hunted by Cromwell's men. She had been on every raid in which Ned had led the buccaneers.

"Leclerc's guns interrupted the legislative council, then?"

"Probably, but Thomas and I had already walked out."

"Walked out? You didn't let the governor . . . ?"

"No, we weren't rude to him. He's going to shut down all the brothels and doesn't give a damn that the buccaneers will leave and go to Tortuga."

She shrugged her shoulders. "I hate Tortuga."

"Aurelia, my dear," Ned said patiently, "so do I. But the buccaneers aren't monks, and if old Luce is going to shut down the brothels here, then the buccaneers are going to take the women on board and go to Tortuga."

"After they've been to Riohacha."

Ned grinned. "Yes," he agreed, "after they've been to Riohacha and rescued Coles and Gottlieb."

"Let's go below," Aurelia said, "it's scorching in the sun. Diana was here."

"And what has Lady Diana Gilbert-Manners got to say?"

"Oh, Thomas got drunk last night and was nasty to her."

"What did Diana do, stamp her foot?"

"No, she poured the rest of the bottle of rum over his head. He didn't mention it?"

"No, but I'd hardly expect him to. Though he did smell of stale rum, come to think of it."

He went to the companionway and shouted for John Lobb, the mate of the *Griffin*. Lobb, a Man of Kent and former poacher, came down to the cabin and stood listening while Ned gave him

Leclerc's news and orders to get the *Griffin* under way within an hour.

As soon as Lobb had gone back on deck, Aurelia asked: "Why has the governor decided to close the brothels? He sounds more like a Puritan!"

"I'm damned sure he was one, until the Restoration," Ned said crossly. "He complains that his wife is offended by the sight of the brothels."

Aurelia laughed softly. "Has anyone told her that both the leader of the buccaneers and his second-in-command have mistresses on board their ships?"

But Ned did not laugh. Instead he said: "Don't use the word 'mistress' like that. I want to marry you; it's you that insist we build a church in Port Royal first. And Diana may be Thomas's mistress, but he can't marry her while that dreadful wife of his stays alive in London."

Aurelia grinned mischievously. "You know, *chéri*, you always get upset whenever I say I'm your mistress, but I love being your mistress. I am free to run away with a handsome man like Leclerc, or I can stay with you. Why, I'd just love to run away with Leclerc: I'd make him clean up that ship, wash and shave himself regularly, wear clean clothes: you'd never recognize him."

"Women are the Puritans: they always want to reform a man," Ned protested. "Leclerc is quite happy, gross and grubby, unshaven and looking as though he has slept in his clothes for a month. He doesn't want to be scrubbed and polished. Probably some wife or mistress in the past overdid the scrubbing, and his present state is a protest."

"Perhaps. Meanwhile," she added, "Port Royal hasn't got a proper church!"

"Oh yes, that came up at the legislative council, too. O'Leary, the chandler, asked Luce if he thought that once the brothels were closed the buccaneers would go to a church, if there was one. That led to Thomas suggesting that Luce should pay for a church."

Ned started to unroll a chart on the table in the cabin. "Thomas pointed out that the buccaneers have brought a lot of treasure into Jamaica, and if old Luce will pay for a church, good luck to him: it'll save me the expense." He began plotting the direct course to Riohacha. With the trade winds usually blowing from the east or north-east, they should be able to stretch over to Riohacha without tacking. And Riohacha was one of the easier landfalls to make on the Main: the big range of mountains with the very high peak in the middle (the Pico Cristobal Colon, the Spanish called it) ended a few miles west of the port.

"I'll be glad to be at sea again," Aurelia said. "We've been in port too long."

"But we've been busy building the house," Ned said crossly. "Damnation, do you want a house or a ship? While we are up in the hills building the house, you want to be at sea. When we are at sea you want to be building a house."

Aurelia laughed and clapped her hands together. "*Chéri*, that's why I fascinate you: you can never guess how I'm going to be. Just think, supposing I was a fat and cheerful wife, always laughing at your old jokes, always wanting the same things, always content, always *predictable*. You would soon be bored, *mon chéri*. Oh so bored."

One by one the fifteen buccaneer ships had weighed anchor in the great harbour, the pawls of their windlasses clunking monotonously as the anchor cables came home, streaming water as the pressure squeezed it out of the strands of the rope.

Lobb gave the orders for the *Griffin*'s mainsail to be hoisted, followed by the foresail, and the ship bore away, running parallel with the low sandy spit better known as the Palisadoes and ending at Gallows Point. As they passed Ned could see bodies hanging in chains from the gibbets on the Point. Not bodies now, with this heat; just skeletons, the remains of Army officers who had tried to overthrow Major-General Heffer when he was acting governor, before Luce arrived. The dissident officers had wanted to be sent back to England: they hated Jamaica and were frightened that they would be struck down by something like yellow fever, so that they would leave their bones in an island they hated. Well, treason had not helped – their bones stayed on the island, even if wrapped in rusty chains, a dreadful warning to any others who might have been nursing, before the Army was disbanded, any ideas of treason.

The *Griffin* sailed easily, skirting the palms along the Palisadoes, and then hauled her wind to round the Point and head out to sea, passing the newly named Fort Charles. In a few minutes she would have to bear up on to a reach which would end on the Spanish Main.

Aurelia walked across the deck and stood by Ned, careless of the heat of the sun, which was now almost overhead, so that it seemed they were growing from small pools of shadow.

"I always love it here: just as the open sea starts making us pitch and roll. It's when I start to live. The ship, too, she comes alive: the creak of the hull and masts. Look, the guns strain at their tackles, as though they're eager."

"You sound bloodthirsty to me," Ned said with a grin, "but I know what you mean. It excites me, too." He turned and looked eastwards, along the Palisadoes. "I wonder if old Loosely's watching us sail?"

"Sir Harold Luce," Aurelia said with mock primness, "must be looking on you as pirates. He hasn't given you commissions . . ."

"We haven't done anything yet," Ned pointed out. "There's no law to say ships can't sail out of the harbour, and that's all we are doing."

"Oh, quite," Aurelia said, brushing back her hair as the wind caught it. "I'm sure that Sir Harold is looking out of his window and thinking what a coincidence it is that fifteen ships all suddenly sail."

Ned shrugged his shoulders. "If he thinks back to what we told him this morning, he'll think we're all going to Tortuga. Probably thinks we've emptied the brothels, too."

"A fleet of floating bordellos," Aurelia said, laughing at the thought. "We must look a fine sight to Sir Harold: he's getting rid of half the buccaneers and all the brothels – at least, he probably thinks he is."

"When poor Lady Luce walks down Cannon Street again she's going to get a shock," Ned said. "All the brothels just as full . . ."

# Chapter Three

Five days later, as Ned stood on deck with the perspective glass to his eye, he said to Lobb: "Well, there's no mistaking them. They're the only landmarks along the coast for a hundred miles, and I can see the two sugarloaf hills clearly. The sun is reflecting off the snow."

Lobb took the proffered glass. "That's them," he announced after a couple of minutes. "The Sierra Nevada de Santa Marta. I can see the highest peak poking up through the cloud. Ah," he exclaimed, "I can just make out La Mesa!"

Ned took the glass back and looked further to the eastward. Yes, he could distinguish the prominent and flat-topped hill. They were too far offshore to make out Cabo San Augustin to the north-east.

Ned nodded contentedly. "Not bad, Lobb. Riohacha is about forty-five miles to the east of the Sierra Nevada and thirty east of La Mesa. We must be steering almost directly for it."

"Yes, and the closer we get inshore the more the east-going current will carry us up to it. The west-going current dies out in another ten miles or so."

Aurelia nudged Ned and pointed towards the *Peleus*, which was bearing up slightly to close with the *Griffin*. "Thomas has seen it too," she said. "He's coming to tell you about it. Are you and Lobb very clever?"

"Oh yes," Ned said with mock seriousness. "Across five hundred miles of open sea, and there's our destination nearly dead ahead."

"We're not there yet! How much farther?"

"It's hard to guess how far off those mountains are. Forty miles to Riohacha, I should think. We should be approaching the town as it gets dark, with us just out of sight of prying eyes."

"It's calm enough for you to go over and see Thomas when he gets nearer. Are you going to?"

"Yes, I want to talk about some details of the attack. I forgot one or two things when we were on board the *Perdrix*."

"Can I come with you? I'd like to see Diana."

Ned laughed drily. "You're bored already with being at sea. You want to see Diana to talk about the houses."

"I don't," Aurelia protested. "But you're the only person I've talked to for days, apart from Lobb . . ."

Half an hour later the *Griffin* and the *Peleus* hove-to while one of the *Griffin*'s boats was hoisted out and lowered. The wind was blowing a fitful ten knots and the waves were less than six feet high.

Ned and Aurelia climbed down into the boat and the six men at the oars rowed briskly towards the *Peleus*.

Thomas and Diana stood at the bulwarks to welcome them on board. As Thomas wiped the perspiration from his brow he said: "Seeing that snow on the tops of the mountains makes me think of cool drinks. What can I offer you, even though it will be warm?"

"Have you any limes left?" Aurelia asked.

"Sacks of them. With rum?"

Aurelia shook her head, and Ned said: "Just a limejuice for me, too: it's too hot for rumbullion: I'll only get a headache."

Diana, like Aurelia, heavily tanned, with long black hair, dark brown eyes and a slim body that warned she would have to watch her weight or she would get fat, said in her deep voice: "If Thomas tells you he has given up drinking hot waters, don't be too impressed. It only happened two days ago and I doubt the resolve will last another couple of days."

Ned, who drank very sparingly and did not approve of Thomas's heavier thirst, raised his eyebrows. "What's this, penitence?"

Thomas looked embarrassed but Diana, with a glance at Aurelia, gave a delighted laugh. "Right first time, Ned. He got beastly drunk the night before the legislative council meeting, and so . . ."

"And so she started sleeping by herself," Thomas growled.

"Yes, it seems Thomas was not built to sleep alone," Diana said. "So we struck a bargain. He can come to my bed providing his breath does not smell of hot waters."

"See he keeps to it," Aurelia said. "Perhaps it will make that great paunch smaller."

"Ah yes, we are working on that too," Diana said. "He's promised to cut down on the vast quantities he eats."

"Seems to me that Thomas has entered into a lot of commitments," Ned said. "Now, can we spend a few moments discussing Riohacha?"

Aurelia and Diana went below while Ned and Thomas walked aft and stood under the awning stretched across the afterdeck.

"I reckon we'll sight Riohacha just as it gets dark," Thomas said.

Ned nodded. "We'll be much too far off for anyone on shore to see us. We heave-to until it is quite dark, and then close the shore to anchor in the river mouth some time before midnight.

"But what I came over to say was, I forgot the *Dolphyn* and *Argonauta*. They'll presumably have small prize crews on board. You have three boats, and I want your second and third ones to take boarding parties to both ships – but after we have landed at the fort: I don't want the sound of shots raising the alarm."

"One boat for each ship?"

Ned shrugged his shoulders. "We'll just have to chance it. I doubt if either ship will have more than half a dozen men on board, and they'll probably be sleeping off a night's heavy drinking."

"Very well," said Thomas. "We're always short of boats. You haven't forgotten the petards have you?"

"No, we've made four, but we'll concentrate on the main door. That'll be easy to find in the darkness. If all goes well, we'll have about half an hour of moon – just enough time for us to get our bearings."

Thomas looked up as a seaman walked over to him. "Ah, our drinks. You know, I'm beginning to like limejuice without rumbullion in it. Bit of a sharp taste, but it leaves your mouth nice and fresh."

"From the look in Diana's eye, you'd better get used to it," Ned said.

21

"Yes, she can be remarkably strong-minded, and I'll be damned if I'm going to sleep alone like some monk!"

Ned looked round at the ships now all lying with their mainsails lowered: only two or three of them would heave-to satisfactorily. "Look at them," he said, "as far as old Loosely's concerned, they're just pirates!"

Thomas laughed heartily and slapped his stomach. "I wish Loosely was here to see us. Still, if we told him where we are bound, he'd faint."

"He's probably prowling round Cannon Street at the moment to make sure all the brothels are closed."

"Might have done him a bit of good to have visited one first," Thomas said sourly. "Being married to that woman can't help much, either."

The two men talked for another five minutes and then Ned and Aurelia returned to the *Griffin*. "You had a good gossip?" Ned asked amiably once they were down in the cabin again.

"This is a hard voyage for Thomas."

"How so?" Ned asked.

"Diana's set up some rules. Apart from not drinking hot waters and eating less, there are others."

"Concerning what?"

Aurelia laughed. "I shan't tell you. I might want to apply them to you."

"Thomas is frightened of Diana. I'm not frightened of you."

"It's not fear upsetting Thomas when he has to sleep alone," Aurelia said matter-of-factly.

Ned took down the chart and unrolled it again. He looked at the small wedge-shaped indentation which was the Hacha River, with the town on the west bank. There were not many soundings and the river emptying into the sea meant mud or sand, so it could be shallow close in. But wherever it was deep enough to anchor the *Dolphyn* and *Argonauta*, it would be deep enough for the other buccaneer ships. But how far were the two captives from the fort? That was the distance that the boats were going to have to row. And they would be close enough in to be seen from the town – if any sharp-eyed inhabitant was awake at that time of the night.

He rolled up the chart. As usual, it depended on luck as much as planning, and in fifteen hours or so it would all be decided one way or the other.

Clouds kept cutting off the moon as though someone was opening and shutting the door of a lighted room, but the breeze was shifting the clouds fast. Ned looked astern and watched the rest of the buccaneer ships following the *Griffin*. Ahead the shore made a heavy, black outline; the *Dolphyn* and the *Argonauta* could be distinguished only by their masts jutting up above the land.

There was the church: he had been able to spot it during one period of moonlight. That black shape on the hills opposite the town was a big patch of trees. And, as clouds slid across the town and then left an opening, he picked out the fort. Square, not very big, its guns covering the town and the entrance to the river. Could be a stone base with wooden wall. And built close to the houses, not that Riohacha was a big town. However, there were very few towns along this coast. Santa Marta and Barranquilla beyond were the only ones of any size. Riohacha was an open anchorage; that was one reason why it had not grown: ships had to anchor in open water where there was no shelter from the strong easterly wind that usually blew along this coast, and always there was the risk of heavy surf springing up, which made it dangerous unloading cargo into boats which then had to go a long way up the river to a small jetty.

Nevertheless, Riohacha was an important little port because of its isolation, but why, Ned asked himself, had the Spanish there suddenly seized the ships belonging to Coles and Gottlieb? Yes, Spain had for years proclaimed that no foreign ship could enter the Caribbean or trade with a Spanish port, but necessity had long ago driven the local Spaniards to ignore the order.

The mayor, or garrison commander, at Riohacha must have been acting under new orders: neither would risk frightening off the smugglers if left to his own devices: the smugglers made all the difference between a comfortable life and one where there was a perpetual shortage of the necessities.

The *Griffin* now had the two captured ships on the beam. It was less than half a mile to the town.

"Anchor as soon as you can," Ned told Lobb. Another loud whisper brought the mainsail down and, as soon as the way was

23

off the ship, grunting from the foredeck showed men were strug-
gling with the heavy anchor. A deep plop indicated that it had been
dropped over the side, and Ned could imagine the cable snaking
after it.

Already a couple of men were hauling on the painters of the
Griffin's two boats which had been towing astern. Quickly they
brought them alongside to starboard.

Ned looked astern: the rest of the ships had furled or lowered
their sails and were anchoring. He looked towards the shore. He
could not distinguish houses – he had only spotted the church and
the fort because they stood alone. With luck, since they were
anchoring on the down-moon side of the town, the ships would be
hidden against the dark northern horizon.

"We're ready to board the boat, sir," Lobb reported, and Ned
turned to Aurelia and kissed her. "You're the captain of the *Griffin*
again. But I should leave more men with you."

"Don't be silly. All we have to do is make sure we don't drag the
anchor, and there are enough of us for that!"

Ned scrambled down into the boat and turned to watch men
carefully handing down the four boxes that were the petards,
making sure not to snag the hooks on anything.

"The men with the slowmatch?"

"They're just coming," Lobb said. "I told them to keep away
from the petards, in case any powder leaks out."

Slowmatch was not very reliable. Made from mangrove bark
pounded into flat strips and dried in the sun, it had the merit of
burning evenly, as long as it stayed alight. And that was why four
men were carrying strips of slowmatch: one of the four pieces
should stay alight, particularly as each of the men from time to time
blew gently on his glowing strip.

Ned could already see boats detaching themselves from the sides
of the ships: they did not have to bother loading petards and he
listened: no, not a sound: they had all made a good job of muffling
their oars. As long as all the men were sober: it just wanted a
drunken man to shout or start singing or some damned thing . . .

And there was the *Peleus*: Thomas had anchored closer to the
Dolphyn and *Argonauta*. In four or five minutes – as soon as he saw
the other boats reach the shore – his boats would be going over to
take them.

Now the *Griffin*'s boats were pulling for the shore, petards carefully stowed, the four men with the slowmatches huddled over their precious strips of mangrove and the rest of the men in the boat straining at the muffled oars.

Ned eyed the river entrance. There were no jetties close in to the town or in front of the fort. Did that mean the water was too shallow? For a moment he almost ordered Lobb to head further to seaward, then he remembered the surf: there was usually too much surf to let a jetty last more than a few hours: they were just lucky that at the moment there was no north in the wind: it was the norther that brought the surf thundering in along this coast.

"Head for the beach directly in front of the fort," Ned muttered to Lobb. He was conscious that at least thirty boats were following – some of the buccaneer ships had canoes as well as boats – carrying about a thousand men. A thousand at least, probably more. And the effectiveness of each of them depended on one of the petards exploding and blowing down the door of the fortress. And the petards depended on the slowmatch. Which in turn – oh, stop that, he told himself impatiently: that way lies madness: the never-never-land of if, perhaps and maybe . . .

The wind was warm and steady. Yes, he could now see where the waves lapped along the shore. Not much phosphorescence – there never was when the moon was up. He looked astern. Yes, the other boats were following closely – in fact the one just astern was within five yards, and he could see the stem cutting a smooth moustache of water.

They were passing the town now as they approached the river mouth. Not one light at a window: the town slept. He hoped a restless individual did not decide to go for a walk, or stand at the door relieving himself . . .

Then it suddenly happened: Lobb wrenched the tiller and hissed an order to the men at the oars, and a moment later the keel of the boat grated as it ran on to the sand. The men leapt out, pulling at the gunwales, and one of them ran up the beach with a grapnel on a line, which he dug into the sand.

Six men still remained in the boat: the four men with the slowmatches and the two guarding the petards. Lobb stood against the gunwale with two men and growled: "Quickly, hand out the first petard!"

The two men standing in the water took the box, turned and hurried up the beach, to be replaced by two more. Within a couple of minutes the four petards were landed and Lobb said: "Come on, you with the slowmatches: carefully now!"

With the petards and slowmatches on the shore, Ned led the way to the fort. The yielding sand which seemed to be trying to trip him soon gave way to harder ground and he risked looking up. The fort now seemed enormous, towering over him, black and menacing in the darkness. Still there were no musket shots, no trumpets sounding the alarm. But the huge double doors were shut and locked. Clearly the Dons relied on a lock and did not bother with sentries.

A ring was fitted to the door beside the big keyhole so that it could be grasped to swing it open. Ned gestured to the two men with the first petard and ran a hand round the edges seeking a hook. He fitted it into the ring and muttered to the men to let the petard hang. He felt carefully for a fuse. It was hanging out of the box but was firmly fixed.

"Go back to the boats," he told the men with the other three petards, and took a slowmatch from one of the four men. He blew on the burning end until it glowed, held it against the fuse and blew again until the fuse began to splutter, and then with a hasty warning he told every man to get clear of the door.

By now the beach was littered with boats and, just clear of the water, several hundred men were crouching ready. Finding Lobb beside him and recognizing the limping man as Saxby, he hurried down to the water's edge, still counting. The petard had been fitted with a four-minute fuse, the shortest time that he dared risk. Two minutes . . . no shout from a sentry, no crash of a musket . . . the Dons could not believe that anyone would dare attack them . . .

Two and a half minutes . . . three . . . three and a half . . .

The explosion blinded him and he staggered up to his knees into the sea: the noise made him lose his sense of balance for a few moments. He blinked and then with a bellow ran towards the door, coughing as the smoke of the gunpowder bit into his lungs.

From the corner of his eye he saw that the arch over the doorway was now jagged, and he ran over the wreckage of the doors beneath it into an open courtyard, followed by several score buccaneers who were now bellowing, shouting threats intended to paralyse the Spaniards with fright.

Hurry, Ned said to himself, imagining the four men with the slowmatches trying to light lanterns. He stopped a moment and then, as a shaft of moonlight swept across the courtyard, saw a single door.

Even as he watched, the door flung open and a man stumbled out, clearly half asleep. Half a dozen buccaneers leapt on him and flung the door wide open. In a flicker of moonlight Ned caught sight of steps: they probably led up to the garrison's sleeping quarters.

One of the buccaneers arrived with a lantern and Ned grabbed it in his left hand, unsheathing his cutlass with the right. He pushed past the buccaneers wrestling with the sleepy Spaniard and started up the steps, shouting to the men crowding into the courtyard to follow him.

He had only just started climbing the stairs when another man blundered down, cursing in Spanish. He was carrying a sword and, without needing to parry, Ned ran him through, wrenching the cutlass free so that the man's body tumbled down to the door.

But in the moments as Ned wrestled with the cutlass, a couple of buccaneers managed to squeeze past him and run up the steps. They met a third Spanish soldier, as sleepy as the first two, and his body spun down the steps.

By now Ned could hear questioning shouts in Spanish coming from what was probably a guardroom at the top of the stairs, and he hurried after the two buccaneers, holding up the lantern.

Then he saw a light through an open door at the top of the steps, which curved round to the left: the Spaniards must sleep with a lantern left burning. He felt many more buccaneers pushing from behind him and he hurried up the remaining stairs. He burst into the room to find the first two buccaneers slashing at a dozen Spaniards who had backed into a corner of the room.

One fell with a gurgle, followed by another, and as Ned jumped forward to attack a Spaniard the rest of the buccaneers burst into the room behind him.

"Don't kill them all!" Ned shouted. "I want a couple of prisoners."

But amid all the shouting no one heard him: every Spaniard had half a dozen buccaneers slashing at him; within a couple of minutes only buccaneers, puffing and laughing with excitement, were left alive in the room.

"Damnation!" Ned bellowed. "I needed prisoners to show us where our men are!"

"Look in here!" shouted a buccaneer, grabbing the lantern and pulling open a door Ned had not seen. It led to a corridor and he followed the excited buccaneer, who was wrenching open yet another door.

And there, standing in a long nightshirt, was a white-faced man who Ned guessed must be the commander of the garrison.

The buccaneer stood behind the man with his cutlass, and Ned said in Spanish: "Are you in command?"

"Yes," the man stammered. "What is happening?"

"Buccaneers," Ned said briefly. "Where are your prisoners?"

The man pointed downwards. "The dungeon. They are all secured down there."

"Get the keys and lead the way," Ned said. "No, you'd better follow me: my men are excited . . ."

"May I dress?" the garrison commander quavered.

"No, you look splendid like that," Ned said, flicking the hem of the nightshirt with the point of his cutlass. "Which way?"

"Along to the guardroom: the sergeant will have the key."

"Your sergeant is certainly dead: I hope the key is somewhere safe."

"It's on a hook; we'll find it," the man said, obviously relieved to find himself still alive and gaining a little confidence with each passing second. Ned turned and led the way along the corridor, calling to the buccaneers that he had a prisoner.

As soon as they reached the guardroom, now lit by more lanterns, the prisoner saw the pile of bodies and groaned. The sight of his men lying dead seemed to paralyse him and Ned prodded him with the cutlass.

"The key," he growled. "Hurry up!"

Even as he spoke he heard the ripe voice of Thomas, who had just arrived at the fort to discover that the fighting was already over.

The prisoner stepped carefully over the bodies and round the wooden frames of the beds on which the guards had been

28

sleeping. He pointed to a locker fixed to the wall. "In there, on a hook," he said.

Before Ned had time to give any order a buccaneer was levering off the door with a pike, and Ned recognized the man as one of his captains, the Spaniard Secco, who had understood what the garrison commander had said.

Ned hurried over with the lantern and as the splintered door of the locker swung open Ned saw several large keys hanging from hooks.

"Which one?"

"We need the large one for the door. And . . ." he hesitated. "Yes, we shall need those small ones too, all four of them."

Ned, not noticing the hesitation, snatched the keys and motioned the prisoner to lead the way to the dungeon.

At that moment Thomas came into the guardroom. "Why Ned, you were in too much of a hurry: you've done me out of a fight. Who's this fellow? Why, you woke him up!"

"Says he's the garrison commander."

"Ah, and he knows where the keys are, I see."

Ned waved the keys. "You're just in time – we're on our way to the dungeon: all our men are down there."

"Must be a damned big dungeon," Thomas commented. "There'll be upward of a hundred men."

Ned led the way with the thoroughly frightened commander closely behind him, followed by Thomas and several dozen buccaneers, disappointed that the fighting in the fort was all over.

"By the way," Thomas said, "no trouble with the *Argonauta* and *Dolphyn*: you were quite right, half a dozen Dons in each ship and all of 'em drunk. Soldiers, they were, and they'd found some rum jars."

"Probably why there were so few soldiers here," Ned said. "I don't reckon there were twenty men, though I haven't counted the bodies."

The commander pointed across the courtyard to a passageway in the far corner. He directed Ned along it until they came to a heavy door which was studded with bolt heads. He indicated the large key.

Ned unlocked the door and swung it back. In the light of the lantern he could see a narrow staircase leading downwards. But

29

the place smelled like a sewer. Ned took a deep breath and started down the steps.

He was almost at the bottom when he realized he was actually in the dungeon, and that crowded on the stone floor were at least a hundred men – the crews of the two buccaneer ships.

He stopped and shouted: "Coles – are you here? Gottlieb?"

"Over on the far wall in irons," a voice said in English, "but they can't talk. That's – that's not Mr Yorke, is it?" the voice added, as though the speaker could not believe his ears.

"Yes it is." In the dim light of the lantern Ned could only see sprawled bodies, men lying on the stone floor so closely packed it was impossible to walk. The stench was almost unendurable.

"Why can't they talk?" Ned demanded.

"Beaten by the Dons and they're slung in irons," the man said. "Wait, I'll lead you."

Ned turned and held the lantern up to the garrison commander's face. The man had turned grey; he stared at the floor, knowing Ned was examining him. "Start saying prayers," Ned said in Spanish. "There are more than a thousand of these men's friends in the courtyard . . ."

Picking his way carefully, Ned followed his buccaneer guide, who was trying to shout, though his voice came out at little more than a croak. "Make way there, it's Mr Yorke and Sir Thomas, make way!"

They found Coles unconscious hanging as though crucified from leg and arm irons on the far wall. The lantern showed his chest still moving, but otherwise the man could have been dead. And ten feet to one side Gottlieb also hung in irons: he too was unconscious.

"The smaller keys," the garrison commander whispered.

Ned passed the lantern to Thomas and knelt by Coles. First he unlocked the irons holding his arms and then unlocked the leg irons. He gently lowered Coles's body and the man groaned.

With the other two keys Ned freed Gottlieb and lowered him to the stone floor.

Thomas examined him with the lantern. "He's alive too, but a few more hours . . ."

Ned felt so cold that he wondered why he was not shivering, although the heat in the dungeon was intense. He stood up and turned to the garrison commander. He pointed to where Coles had been hanging. "Lean with your back against the wall," he said.

The puzzled Spaniard turned and leaned against the wall.

"Raise your arms."

Before the man fully realized what had happened, Ned had shut the arm irons round his wrists and locked them.

Then he crouched and fitted the leg irons and locked them. He put the keys in his pocket and Thomas said angrily, waving his cutlass: "I'd spit him, Ned!"

Ned shook his head. "We have a lot of questions to ask him. Leave him there while we get these men out of here. Send some of our men down – we're going to have to carry Coles and Gottlieb up to the fresh air. Then we'll come and have a chat with our Spanish friend."

Before anyone could move, one of the buccaneers staggered over to where the prisoner was held in the irons and kicked him in the stomach amid a torrent of what Ned took to be Dutch. The man was swaying from the effort and Ned waited to see if he was going to repeat it, but he seemed satisfied and turned away, while the prisoner writhed in the chains.

"That'll get him in the right frame of mind for our chat," Thomas commented grimly.

As soon as Ned reached the top of the steps and found himself in the courtyard he shouted for Saxby, who limped across. Quickly Ned explained that Coles and Gottlieb were below. "Take them out to the *Phoenix*: they're in very poor shape and in need of some treatment from Mrs Judd. Tell your men to be gentle with them."

He turned to Lobb, who had just walked up. "All the men from the *Argonauta* and *Dolphyn* are down there in the dungeon, starved and parched. Have them taken out to their ships so they can get some food and water."

Ned turned to Thomas. "Can you spare your mate, Mitchell? Neither Coles nor Gottlieb will be much use for a few days."

"I can spare Mitchell. Which ship do you want him to go to?"

"Let him take the *Dolphyn*." He spoke to Lobb. "You'd better take command of the *Argonauta* when it's time to sail. I reckon by then the men will have recovered enough to get the sails up."

What next? The fort, of course; it had to be secured; the

explosion would have been heard everywhere, but people must have pulled the bedclothes over their heads. He saw Leclerc bustling about with a lantern, trying to sort out his men. "Ah, take a hundred or so men and cover the fortress from outside: I don't think we need fear an attack from the townspeople, but we'd better be on our guard."

He waited as both Saxby and Leclerc shouted to the men milling about in the courtyard and then watched as the first of the buccaneer prisoners stumbled up from the dungeon, gathering round listlessly at the top, uncertain what to do. The sudden change from being prisoners in that stinking dungeon to being free men in the courtyard, Ned realized, had happened so quickly that the men were bewildered.

He walked over to them. "You're now going to be taken out to your ships, where you'll have to feed yourselves because I can't spare men to help you. Your captains are being taken to the *Phoenix* for treatment; in the meantime the mates of the *Peleus* and the *Griffin* will command your ships."

Two or three of the men gave a weak cheer, and Ned waved his lantern, pointing towards the beach. "Boats are down there waiting for you."

He turned to Thomas. "Once all these men are out of the dungeon, we'll continue our chat with that garrison commander."

"You're not turning the rest of the men loose to raid the town?"

"Not yet. We've plenty of time, and the most important thing is to find out why the Spanish seized our men. Ah," Ned said, "here they come with Coles and Gottlieb."

Preceded by a man with a lantern, three men came out carrying the Englishman and Dutchman. Although the lantern was dim, Ned saw that Coles's eyes were open.

He hurried over to the man. "How are you feeling?"

"Sore," Coles murmured. "But glad to see you. Wouldn't have lasted much longer."

"What were the Spanish after?"

"Don't know; just seized us when we were selling 'em some piece goods. Kept asking us about paying off the Army in Jamaica. Gottlieb and I didn't know much about it, but the Dons wouldn't believe us and kept on with the bastinado."

The man's eyes closed: those few words had exhausted him.

Ned bent down and said: "Mrs Judd in the *Phoenix* will soon put you right."

Gottlieb was too exhausted to speak English; clearly his brain was working in Dutch, and Ned signalled to the three men carrying him to take him down to the boats.

Thomas grunted and said to Ned: "Paying off the Army in Jamaica, eh? Why are the Dons suddenly interested in that?"

"No Army means the island's undefended on land," Ned said crisply. "And if the buccaneers move to Tortuga . . ."

"Yes, old Loosely could find he has the crazy King Carlos as a new landlord," Thomas said.

Lobb came out through the doorway carrying a lantern. "That's all our fellows out. Phew, what a stink down there. There's just someone in a nightshirt chained to the wall, but I expect you know about him. He's mumbling in Spanish."

"Yes, he's responsible for all this trouble. Now, you hurry with those men and send the boats back."

"Aye, but the men are right poorly," Lobb said. "They've only been fed a little thin soup each night. No water during the day." With that he followed the last of the freed prisoners out through the shattered archway and down to the beach.

"Come on," Ned said to Thomas. "Let's go down and question our man."

At that moment Secco appeared out of the darkness. "You need help," he said, making it a statement, not a question. Realizing that a Spaniard could best deal with a Spaniard, Ned led the way down into the dungeon.

33

# Chapter
Four

The garrison commander, stretched out against the slimy wall by
the chains, grey-faced with fear and looking absurd in his
nightshirt, watched the three men nervously.

"What is your name?" Ned asked in Spanish.

"Balliardo. Francesco Balliardo."

"You questioned our men; now it's our turn to question you,"
Ned said heavily, "and you will answer truthfully. If you do not
survive, we'll simply start on the mayor, and then the customs
officer, and the priest . . . Do you understand me?"

"Yes, yes," the man stammered.

Ned turned to Secco and said in English: "You question him.
We want to know first why he took the *Argonauta* and *Dolphyn*
people prisoner."

Secco spoke rapidly, idly tapping his foot with his cutlass, a
gesture which Balliardo watched warily.

Ned understood the halting reply. He had received orders from
the provincial governor at Barranquilla.

What had the orders said?

That any buccaneers and smugglers along the coast were to be
seized.

Why seize them now? Smuggling had been going on for years.

Yes, Balliardo said, he knew that; but his orders had been
definite: seize any smugglers and buccaneers – indeed, any foreign
ship – that came along the coast.

"And having seized them?" Ned asked.

"I was to ask their captains some questions, if the ships came from Jamaica."

"What were the questions?"

"I cannot tell you," Balliardo said, staring fixedly at the floor. Ned looked significantly at Secco, who slapped the man's face. "Answer!"

"I can't; it is more than my life is worth."

"Why?" Ned asked innocently. "Will the authorities kill you?"

"I expect so," the man said brokenly.

Ned gave a bloodcurdling laugh. "*What* an unlucky man you are. You think there is a possibility your people will kill you if you answer my questions. Just a possibility. But let me assure you, I am certainly going to kill you if you don't answer me. Now, *what* questions?"

The man looked up like a trapped animal, sighed and then whispered, as though afraid of being overheard, "What ships there were in Jamaica. How many frigates. If more were expected."

Ned guessed the Spanish authorities would never believe the correct answer – that there were no British frigates and none was expected, unless carrying despatches for the governor. "What else," he said to Secco in English, leaving the Spaniard to ask the question, guessing that Balliardo might need persuading to answer.

"Nothing else, I swear."

Secco did not bother to translate: instead he kicked Balliardo's shin. The man said nothing.

"What else?" Secco repeated, his voice quiet but menacing.

Balliardo shook his head and Secco punched him in the stomach, leaving him winded and gasping for breath. As soon as Balliardo had recovered, Secco said once again: "What else?"

The man shook his head helplessly. Secco said coldly: "Our lives are at stake." His cutlass flashed and a piece of Balliardo's nightshirt fluttered to the ground.

"The rack . . ." Balliardo gabbled. "If I tell you anything they'll put me on the rack!"

"How will they know?" Secco asked.

"But they're here now!" Balliardo had blurted it out and a moment later realized what he had said.

"Who is?"

35

Balliardo shook his head but a moment later Secco was standing close to him, doing something with his left hand. Balliardo screamed with pain and tried to cover his groin with his hands, clanking the chains of the metal bands round his arms.

"I know a thousand painful and slow ways to kill you," Secco said calmly, "and I have all night. I repeat, who is?"

This time Balliardo was taking no chances: he had obviously made up his mind that he preferred risking the rack administered by his own people to the certain death he inevitably faced at the hands of these heretics.

"The provincial governor from Barranquilla. He is here."

Balliardo's voice had again dropped to a whisper, and clearly the thought of the provincial governor terrified him.

Secco glanced at Ned to make sure he had understood. Ned nodded.

Secco said: "Where is he staying?"

"With the bishop. No, I mean with the mayor."

"The bishop? Riohacha does not have a bishop!"

"No, of course, but he is here too, the provincial bishop. He and the governor are staying for several days."

"Where?"

Balliardo was no longer even pretending to be reluctant to answer the questions. "The governor is at the mayor's house; the bishop with the priest."

Ned asked: "Are there any more important people staying here in Riohacha?"

"No, only the staff of the governor, who are lodged in some other house – I don't know which one – and the bishop's chaplain, who is also lodging eleswhere: the priest's house is quite small."

Then Ned said suddenly: "Why did you ask about the Army in Jamaica?"

Balliardo shrugged his shoulders and set the chains clanking. "We heard that the Army was being disbanded. Had been disbanded, by the new governor who had just come out from England."

"Why are you interested?"

"Me?" Balliardo exclaimed. "I am not interested. It was the governor."

"Why did you torture the two captains?"

36

"Why are you torturing me? The same reason. To get answers."

"But they knew nothing," Ned said.

"How was I to know? They are brave men. They said nothing. One of them spat in my face."

There was a flash of steel and the flat of Secco's cutlass hit Balliardo across the face. "I spit in your face, too," Secco said angrily. "Why was the provincial governor from Barranquilla interested in the disbanding of the Jamaican Army? Make a guess!"

Balliardo turned his face away from Secco, spitting blood. He coughed a few times, shook his head and then muttered: "There have been rumours that the English governor has gone mad. I suppose the governor at Barranquilla is curious. The Viceroy in Panama even. It is a strange thing to do, you must admit."

Secco laughed drily. "The English do strange things from time to time. But never rely on it."

"I will not," Balliardo said politely, "and thank you for the advice."

"Where is the mayor's house?" Ned asked.

"The big white building past the church."

"And the priest's?"

"Just before the church there are three big kapok trees. The priest's house is right beside the middle one."

"This comedian knows nothing," Ned said in English. "He is just a parrot repeating words put in his mouth. I think we'll call on the governor."

Thomas nodded. "Just a moment. The governor wants to know about disbanding the Army, so do you think Spain intends to make our King give the island back – make him keep to that secret treaty?"

"Perhaps, though I can't see the merchants in London staying quiet about it: they are investing money out here, and Jamaica is the key to the Caribbee."

"Who does the governor of the province get *his* orders from?" Thomas asked.

"The Viceroy, I suppose, who hears direct from Spain."

"I wonder how much the Viceroy told the governor."

"Well, we can't get the Viceroy, but the governor is ours for the taking. He's an important figure: there aren't many provinces, and this is the one nearest Jamaica."

"Let's hope he talks," Thomas said.

"There's no rush," Ned said bluntly. "We can take him with us."

"Yes, and the bishop; they would make good hostages. I wonder how much ransom they're worth? What about this apology?" he said, gesturing at Balliardo.

"We'll leave him here. Somebody will find him. What he did to Coles and Gottlieb – what he would have done to them in the end – doesn't make me want to unlock him. In fact, I'd sooner throw the keys into the sea. Come on, let's go."

He led the way out of the dungeon, up to the courtyard and out to the shattered gate. "Leclerc," he bellowed. "Where are you?"

The Frenchman answered from further along the wall of the fortress.

"It seems the governor of the province is here in town: I want fifty men to come with me and find him. And the bishop, too: he is staying at the priest's house, which is beside three big kapok trees next to the church. Send another fifty men to surround the house, but don't disturb the bishop: we'll call on him after we've seen the governor."

Leclerc laughed cheerfully. "All we lack is the Viceroy," he said as he called to his men. "Shall I stay here?"

"Yes, guard the fort. The garrison commander is down in the dungeon."

"From what I hear, that's a good place for him."

"Yes, you can go down and kick him when you feel bored."

Ned waited until the men were ready and then led the way towards the mayor's house. It was a wide track rather than a road and, from the smell, lined with rotting cabbage and heavily traversed by donkeys and pigs.

The air was hot and very humid: the high land and the trees on the other side of the river seemed to be blocking any night wind that might have cleared away the smell, which seemed to hover in the air, sticky and clinging, catching the back of the nose.

There was the church – and yes, the three kapok trees. Ned turned and called to the second group of men: "That's the house. Don't let anyone leave."

A hundred yards further a high wall surrounded what was obviously the mayor's house.

"Do we expect any shooting?" Thomas said.

"I doubt it. The explosion of that petard didn't bring the townspeople rushing down to the fort with the mayor leading them . . . The sound of us forcing his gate open will by comparison sound like music. As soon as he heard the petard the mayor must have guessed what was going on."

As they spoke three buccaneers were smashing down the wooden gate and as it collapsed inwards, it left a black hole in the wall.

Ned walked through the entrance and could see the house set back thirty yards from the wall. There were lights at several windows.

He walked along the path and up half a dozen wooden steps to the front door, banging on it with the hilt of his cutlass.

A man's voice asked nervously in Spanish: "Who is there?"

"The buccaneers. Open up, or we smash the door down," Ned answered in Spanish.

"But what do you want? What was that explosion?" the voice persisted.

"Open this door or we'll cut your throat," Ned said harshly.

The door creaked open and a man with a lantern cringed against the door jamb. "What do you want?" he repeated, unable to keep the despair from his voice. "That explosion – what is happening?"

Ned pushed into the house, seizing the lantern from the servant with his left hand and holding his cutlass in his right. "Fetch the mayor!"

"I am the mayor," a voice said from the darkness at the back of the first room. Ned held the lantern higher and could just make out a figure standing beside another door. "What was that explosion? Was it the magazine of the fort?"

"You have the governor staying here. Fetch him!"

"I – er, well – "

"Fetch him!"

The figure scurried off.

Ned turned and asked: "Is Secco there?"

The buccaneers behind Thomas turned and called the Spanish captain, who hurried into the room.

Quickly Ned explained what was happening. "We can take this man – the governor of the province – back with us, but I want to get him to talk now: it may save us time."

"At your service," Secco said with a flourish. "I can guarantee that he will give no more trouble than that garrison commander. But it's a pity we have no arm and leg irons. A man in irons feels very vulnerable . . ."

The mayor hurried back into the room, followed by a tall man fully dressed, with lace at throat and wrists and a heavily embroidered coat.

"Well?" the man demanded haughtily.

Ned stared at him for a minute or more, realizing he must have dressed after the explosion.

"Who are you?" he said casually.

"Don Esteban Sanchez," the man said. "And you?"

"I am the Admiral of the Brethren of the Coast," Ned said quietly. "We are the people who have just captured Riohacha. No doubt you heard us."

"I heard an explosion, certainly," the governor agreed. "The mayor thought there had been an accident at the fort."

"No, that was a petard blowing down the doors. All the prisoners have been released. The only person left in the dungeon," Ned added, "is the garrison commander."

The governor shrugged his shoulders: it was a matter of indifference to him, he seemed to be saying.

Ned put down the lantern, as if indicating the preliminaries were over.

"Now we come for you."

"Come for *me*? But I am the governor: you can't bother me. After all, England and Spain are at peace."

"But 'No peace beyond the Line'," Ned said ironically. "If we are all at peace, why did you give orders that my people should be captured and tortured?"

"I gave no orders about torturing."

"You gave orders that they were to be taken prisoner and asked certain questions. The torturing just followed as a matter of course."

Again Don Esteban shrugged his shoulders.

Ned tapped the floor with the point of his cutlass. "Don

Esteban," he said coldly, "I hope you have made your peace with God, because you are close to death."

The mayor – who Ned saw was a chubby little man, greasy of face with darting eyes – gave a gasp. Ned turned to him. "And you, too. I'll probably let the bishop live, because he had nothing to do with the torturing of my men. At least, I assume he did not."

Don Esteban's face was now grey in the light of the smoky lantern: he seemed to Ned to have shrunk a little. His shoulders were now hunched and he was looking down, so that he seemed less tall than when he walked into the room.

Ned turned to some of the buccaneers standing in the room behind him, and said in English: "Seize that man – the tall one."

Don Esteban tried to cling to a semblance of dignity as two burly buccaneers seized him, one twisting his arm behind him and the other putting an arm round his throat.

"This is an outrage!" Sanchez spluttered, gasping for breath.

"Don't use childish phrases," Ned said coldly. "You are facing death, so don't pretend to be offended." He turned to the mayor. "Sit down on the floor out of the way; your turn will come."

He faced Sanchez and said formally: "I am going to question you here, but there is a spare set of irons and chains in the dungeon of the fort. I have the key for them in my pocket. Which do you prefer, here or the dungeon?"

Sanchez shrugged his shoulders, as best he could. "It makes no difference to me; I am not going to answer your questions."

"We shall see," Ned said, looking round to Secco, and gesturing towards the governor.

Secco moved over until he stood a yard in front of the governor and tapped the wooden floor with the point of his cutlass. "You ordered the garrison commander to seize anyone in foreign ships who visited Riohacha. Why?"

Again the governor shrugged his shoulders as best he could. "The same order went out to Santa Marta, Barranquilla, anywhere there were likely to be smugglers."

"What was the reason?"

"Orders from the Viceroy," the governor said without hesitation, obviously glad to shift the responsibility.

"Why did the Viceroy give that order?"

41

"How do I know?"

And that is what he is going to do, Ned realized: answer the obvious questions and shelter behind the Viceroy for the rest: Sanchez has realized that his life is dangling on a thread.

"You wanted to know if the Army in Jamaica has been disbanded. Why?"

"Curiosity. We had heard rumours that the new governor was paying off the soldiers. This seemed a strange decision, so we wanted to know more about it."

"And curiosity was the only reason for the question?"

"Of course."

Secco took a step forward and slapped him across the face. "You lie."

Sanchez said nothing.

"Now give us the true answer. It wasn't just curiosity, was it?"

"The Viceroy wanted to know. He gave no explanation."

So we get the Viceroy again, Ned thought. The perfect excuse – at least, so Sanchez thought.

"Why seize our ships?"

For the third time Sanchez shrugged his shoulders and almost immediately doubled over as Secco punched him in the stomach. His arm would have been dislocated had the buccaneer holding him not eased his grasp.

Sanchez was gasping for breath and he looked round at the buccaneers, who were just staring at him.

"We have the whole night," Ned said helpfully. "And tomorrow, too. In fact even longer; no one is going to come to rescue you."

"Pay attention," Secco said. "Why seize the ships?"

Sanchez shook his head and Secco hit him again.

The man began to wheeze, dragging in each breath as though he had a cloth in his mouth.

"Why?" Secco repeated, drawing back his arm once more.

"To stop them sailing again."

"Obviously," Secco said. "Why did you not want them to sail?"

Yet again Sanchez shrugged his shoulders and yet again Secco hit him. This time the governor collapsed, like a punctured bladder, and slowly enough that the two men holding him could let him go.

Secco turned to Ned. "No stamina, this one. A pity there's no rack in the dungeon. Still, this might help," he said, sliding a dagger out of a sheath at his waist. "We'll see how he likes being used as a pin cushion."

They all waited for the man on the floor to recover his breath. The lace collar at his throat was now creased and soaked with perspiration; his embroidered coat was riding up and tearing the buttons from his breeches; his breeches were marked with dust from the floor.

"Hoist him up," Ned told the two buccaneers. There was no point in giving him too long to recover.

Once on his feet and held by the buccaneers, the man's eyes moved slowly from Ned to Secco, obviously unable to work out the relationship and puzzled because Ned had spoken to him in good Spanish.

Secco resumed his position a yard in front of Sanchez, only now he deliberately sheathed his cutlass and held the dagger in his right hand. The blade was less than a foot long, and the metal glinted in the light of the lantern so that Sanchez now stared at it like a rabbit watching a ferret.

"I was asking you why you didn't want the ships to sail . . ."

Sanchez said nothing, still staring at the dagger.

Suddenly the blade snaked out, stabbing Sanchez lightly in the left arm.

"So that they would not report movements of our ships."

"Ships?" repeated a startled Secco. "What ships do you have?"

Watching the governor's face, Ned thought: he let that slip. He did not mean to say that, but he is frightened of that dagger.

The dagger flashed again and Sanchez recoiled as the blade jabbed the fleshy part of his upper arm.

"We – we have a few ships in the coasting trade."

"Have any ships come recently from Spain?" Ned asked casually.

"No, no, of course not," Sanchez stammered.

So, Ned thought, ships *have* arrived from Spain. And they would be in the main port of Cartagena. What kind? Ships of war or a few trading ships with some long overdue cargoes?

"Why are you here?" Ned asked. "What made you leave Barranquilla?"

Again Sanchez looked at the dagger before answering. "The Viceroy ordered me to inspect the ports."

"Inspect the ports?" Ned repeated dubiously. "What is there to inspect here?"

When Sanchez hesitated, Secco twirled the dagger and the governor said hurriedly: "It is just routine: inspect the fort, talk to the mayor and the garrison commander."

"And tell them to prepare to receive some ships?" Ned asked on the spur of the moment.

Sanchez looked down at the floor and to Ned, who was watching him closely, the man seemed to have aged several years in a matter of moments. "No," the governor muttered, "just the usual. Inspect the guns, look at the mayor's accounts, see if there is any damage to the sea wall that wants repairing – the surf is bad along this coast."

"Ask him again about disbanding the Army," Ned told Secco and then took Thomas by the arm and led him outside.

"That was a good shot," Thomas said. "My Spanish isn't much good, but you have him worried with that last question about receiving ships."

"Yes, but it's all a puzzle. I think some ships have come out from Spain, and I expect they're in Cartagena. And it looks as though this fellow is visiting the ports along this coast to get them ready to receive ships."

"That means one of two things," Thomas said. "Either the Dons are getting ready to make a bolt for Spain with a plate convoy – or else they are going to make some move against Jamaica."

"That would explain the interest in disbanding the Army," Ned said thoughtfully. "But they've never had enough ships to make any move . . ."

The mosquitoes were whining round their heads and Ned brushed them off his neck. Out here it was humid and in the night air the perfume of the flowers and shrubs hung heavily, almost oppressive.

"Look at it from the Viceroy's point of view," Thomas said. "He's heard that the Jamaica Army has been disbanded, which means his own troops wouldn't meet any opposition. He's probably heard that the buccaneers have had their commissions withdrawn by this same governor and intend going to Tortuga. That leaves Jamaica helpless. So just a few Spanish ships crammed with soldiers . . ."

"I wonder . . . that's strange: Coles and Gottlieb were ques-

44

tioned about the Army: they weren't asked about us and commissions being withdrawn."

Thomas sniffed. "Maybe the Viceroy knows for certain about the commissions: don't forget, no one made much secret about them. In fact, you went round to every ship and collected them up for old Loosely."

"Come on," Ned said, "we'll ask the governor!"

Sanchez was lying on the floor again, curled up, and Secco and the two buccaneers were standing over him. The mayor, wide-eyed, was watching still squatting on the floor.

Secco gestured at Sanchez and said contemptuously in English: "The man has started fainting. His arm is a bit bloody but only from pinpricks."

"There's no hurry," Ned said, thankful that Secco had not been too enthusiastic with the dagger, "but I have a particular question I want to ask him."

"He hadn't any more to say about disbanding the Army," Secco reported. "But I'm sure some ships have arrived from Spain. The way he answered that question – tried to avoid it, rather. More ships from Spain, and they're afraid some of the smugglers will see them and report them in Jamaica."

Ned nodded as Sanchez groaned and stirred. When he is asked questions in Spanish by Secco, he answers immediately, without pausing, Ned reflected. When I ask him a question in my not-so-good Spanish, he pauses, and that gives him time to think up an answer.

Ned told Secco: "When he recovers, ask him when he heard that the governor of Jamaica had withdrawn the commissions of the buccaneers. Try to trap him into a sudden answer. I think the Viceroy already knew, but he wasn't sure about disbanding the Army."

Secco grinned. "I understand perfectly." He pushed Sanchez's body contemptuously with the toe of his boot. "He's a very frightened man. He thinks he is going to be killed any minute, when we have finished questioning him."

Finally Sanchez was back on his feet, supported by the two buccaneers, and before Secco resumed his former position, Ned said: "Can you understand me?"

Sanchez nodded.

"You are not answering our questions properly, so you're no use to us," Ned said harshly. "There is no point in keeping you alive. I warned you to make your peace." A sudden thought struck him. "Would you like a priest?" he asked innocently. "Isn't there some ritual you Catholics have when a man is dying?"

"I . . . I'm not dying," Sanchez protested feebly.

"Oh, but you are," Ned said, summoning up a fiendish laugh which left him wanting to giggle. "Oh, yes, you are a dying man. The Last Rites, isn't that what the priest administers?"

Sanchez fainted again, sliding to the floor like a collapsing sack.

"Ned, you're being nasty to the poor man," Thomas said lightly. "My Spanish isn't very good, but you're frightening him."

"I don't know what I said that upset him," Ned said. "I just told him that he was dying, and asked him if he wanted a priest."

Thomas roared with laughter. "Masterly, he's dying and does he want a priest! Oh, wait until I tell Diana. She'll love that! Very droll, Ned, very droll."

"Our friend on the floor doesn't seem to appreciate the drollery," Ned said. "I do wish he'd stop fainting."

Secco gestured to the two buccaneers, who hauled the governor to his feet. Secco looked at Ned with raised eyebrows, and when Ned nodded said immediately in Spanish: "When did you hear about the commissions?"

"A man in Port Royal – what commissions?"

Secco turned the dagger, his thumb along the flat of the blade.

"What man in Port Royal?"

Sanchez shook his head muzzily. "I don't know; an agent of the Viceroy, I suppose."

The dagger flashed again and Sanchez recoiled, trying to wrench his right arm from the buccaneer's grasp so that he could protect his left. The dagger moved a second time and Secco said quietly: "What did you hear about the commissions?"

"Oh my God, that they had been withdrawn!"

"And then what did you hear?" Secco asked relentlessly.

"That the buccaneers were going to Tortuga."

"The Viceroy knows all this for certain?"

"For certain," Sanchez agreed hurriedly, as though anxious to avoid another jab from the dagger.

"So there'd be no buccaneers and no soldiers?"

"I suppose not," Sanchez said wearily, and fainted again.

"We're wasting our time," Ned told Thomas. "Let's collect the bishop." He told Secco: "Take the governor and the mayor out to the ships, we'll keep them with us, along with the bishop. You never know when a trio of hostages might come in useful."

Thomas said: "Why not send the governor and this greasy mayor to the *Dolphyn* or the *Argonauta*: those fellows will guard them carefully!"

"I was going to ask you to be host to the bishop!"

"No Papist on board the *Peleus*," Thomas said firmly. "Not even sitting in a boat towing astern."

"All right, we'll let Secco guard him." He turned to the Spaniard. "How do you feel about having a bishop on board?"

"I have two murderers, a coiner, a triple bigamist and four thieves among my crew, so I'd hardly notice a bishop."

"Chat with him," Ned said. "You never know what information you might pick up."

"Search the priest's house thoroughly," Secco advised. "The bishop is probably travelling with all his finery: these fellows like their comfort."

The bishop, when they had hammered on the priest's door and demanded that he produce him, turned out to be a man who made the mayor look like a fine upstanding example of the human race. He was almost as wide as he was tall; his eyes were so close together they seemed to touch; his mouth reminded Ned of a squashed banana. His hands kept moving, as though he was washing them. He was a man, Ned decided, who could never be trusted to give a straight answer about anything: to him the shortest distance between two points was the most devious way.

Ned had wasted no time: he had introduced himself as the leader of the buccaneers, agreed he was responsible for the explosion which had brought them all out of their beds in alarm, and asked the bishop: "Why are you here in Riohacha?"

"Just visiting my flock," the bishop said ingratiatingly.

"Why are you travelling with the governor?"

"Because of the danger from bandits," the bishop admitted. "Bandits commit any outrages against the Church."

"So you and the governor have been warning the ports?"

The bishop's eyes flickered. He was gross, as repulsive a man as a busy person would meet in a month, but he was shrewd.

"Visiting the ports. Why should we be warning them?"

"To keep a lookout for buccaneers."

The bishop shrugged his shoulders, a gesture which started his stomach swinging from side to side. "I know nothing of buccaneers – except for you."

The man was too quick to be trapped and too pathetic to be forced. "You will come with us," Ned said, and turned to the buccaneers standing behind him. "Search the house."

"But that is an outrage!" exclaimed the bishop. "I am a man of God engaged on his pastoral duties."

"And particularly the bishop's room," Ned added.

Chapter
Five

Aurelia was waiting for him on board the *Griffin*, and the first hint of dawn was lightening the eastern sky as he climbed on board. As she kissed him she murmured: "You've been such a long time!"

"We had to ask many people many questions."

"That explosion! How it echoed! But I didn't hear any musket shots afterwards."

"Not a musket or pistol was fired," Ned said. "We took the fort by complete surprise; even the garrison commander was still in his nightshirt."

"Did you find out anything from him?"

"Not really; we found out more from the governor of the province," Ned said airily.

"The *governor*? But where . . .?"

"He's on a visit to Riohacha. Or he was; he's on a visit to the *Dolphyn* or the *Argonauta* now, on his way to Jamaica."

"And our men? A boat passed nearby taking Gottlieb and Coles out to the *Phoenix* for Mrs Judd to nurse. What happened to them?"

"Torture," Ned said. "The garrison commander was asking them questions – using a bastinado."

"And the rest of their men?"

"Locked in the dungeon without water and with very little food, but they'll be all right. And we found a bishop, too."

"Ned – what do you mean, a bishop?"

"He was travelling with the governor. The bishop of the province. He was staying with the town's priest."

"Where is he now?"

"Being held on board Secco's ship. He's a little fat toad; I've seldom seen anyone so repulsive. Do I get some breakfast?"

Aurelia sat opposite Ned at the table in the saloon as he ate his food. "Did you find out much from the governor?" she asked.

Ned shrugged his shoulders. "Not much. He didn't know anything really. He was just carrying out the Viceroy's orders."

"What were they?"

"That's the part that wasn't too clear. We spent some time trying to get him to tell us more."

"What were you trying to get him to tell you?"

"Well," Ned said, "it looks as though the *Argonauta* and *Dolphyn* were seized because the Spanish had some more ships arrive recently, and they're afraid that buccaneer ships might see them and report back to Jamaica."

"Why should it matter?"

"That's the puzzle. The garrison commander was trying to find out for sure if it was true that the Army has been disbanded in Jamaica. The Viceroy already knows that old Loosely has withdrawn the buccaneers' commissions. As far as I could make out from the governor, the Viceroy must know – or think, anyway – that Jamaica is defenceless, or soon will be: no army, no buccaneers. So if more ships have arrived from Spain, he might be planning to invade the island. Or he might be planning to send home a plate convoy . . ."

"You couldn't get the governor to talk about that?"

"No, Secco did his best."

"What do you mean – you tortured him?"

"Well, we tried to persuade him to help us."

"You tortured him!" Aurelia said accusingly.

"What if we did? We didn't kill him. And we are trying to find out something concerning the very safety of Jamaica."

"But if you tortured him, you're no better than the garrison commander who tortured Coles and Gottlieb."

"They started it," Ned said lamely. "They seized our ships and men. The garrison commander chained Coles and Gottlieb to the wall of the dungeon and went to work with the bastinado. Both were in a terrible state when we arrived. So the garrison commander and the governor can't complain if we use a little persuasion as well."

Aurelia sighed. "You men. You'll always have excuses. And anyway, you didn't succeed: you still don't know anything for sure."

"At least we know the Dons think they can take Jamaica," Ned said. "It's either an attempt on Jamaica or a plate convoy."

He pushed away his plate. "It's time we got under way. Lobb won't be coming with us – he's commanding the *Argonauta* or *Dolphyn*. Thomas has given up Mitchell, too."

Aurelia sighed again. "Not much sleep for us, then, with no mate."

"At least we don't have two sick captains to nurse."

"Ha, Martha Judd will be loving it. Nothing she likes better than nursing people. It's something she knows about."

Up on deck, Ned sent men to the windlass, and soon they were heaving down on the bars, bringing home the anchor cable. Water spilled across the foredeck, squeezed out of the cable along with sand which it had brought up from the bottom mixed with foul-smelling mud. Ned quickly had men with buckets swilling off the mud with sea water before the cable went below: it would attract enough flies without being coated with mud.

The clunking of windlasses came from all the ships as they followed the *Griffin* and began to weigh their anchors. The *Griffin*'s mainsail was soon hoisted and sheeted home, followed by the foresail.

Aurelia, standing beside Ned on the afterdeck, gave a shiver. "I wonder what waits for us in Jamaica this time," she said. "There always seems to be some nasty surprise."

Light winds gave them a slow passage: it took five and a half days to reach Port Royal, when the *Griffin* led the squadron of ships past the Three Fathom Bank and Salt Pond Reef to cross Green Bay, leaving Fort Charles and the Palisadoes to starboard. They passed the battery to larboard which had for obvious reasons been called the Twelve Apostles, and passed through the Port Royal anchorage before turning to windward to get up to the governor's jetty.

Slowly the *Griffin* began tacking up the anchorage. Ned saw that the buccaneer ship left behind because she was being rerigged was now ready for sea. And there, close in off Plumb Point and the governor's house, a small frigate was at anchor.

51

He examined it with the perspective glass. "Either the *Convertine* or a sister ship," he told Aurelia. "So the Committee for Foreign Plantations has sent out more despatches for Sir Harold. I wonder what nonsense it is this time." He thought a moment. "I hope it's not telling old Loosely that the King is carrying out his agreement to hand over Jamaica to the Dons . . ."

"Do you really think that London merchants would let the King do that?"

Aurelia sounded both puzzled and alarmed. On the north coast, at the top of some cliffs, they had just built their house: large, airy, surrounded by trees and rich land, and not far from a similar house that Thomas and Diana had built. They now had a stake in the island: no longer was their only home their ship: the house was there, cared for by servants, bulletwood shutters covering the windows should it be attacked, two wells providing more water than they could ever want. But if the island was handed back to the Spanish . . . I would burn it down, Aurelia told herself. I would rather flames had it than the Spanish.

Ned noticed her withdrawn silence. "What are you thinking?"

"About the house and the Spanish coming."

Ned laughed lightly. "The Spanish aren't here yet, whether the King gives them the island or they try to invade. Cheer up, the merchants and the buccaneers will be on your side."

Aurelia gave a weak smile. "What is Sir Harold going to say about your hostages?"

"I haven't talked to Thomas yet, but my own feeling is that corsairs don't have to account to the governor!"

"Corsairs? Why are we corsairs?"

"Well, we've no commissions and we have just acted against the Spanish: I'm sure Sir Harold would rate that an act of piracy. I think Sir Harold would prefer to know nothing about it. That way he can't be blamed for anything."

"But Ned, you can't keep a Spanish governor, a bishop and a mayor prisoner in Port Royal without telling the governor!"

"I can, but if it worries you let's take 'em to Tortuga. There we can hang 'em from a kapok tree, if we feel like it."

Aurelia thought a few moments, rubbing her brow, obviously perplexed.

"You're probably right," she said finally. "I agree that it's nothing to do with Sir Harold. But can you keep it secret?"

"Not many of the men know about it, but does it really matter? If old Loosely makes a fuss, then we'll go to Tortuga."

"But what are you going to do with them? You can't hold them hostage indefinitely."

"They're useful to have around," Ned said with a grin, "but the chance will come to ransom them. A governor and a bishop should fetch a fair price!"

"What about the mayor?" Aurelia asked mischievously.

"We'll throw him in as a make-weight," Ned said.

By now the *Griffin* had tacked up almost abreast of Plumb Point and the anchored frigate, and Ned gave the signal to luff up, anchor, and back the mainsail before furling it. As soon as the ship was anchored he gave the order to hoist out one of the boats.

By the time the boat was in the water and Ned was ready to climb down into it, Aurelia was ready: her hair was combed and tied with a fresh ribbon, she had changed into a blue jerkin and a white split skirt, and she was wearing a wide-brimmed straw hat.

Thomas and Diana greeted them cheerfully, Thomas gesturing at the frigate. "Any bets?"

"The King is handing over the island to the Dons," Ned said.

"Don't joke about it," Thomas said with a shudder, "although I must admit that was the first thing that crossed my mind when I saw the frigate at anchor."

"Well, she's carrying instructions, that's for sure," Ned said, "and nothing has ever arrived from London – including old Loosely – that was good news for us."

"Your luck must change some time," Diana said lightly. "Why, your brother might send you a packet of sweetmeats."

Ned gestured towards the *Phoenix*. "Thomas, let's leave the ladies to gossip while we go over and see what Martha Judd has done for Coles and Gottlieb. They've probably recovered enough to go back to command their ships."

Saxby was waiting on board the *Phoenix*, and he immediately commented on the frigate, saying gloomily: "More trouble for all of us . . ."

"At least her ship's company haven't any brothels to visit," Thomas commented. "They've probably been thinking about nights of sin all the way across the Atlantic, and now they've found a Puritan has sneaked back!"

"Let's hope they riot," Ned said sourly. "Come to think of it, we ought to have let our chaps riot in the streets. A few bottles through the governor's windows might have worked a treat."

"Bit late to think about that," Thomas muttered. "All the whores have become nuns by now."

Ned laughed sourly. "That's what puzzled me about old Loosely. Did he think that shutting down the brothels would change anything? A whore's a whore, whether in a house or out in the street."

"Just go to the door of a tavern and whistle," Saxby said unexpectedly.

"How are the patients?" Ned asked.

"Both up and walking about," Saxby said. "Both anxious to get back to their ships."

"So Martha's sorted them out?"

"She's been enjoying herself. I think both Coles and Gottlieb have enjoyed their convalescence, too. Special soups, hot poultices, tots of rumbullion – they haven't been looked after like that for years!"

At that moment Martha Judd, a large woman with breasts like sacks of potatoes and a cheery red face, came on deck, took one look at Ned and said: "She's not feeding you right: you look thin."

"It was all the chasing about building the house," Ned said defensively.

"Sir Thomas was chasing about just as much, but he looks as plump as ever."

"I'll tell Aurelia," Ned said. "How are your two men?"

"They were right poorly when they arrived. That Dutchman was worst. But they're both all right now. I have a sovereign remedy for men in that condition, and it soon put them right."

Ned wondered what the "sovereign remedy" was but decided not to ask: it had worked and that was all that mattered.

"Well, we'll get our mates back, then," Thomas commented.

Saxby looked round for the *Argonauta* and *Dolphyn*, spotted them and said: "I'll send 'em off in one of my boats and deliver Lobb and Mitchell on the way back."

He suddenly pointed to a boat which had left the jetty at Plumb Point and was heading for the *Griffin*.

Ned groaned. "It'll be that damned secretary to the governor."

"Your men will send him to the *Peleus*. We'd better say hello to Coles and Gottlieb, and then be getting back to wait for him."

Ned shook hands with the two men and, after being assured that both had fully recovered, asked Coles: "What do you remember of the questioning by the Spanish garrison commander?"

"The Army here," Coles said. "He just kept on asking about the governor disbanding the Army. If it was true."

"What did you say?"

"Well, it seemed important to him to know, so I didn't tell him: I just said I didn't know what the Army did, though I did say there always seemed to be plenty of soldiers in the taverns . . ."

"You didn't say the governor was paying off the soldiers?"

Coles shook his head. "As soon as Gottlieb and I worked out what the Dons wanted to know, we didn't give 'em any answers. Not the right answers, anyway. If they went on what we said, then the Army was still marching up and down during the day, and getting drunk in the taverns at night."

"That was fine," Ned said. "I'm sorry you were beaten so badly."

"We'd have been beaten whatever we said," Coles commented cheerfully. "That garrison commander wouldn't have known what to believe. Just supposing we'd told him the truth – that the governor had disbanded the Army and withdrawn our commissions: the Spaniards would never have believed that!"

Ned thought of the Viceroy in Panama. Was he at this very moment trying to make up his mind about the same thing? Neither disbanding the Army nor withdrawing the commissions of the buccaneers *sounded* likely: they would seem to be rumours that had become distorted in the telling.

Ned shook Coles and Gottlieb by the hand. "I'm sorry it had to be you, but thanks for keeping your mouth shut."

Back on board the *Peleus*, Ned and Thomas found the women sitting side by side on a hammock underneath an awning which had been rigged for them.

Diana waved towards the *Griffin*. "A man has just gone on board – he was rowed out from the jetty. Our men are now telling him he's at the wrong ship if he wants Mr Yorke."

55

"He does: he's the governor's secretary," Thomas said. "He's about as useless as the secretary old Heffer used to have when he was acting as governor. There's something about governor's secretaries . . ."

The secretary arrived on board ten minutes later and minced across the deck to Ned. He gave a stiff bow and introduced himself as William Hamilton, although Ned remembered him from the legislative council meeting.

He was wearing a sabretache and he opened it, removing a sealed letter, which he gave to Ned. "From the governor. Would you be kind enough to give me the answer."

"Wait here," Ned said. "I am going to the cabin. You'd better come with me, Sir Thomas."

"Yes indeed," Thomas said formally. "A letter from the governor . . ."

Ned sat at Thomas's table, broke the seal and unfolded the letter. "Just as I thought," he said disgustedly. "He's calling a meeting of the legislative council for tomorrow morning at half past eight, and will I attend and bring you."

"That doesn't warrant a written answer," Thomas growled. "Tell that clown up on deck that we'll be along."

When Hamilton had left to return to the jetty, Ned said to Thomas: "We'd better decide on what we do, if we can guess what the meeting will be about."

"I can't help thinking it's about handing the island over to the Dons," Thomas said gloomily. "What do we do then?"

"There's not much choice. Aurelia is determined to burn down our house. We take the buccaneers to Tortuga and just raid the Spanish: there'll be no one to say whether or not we should have commissions: the nearest English authority will be at Antigua, and we don't give a damn about them."

"Well, I agree with all that. What other surprises could old Loosely spring on us?"

Ned shrugged his shoulders. "Well, he's disbanded the Army and withdrawn our commissions. He's shut the brothels on his own authority. Not much else left, is there . . .?"

Thomas asked: "What do we do about our hostages?"

"If we hand Sanchez over to Loosely, he'll probably hold a banquet for him – and the bishop, too. There's nothing old

Loosely won't do to get snug with the Dons: he'll never believe anything we say."

"I can just imagine," Thomas said. " 'Well, Sir Harold,' we tell him, 'the Dons are getting ready to invade Jamaica.' 'Oh no, no, no,' says Sir Harold, 'the Spanish are our friends: why, they're so friendly I've been able to pay off the Army and I've told those naughty buccaneers to go away . . .' "

"Or else," Ned said, "Sir Harold will say, 'Let us all be friends – I'm just giving the island back to the Spanish, from whom we wickedly took it, much to the embarrassment of our King, even if he was in exile at the time and the country was being ruled by Sir Thomas Whetstone's impetuous uncle, Oliver Cromwell . . .' "

Thomas ran his hand through his beard, curling the end of it outwards and giving himself a satanic look. "The fact is, Ned, we don't have many friends. If we move to Barbados, or Antigua, or one of the other Windward or Leeward islands, we're a long way from the Main, and thus a long way from our targets. Tortuga is going to be no use with the Dons at Jamaica . . . where will we get stores?"

Ned folded the governor's letter into a ball. "So for the time being we keep the Spanish governor, the bishop and the mayor on board the ships – "

"Yes, we might need them as hostages," Thomas interrupted.

" – but we don't make any secret of it, do you agree?"

"No secret at all," Thomas said. "After all, as far as old Loosely is concerned we are pirates, and holding some Dons as hostages is just what you'd expect pirates to do, isn't it?"

Ned nodded. "Not that we shall be staying here long."

Thomas held up a hand. "Supposing we heard for certain that the Spanish are coming – do we still leave the island to its fate, or do we stay and fight?"

Ned shook his head ruefully. "I'm just muddled," he said. "We leave for Tortuga – for the time being – if Loosely is handing over the island to the Dons. But if he isn't and there is a warning that the Spanish are coming, then I suppose we stay and defend the island. But," he reminded Thomas, "supposing all the Dons intend to do is run a plate convoy to Spain what then?"

"We go after it," Thomas said promptly. "No doubt about that."

Ned nodded contentedly. "What a handful of alternatives," he said. "The trouble is, we don't know whether Sir Harold is our friend or our worst enemy."

"I'm sure Sir Harold isn't very sure, either. Unless of course that frigate brought him news that lets him make up his mind. Certainly he hasn't many friends in the legislative assembly. I hope that chandler, O'Leary, will be at this meeting tomorrow – he's the one that has all the common sense."

 # Chapter
Six

Sir Harold Luce came into the small, airless room, where the members of the legislative council were sitting waiting for him, like a ferret coming out of a rabbit hole without having chased a rabbit. He had a smug look about him that made Ned glance across at Thomas, an eyebrow raised.

"Good morning gentlemen," Luce said, "please be seated."

This was an unnecessary remark since no one had risen, even though Sir Harold had been preceded by his secretary, who had announced him to a council that went on chatting.

Luce took his chair at the head of the table and put down some papers he had been carrying. His tiny eyes flickered round the table and he hunched forward as if about to make a speech. "I expect you wonder why I have called this meeting of the council," he said.

"Well, I don't," O'Leary said flatly. "It's a damned nuisance. I've enough work to do, with the buccaneers just back in port. They all want cordage and things. Wish I wasn't a member of this council," he growled. "All talk and no do, unless it's debating brothels."

"Yes, quite," Sir Harold said uncomfortably, "but I expect most of you have seen that a frigate's arrived from England. It brought me instructions – "

"Well, I'm damned," O'Leary interrupted sarcastically. "I thought she was laden with lace for the ladies and sweetmeats for the children."

"Yes, quite," Sir Harold repeated, unable to deal with O'Leary. "No, well, instructions for me, from the Committee for Foreign Plantations."

"So now you reopen the brothels, eh?" O'Leary inquired.

Luce could not think of an answer and ended up by appearing to ignore him, his sallow face flushing as though he had just been slapped a couple of times.

"When I read the instructions, I knew it was my duty to call the legislative council," he said pompously.

"Bravo," said Thomas. "Can we go home now until the next frigate arrives?"

"Ah, Sir Thomas," Luce said, shaking a finger, "you must not tease the governor, you know!"

It was said lightly and helplessly, but Thomas growled: "We've no one else to tease."

Luce tapped the papers in front of him. "As I was saying, I have instructions from the Committee for Foreign Plantations: important instructions."

Ned saw another opportunity to throw Luce off his stride.

"Tell us, Sir Harold, if they are instructions to you, why are we sitting here? Obviously they don't concern us. They're instructions to you. Secret, too, I've no doubt."

Sir Harold looked like a man whose aces had all been trumped. "Well, no," he said lamely. "I called this council because the instructions concern the future of the island, particularly the men of business."

"Ah, then you'll excuse us," Ned said. "We are not involved with business. At least, only as customers."

"No, please stay, Mr Yorke. This does concern you."

"But you said 'business'," Ned said, as though Sir Harold had just insulted him.

"Please, if you'll just listen," Luce said almost desperately. "If only you'd listen, you'll see how you're affected."

"You haven't said anything yet," Thomas said, his deep voice filling the room. "You keep on saying you have instructions from that damned Committee for Foreign Plantations, and as far as we're concerned we certainly didn't think that frigate was just cruising, calling in for a few casks of rumbullion to take back to England."

"I haven't had a chance," Sir Harold wailed. "I have the instructions here in front of me, and I'm trying to explain."

"These sound the sort of instructions we don't want to hear about," O'Leary said warily. "A frigate brought you the news that anyone not actually convicted of murder can be sent out here as a settler. Do the new instructions say now it's all right for murderers, too?"

"Oh please let me start, gentlemen," Sir Harold pleaded. He took a deep breath and said hurriedly: "The Spanish either have to permit trade or we force it."

There was at least half a minute's dead silence, and then Ned, Thomas, O'Leary and a couple of other men sitting at the table began to roar with laughter, Thomas slapping his hand down on the table as though keeping time.

Luce waited for them to stop laughing and then said lamely: "What's funny about that?"

Ned looked at him incredulously. "Just pause and think, Your Excellency," he said. "Just start at the beginning!"

"The beginning? What do you mean?"

"How is Your Excellency going to ask the Dons to permit a trade?"

"Why, send an envoy in a ship, of course!"

"What envoy in what ship and where to?" Ned asked.

"Well, General Heffer can go. I'll charter a ship."

Ned shook his head. "That will be a problem. There are none to charter."

"But surely I can charter one of your ships?"

Ned shook his head regretfully. "Apart from the fact that you regard them all as pirates, it would be tactless for your envoy to arrive at a Spanish port in a ship owned by a former buccaneer."

"But – well, you'd be sailing under a flag of truce."

Again Ned shook his head. "I don't think any former buccaneer would risk sailing into a Spanish port under a flag of truce. But quite apart from that, surely such a decision – to allow trade – would have to be made in Spain. After all, 'No peace beyond the Line' has been Spanish policy for more than a hundred years. So the governor of whatever port or city your envoy went to would have to apply to the King of Spain and wait for an answer. Six months," Ned said, "that's how long it would take to get an answer – and, anyway, I can tell you the answer now."

"You can?" Sir Harold said incredulously.

"Of course; any of us can. The answer will be 'No'."

"But supposing we force a trade?"

"*Force* a trade?" Ned laughed drily. "With no ships and no Army, you are going to *force* a trade?"

"I shall do the best I can to carry out my instructions," Sir Harold said stiffly.

Thomas muttered: "The best thing you can do is carry those orders to the window and throw them out."

"Come now," the governor said, "I expected more cooperation from the buccaneers."

"There are no buccaneers," Ned said. "You called in their commissions."

"But the buccaneer fleet sailed together the other day and came back yesterday!" Luce protested.

"Oh no," Ned corrected him. "That was not the buccaneer fleet. That was just a collection of ships that had a job to do, and they all sailed together."

"But they were buccaneers," Luce protested.

"Sir Harold," Ned said sternly, "the buccaneers do not exist. You cancelled their commissions. If they take any action against another ship or country, you will – you've already made this quite clear – call them pirates. And none of us," he said innocently, "would want to be called pirates."

"Where were your ships going the other day?" Luce asked suspiciously. "You sailed in a hurry."

"Oh, just fishing," Ned said airily. "We had plenty of bait."

"Did you catch any fish?" asked an unbelieving Luce. "I didn't hear of a lot of fish being on sale in the market."

"We caught some big ones," Ned said. "Kept them ourselves."

"Very well," Luce said, "let's get back to our business. You've heard the instructions of the Committee for Foreign Plantations, and I must say I expected a more helpful attitude on the part of the council."

Kinnock, Port Royal's pawnbroker, tugged his red nose and then twisted his tobacco-stained moustaches. "Helpful attitude?"

he repeated scornfully. "The council roared with laughter. What more do you expect?"

"Well, here I am without a ship to use to send an envoy," Luce said, his voice suddenly querulous.

"You get rid of our ships and your soldiers, and then start talking wildly about 'forcing' the Spaniards to do things," O'Leary said contemptuously. "You're doing things in the wrong order. Force the Dons to do what you want – if you can – and *then* disband your army and send away your ships. But if you insist on doing things backwards, don't come whimpering to us!"

"I'm not whimpering," Sir Harold protested. "But you must admit I have a difficult task."

"Difficult task?" O'Leary repeated incredulously. "You have an *impossible* task. Can we now turn to 'other business'?"

"There is no other business," Luce said. "I have decided what we are going to do and I will send a despatch back to the Privy Council with the frigate, which sails tomorrow."

"Use the frigate to carry General Heffer to whatever governor you intend to persuade or force," Ned suggested. "Surely you have the authority to give orders to one of the King's ships."

"I don't think I have," Sir Harold said nervously. "Anyway, sending an envoy in one of the King's ships might be regarded by the Spanish as provocation."

"Well, you *are* in a pickle," Ned said sympathetically. "General Heffer would never make it in a canoe or a fishing boat, and that's all you'll find in Port Royal."

Luce picked up his papers and began to sort through them nervously, and every man in the room except the secretary knew that the governor now realized he was trapped by his own actions: he had cancelled the commissions of the buccaneers, regarding them as pirates; and now, when he needed their cooperation, they were refusing.

What could he tell the Privy Council's Committee for Foreign Plantations? With the frigate sailing tomorrow, he had to write the despatch tonight. But to say what? Thank you, gentlemen, I have received your orders to ask the Spanish to permit a trade, or to force it, but I can't send anyone from Port Royal because I do not have a ship, and anyway I could not force a trade as I have neither ships (my fault) nor soldiers (your fault, since you ordered me to pay off and disband the Army) . . .

The next frigate, Luce decided, would bring out a new governor. Not that a new governor could achieve more than he had done. Or, at least, tried to do.

He gave Ned a despairing look. "Can't I prevail on you to provide a ship?" he asked.

"Your Excellency," Ned said patiently, "although I have explained it all several times, you still do not understand what the buccaneers were. I was their elected leader, yes; but I could not order a particular ship to do this or that. I could only lead and hope they all followed. But now they have no commissions signed by the governor, there are no buccaneers, so I have nothing to lead. I have no influence; I command only my own ship, just as Sir Thomas commands his."

"But won't you take your own ship?" pleaded Luce, grasping at a straw.

Ned shook his head. "My ship is too well known in all the Spanish ports. If she came in waving a dozen flags of truce, the Spanish would still open fire on her, and I couldn't blame them. They would suspect a trick."

Luce sighed. "If General Heffer would take a chance, then I can't see why you won't."

"No one's asked General Heffer," Ned pointed out, "but anyway, it's my decision that counts where my ship is concerned."

Luce shrugged his shoulders and looked round the table, suddenly seeming to have shrunk. "That concludes this council meeting, gentlemen," he said.

Chapter
Seven

Thomas went back to the *Griffin* with Ned to collect Diana, who had called on Aurelia. With the sun almost vertically overhead but a slight breeze blowing across the anchorage to keep them cool, they sat on the afterdeck under a small and heavily patched awning.

Aurelia handed them all lemonade, explaining that the last of the limes had already been squeezed and only lemons were left.

"Well, now," she said to Ned and Thomas, "tell us what happened at the council meeting."

Ned sighed and then sipped his drink. "I'm not sure whether it was funny or tragic. Sir Harold has received instructions from the Committee for Foreign Plantations to get the Spanish to permit trade –"

"Well, that's good!" Aurelia exclaimed.

"– or force a trade if they refuse."

"Oh dear," Diana said. "With what does he 'force' it?"

"Exactly," Thomas said. "He hasn't even a ship in which to send an envoy to talk to the Dons; he has neither ships nor soldiers to force anyone to do anything."

"But you will let him use a ship," Aurelia said matter-of-factly.

"We won't," Ned contradicted grimly. "Not after he cancelled all our commissions. Don't forget we're pirates, darling; he doesn't know that you returned from a piratical raid when you arrived back yesterday. He'd have a fit."

"Then you ought to have told him all about it," Aurelia said.

"Obviously the attitude of the Spaniards at Riohacha – in that whole province – has a great bearing on how Sir Harold acts."

Ned made an impatient gesture. "Very well, we know from what we found at Riohacha that the Spanish will never agree to allow trade, and we don't have a chance of forcing it – how the devil does one *force* somebody to trade? Very well, that being so, what's it matter that Sir Harold hasn't a ship to carry an envoy anywhere?"

"All you know," Aurelia said, "is that in the province of Colombia there can be no trade. But what about Cuba? Or Hispaniola? Puerto Rico? Their governors might allow it."

"It's not what governors or viceroys will allow," Ned said stubbornly. "It's what Spain says. The Privy Council should have started negotiations in London, through the Spanish ambassador. This is a matter between London and Spain, between kings, not between a fool like Loosely and the governor of somewhere like Puerto Rico."

"I still think you should help Sir Harold," Aurelia said.

"So do I," Diana said. "Old Loosely's a fool, yes, but he has instructions from the Privy Council and it's up to him to try to carry them out. Don't forget it takes six months to get fresh instructions from London – three months for London to hear from Loosely that he can't do something, and three months for fresh instructions to arrive."

"And you may get a new governor," Aurelia said. "If Loosely annoys the Privy Council, they will replace him. Who knows who you might get then? This man is a disaster, but at least you now have him listening to you. A new one might make even bigger mistakes and ignore you."

Ned sniffed crossly. "So what do you want me to do? Take Heffer on a cruise, asking the Dons politely if we can sell them a few yards of cloth and a gross of needles?"

"Very well, supposing the Dons say no," Aurelia pointed out, "what have you lost? They say no and you come home. It isn't as though you've lost a battle."

Ned looked over at Thomas, who grimaced. "The only place we've never raided is Santo Domingo, so I suppose we could take old Heffer there for him to talk to its governor. It's not far to go, and we wouldn't have to wait long for the governor's answer, apart from the fact we won't be recognized."

Aurelia brushed back her long, ash-blonde hair with her hand, a gesture which could mean either that she was impatient or too hot. "You're just being stubborn Ned. You're refusing to help the governor when you should be thinking about the island. Just suppose the Spaniards *did* allow a trade – what an enormous difference it would make to Jamaica. Why, the merchants could do ten times the trade. Five times as many ships would call here . . ."

Ned said: "I can't forget the buccaneers will end up starving because of that damned governor . . . The Dons regard them as pirates anyway, commissions or not, but commissions meant they could still use Jamaica as a base, and get their prizes properly condemned in the court."

"The buccaneers won't end up starving," Aurelia said crisply. "They're all rich men. They could all buy enough land to start estates, just as we have done."

"Yes, they could," Ned agreed, "and they'd be just as unhappy: never knowing whether to be on their estate or on board their ship."

Aurelia nodded: that was an argument she had to concede because, when she was up at the house she dreamed of being at sea in the *Griffin,* and when she was on board the *Griffin* she thought only of the cool house, the gardens now being cultivated, the flowering shrubs and trees growing, spurting higher with every shower of rain. She liked walking along the corridors; she enjoyed being in the kitchen discussing dinner with the cook. Yet there was the thrill of the *Griffin* pounding to windward, sheets of spray hurling back across the deck, the thrill of new landfalls, the thrill of wondering what new adventure was waiting over the horizon.

But the governor was over there, in that house, which had been taken over as the governor's residence, and he was a defeated man; defeated because he could not carry out his orders, and defeated because the former buccaneers would not help him.

"Although you refused him a ship," Aurelia said, "you don't know that one of the ships wouldn't agree to be chartered."

"That's true," Ned said. "Who do you think would want to go – Secco, and be garrotted as a traitor? Or Gottlieb or Coles, with the bruises still showing?"

"No, I think you should take Heffer in the *Griffin.*"

67

A startled Ned stared at her. "Take the *Griffin?*" he repeated incredulously.

"Yes. Make the governor agree that you will take Heffer to Santo Domingo and nowhere else, so there's no risk. Obviously you can't go to Santiago or anywhere on the Main because they know you, but Santo Domingo is safe enough: safe in the sense the Spanish would accept a flag of truce."

Ned looked questioningly at Thomas. "It's the sun," he said lamely. "It's deranged her."

Thomas twiddled the end of his beard and then slowly shook his head. "No, she may be right, if you look at it from the point of view of what it might mean for Jamaica."

"So you think I should take Heffer to Santo Domingo?"

Thomas nodded slowly. "I'll come with you in the *Peleus*. We'll toss up to see who carries Heffer – the man is a bore, and he'll probably be devilishly seasick the whole way."

"All right," Ned said reluctantly, "but let's be quite clear: all we do is carry Heffer there: once in Santo Domingo all the negotiating is up to him. Translators, transport, and all the rest of it – Heffer and whoever he takes with him deal with that."

"Yes," Thomas agreed. "After all, Heffer is the deputy governor. He'll have his instructions from old Loosely, so we are simply shipmasters."

Ned said to Aurelia: "Being fair to governors will get us all into trouble one of these days."

Ned and Thomas went on shore the next morning to see Sir Harold, who met them in the council room looking uncomfortable and nervous, troubled by the heat and puzzled over their request to see him.

"A humid sort of day," he began nervously. "I haven't got used to the heat yet, and Lady Loosely suffers cruelly."

"It's always harder on the women," Ned said, thinking ironically of the deeply tanned bodies of Aurelia and Diana, who gloried in the sun. He could picture Lady Loosely – withered, sharp-eyed and with a querulous voice. He pictured her sitting tight-lipped in a rattan chair, anxious to catch every cool draught of wind coming through the window, calling for more lemonade, and never leaving the house without the enormous parasol which was already becoming famous in Port Royal.

"Now what can I do for you gentlemen?" Sir Harold asked ingratiatingly.

"Nothing," Ned said firmly. "We were going to offer to do something for you."

"Oh, indeed?" Sir Harold said warily. "What had you in mind?"

"There's just one question first," Ned said. "Where do you want to start negotiating with the Spaniards?"

"Bless my soul," Luce said in surprise, "I hadn't thought about it. Where do you suggest? Santiago de Cuba? Santa Marta? Or even Cartagena?"

"What about Santo Domingo?" Thomas asked.

"That would do as well as anywhere," Luce said. "It seems an excellent place. But why do you ask?"

"We might be able to find you a ship to carry General Heffer," Ned said cautiously. "All negotiations with the Dons would be up to Heffer. We just provide a ship."

"But that would be capital, just capital," Luce exclaimed, hardly able to believe his luck. The frigate was sailing in five or six hours: there would just be time to write another despatch for the Privy Council and get it out to the frigate captain, and substitute it for the one he had written last night, reporting his inability . . . Luce shuddered: it would be a close-run thing.

"When would this ship be ready to sail?" Luce inquired.

"Three or four days – just as soon as she has taken on water and provisions. How many would there be in General Heffer's party?"

"Well, the General, and I expect he would like a couple of ADCs, and a secretary, and a translator. I assume there's someone available who speaks fluent Spanish. We don't want to rely on the Spanish trying to find someone who speaks English."

"There are many who speak Spanish in Port Royal: that's no problem."

"Then I will tell General Heffer," Luce said. "What ship have you chosen?"

"Perhaps my own ship, the *Griffin*," Ned said. "Sir Thomas will be coming in the *Peleus*. General Heffer will go in one or the other."

"What sort of fee had you in mind for this – ah, this charter?"

Ned shrugged his shoulders. "We've never done anything like this before, so there'll be no charge."

"Tell me," Luce said unexpectedly, "do you think General Heffer will make a good envoy?"

"You haven't much choice," Ned said bluntly. "Anyway, there's no negotiating to be done. Just a straight question to be asked. I should have thought Heffer could do that."

"I had in mind . . ." Luce hesitated, as if trying to pluck up courage. "I was thinking that if you are prepared to take your ship to Santo Domingo, perhaps you would do the negotiating."

"No," Ned said firmly. "I'll take whoever you choose as your envoy, but he does the negotiating."

And takes the blame, Ned thought. It would be very useful for Luce to have someone else to blame for failure – someone who was not himself or his deputy. If the former leader of the buccaneers came back to report failure (whoever came back would be coming empty-handed, there was not much doubt about that) then Luce would very soon twist the story round to imply that the failure was deliberate; intended to make sure there was no friendship with the Spanish. Ned felt quite pleased with himself: he was (thanks to watching Heffer over the past years) now able to think like a politician or a diplomat: at last he could understand duplicity, and although he was never going to practise it himself, it enabled him to spot it in others. Luce breathed duplicity as other men breathed fresh air.

"I hope that you'll act as an adviser, then," Luce said lamely. "Not many people on this island have your experience in dealing with the Spanish."

Ned shook his head. "I've dealt with the Spaniards from behind a sword or musket; I've never negotiated with them."

He almost laughed at the thought of telling Luce about the recent voyage to Riohacha: supposing Luce was told that the governor of the province of Colombia, the bishop of Colombia, and the mayor of Riohacha were all within a mile of this room, on board the *Argonauta*, *Dolphyn* and Secco's ship?

Ned stood up. "Very well, Your Excellency; tell General Heffer and his staff to be ready to embark in three days' time."

A week later Ned stood with Aurelia and Lobb, the mate, on the afterdeck of the *Griffin* as she surged to windward with Hispaniola passing close on the larboard hand and the *Peleus* a mile astern in her wake.

The sun was bright; the clouds were startlingly white; the sky was so blue that many men knew they would make a fortune if they could create just the dye to produce a cloth of that colour. Blue, Ned thought; curious that it is the hardest colour to create. Good red dye came from the cochineal insects that lived on the cactus; but blue – that always created problems. Hard to dye cloth blue – and even harder to stop the blue fading in the sun.

How was old Heffer? Was he capsized in his hammock, white and perspiring, wishing he could die instead of being seasick? Or was he on his feet, chattering away and boring Thomas and Diana, straining poor Thomas's self-control?

He was thankful that when they had flipped a piece of eight Thomas had lost the toss, so that he had to take Heffer and his party. Fortunately there had been no question of splitting Heffer's party into two – Ned felt almost guilty at having pointed out that they all had to stay together in case something happened to the *Griffin* and Heffer would find himself without his translator and ADCs, or other members of his mission.

Thomas had not been shrewd enough to counter that with the argument that the *Peleus* might be lost or delayed. Still, that was Thomas's fault, and now he was paying the price: five days of Heffer's company.

"Why are you grinning to yourself?" Aurelia asked.

"I was thinking of Thomas having to listen to Heffer!"

"Spare a thought for Diana. She has to listen to Heffer, then all his staff agreeing with every word he says, and then Thomas trying to be polite. And no doubt all the time she's afraid Thomas will explode."

"Thomas has more patience than me, so be thankful I won the toss and you don't have Heffer under your feet."

Lobb coughed and Ned looked up. "That chart of Santo Domingo – do you think it is accurate?" the mate asked.

"It's old, that's all I'm sure of, and we must allow for more coral growing on those reefs. What do they reckon – a couple of feet a year, for some of the corals? Best to trust your eyes and hope the sun is behind us when we go in."

71

The chart had come from Secco – a man who disapproved of the whole idea of the mission to Santo Domingo, though he had found the chart among his papers.

Ned said: "The flags of truce – you have them sewn up ready?"

"One for each yardarm, almost as big as the mainsail; and four for the two boats, bow and stern."

"I wonder if the Dons will take any notice of them," Ned mused.

"Why shouldn't they?" Aurelia asked. "If a Spanish ship arrived off Port Royal and came in with a flag of truce, or sent in a boat, we wouldn't shoot at it."

"Darling," Ned said affectionately, "sometimes you are so reasonable I could hit you."

"The fact is," Aurelia said patiently, "that you want old Heffer to fail. You'd hate it if he came back from the Spaniards and said everyone was free to trade."

"That's not true," Ned protested. "There's nothing I'd like better than taking Heffer back with that news. It's just that you know as well as I do that there's isn't a hope of the Spanish agreeing to trade, so we're just wasting our time."

"Is that the last headland before Santo Domingo?" Aurelia asked.

"Yes – one tack out, and the next tack back should bring us in."

"The flag of truce is going to work," Aurelia said. "I can feel it in my bones."

"If it doesn't you'll hear roundshot whistling around your ears," Ned said feelingly. "They say Santo Domingo is heavily defended."

Ned gestured to Lobb, who gave orders to put the ship on the other tack, so that the *Griffin* started out on the first leg of a zigzag which would take her away from the land and then, with the second tack, bring her back.

"You can see Santo Domingo's at the mouth of a big river," Lobb said, pointing over to the larboard side. "Look, the water is getting muddy already."

"Probably there's been a lot of rain up in the mountains," Ned said. "I hope we'll be able to see the bar."

"Once I can see the banks of the river, I'll find the bar," Lobb said. "Anchoring is going to be our problem. There's a lot of

72

mud, and the river flows out strongly – there's a note on Secco's chart that says it's a couple of knots, and thrice that in the rainy season."

After about fifteen minutes Ned looked back to the north-east. "That must be the city coming clear of the headland," he said. "There's the savannah and the amphitheatre of hills that Secco said was to the west of it."

"I wonder if the Spanish are watching us yet?" Aurelia said.

"I doubt it – it must be pretty quiet along here. The last time they had any excitement was when Cromwell sent Penn and Venables."

"Tell me about them; I forget," Aurelia said.

"Well, General Penn and Admiral Venables were sent out by Cromwell and they were supposed to capture Santo Domingo. They came from the east and for reasons no one ever explained properly, let themselves get swept past, landing twenty or thirty miles down the coast. They then tried to march back to attack Santo Domingo, but yellow fever, ague and the Spanish beat them, so the survivors went back to the ships and they went on to Jamaica, which they captured instead."

"Well, they achieved something!"

"The last person to capture Jamaica was a privateer, so taking the island with a force of thousands of men wasn't so remarkable."

"Anyway, you think the Spanish have forgotten that by now?"

"It's one of the few victories they've ever had," Ned said caustically, "so perhaps they still celebrate it."

Two hours later the *Griffin,* a large flag of truce streaming out at each yardarm, and closely followed by the *Peleus,* bore away and began to reach into the anchorage of Santo Domingo, both Lobb and Ned anxiously eyeing the muddy waters of the River Ozama.

The harbour was easier than Ned had expected: the entrance to the river was wide and where it narrowed the city was built on each bank. The chart showed deep water close in to the land, and Ned took the *Griffin* in to the east bank and anchored to leeward of a square fort. The *Peleus* followed and anchored to windward of her.

Through the perspective glass Ned had already seen that the fort had a small jetty, with a couple of boats secured to it. Further inshore there was a beach with twenty or more open fishing boats pulled up out of the water, each boat painted in bright colours, in contrast to the drab grey of the stone fort and the sun-bleached wood of a small shed from which were strung nets.

With the anchor down and holding in six fathoms of water, Ned said to Aurelia, who was examining the coast curiously, "Now we have to wait."

"Will the Spanish come out to us, or do we send in a boat?"

"Well, I deliberately anchored close to the fort. If the Spanish don't come out soon, I imagine Thomas will send in a boat."

They waited an hour and nothing happened. Through the glass Ned could see Spaniards on the parapet of the fort, obviously curious about the two ships that had come in with white flags and anchored.

"The trouble is that no Spaniard likes to do anything without orders," Ned commented. "I expect they've sent a man on horseback to report to the governor and ask what to do."

Then Ned saw that Thomas's patience had obviously given out: both boats were hoisted out in the *Peleus,* and oars were lashed vertically at bow and stern so that the white flags secured to them were unmistakable.

The first boat left the *Peleus,* rowing for the fort, with four men sitting in it, among the rowers. "The translator, the two ADCs and his secretary," Ned commented after inspecting it with the glass. "Heffer isn't taking any chances."

It took ten minutes for the boat to get alongside the jetty, and by the time it arrived twenty or more Spanish soldiers were there to meet it, armed with muskets and pikes, and wearing helmets and breastplates. They stood back while the four men clambered out of the boat, and Ned watched them obviously listening while the translator made some sort of explanation. Then they escorted the four men into the fort.

"Looks friendly enough so far," Ned commented to Aurelia. "I suspect they arrived before the horseman has returned from the governor. Now they'll have to send a second horseman!"

He continued watching the fort and discovered a track leading from the fort and going towards the city. Fifteen minutes after the four men had gone into the fort he saw a man on horseback galloping up to the fort from the direction of the city.

74

"Ah, here comes the messenger from the governor. Either the fort will open fire on us and toss the bodies of our four men over the parapet, or our fellows will come out and fetch Heffer."

An anxious Ned had to wait half an hour before soldiers streamed out of the fort and marched down the jetty again. Ned could just make out Heffer's four men, who climbed back into the waiting boat and were soon being rowed back to the *Peleus*.

"You worry too much," Aurelia said. "I knew everything would be all right."

Ned grunted doubtfully. "You felt it in your bones, no doubt. You have the most sensitive bones in the whole Caribbee!"

The boat reached the *Peleus,* and ten minutes later the second boat left her and started pulling towards the *Griffin*. Ned recognized Thomas's bulky shape sitting in the stern.

He climbed on board the *Griffin* and greeted Ned. "I thought I'd come over and tell you what's happening. The translator's just come back and Heffer is to go to the fort at noon tomorrow to be taken into the city to see the governor. At least, I presume it'll be the governor. He's to take a translator with him, but the Spaniards say only two people."

"What does Heffer think about it?"

Thomas laughed and waved towards the land. "Heffer hates being at sea so much he can't wait to get his feet on dry land again, even if the land is Spanish!"

"What sort of voyage did you have with him?"

"Oh, he was sick for a couple of days, but once he'd recovered we couldn't stop him talking. He had to tell his fellows all about meeting us when we first arrived in Jamaica, then the raid on Santiago to get him guns . . . the man's a bore; even Diana was losing patience at the tenth telling of every story."

"The poor man," Aurelia said unexpectedly. "This is the first time for years that he's been able to talk freely and he's been thoroughly enjoying himself."

"He'll soon be able to talk his head off with the Spanish," Ned said sourly. "Let's hope the governor of Santo Domingo has as much patience as Diana. Maybe he's like Heffer – has no one to talk to."

"By the way," Thomas said. "I thought you anchored rather close to the fort – if they get cross with us, we're well within range of their guns."

"I did that deliberately," Ned said. "The fact that we're right under their guns should persuade the Spanish that we're not planning any tricks. Anyway, the fort is to windward so if we cut our anchor cables we'll soon drift out of range."

Thomas nodded. "Yes, and there's quite a strong current, too. I reckon a couple of knots, so even if it was windless we'd soon be clear."

"Has old Heffer with all his gossip indicated he's prepared what he's going to say to the Dons?" Ned asked.

"No. That meeting is about the only thing he's not talked about – at length! But presumably Luce told him what to say."

"I wouldn't rely on that," Ned said. "My impression was that Luce is very anxious to carry out his instructions but hasn't much idea how to do it."

"All that energy," Thomas said. "It's a pity we can't point him in the right direction; he might then turn into a good governor."

"The brothels are going to be the death of him," Ned said soberly. "I think we'll get back to find the first of the buccaneers have already left for Tortuga, taking some ladies with them. Luce will find his kingdom comprises a row of closed down bordellos."

"Although I'm sure that his wife was behind the bordellos affair," Thomas said, "one mustn't forget that Luce was a Puritan. He probably still prays to my sainted uncle; closing down some brothels in memory of Oliver Cromwell is just the sort of thing one would expect from a reformed Roundhead."

Thomas pulled out his watch. "I told Diana I wouldn't stay long, because she wanted to come over. By the way, one of Heffer's party was so seasick all the way that we had to throw a bucket of water over him after we anchored."

"Who was that?" Ned asked.

"One of his ADCs, a Captain Irons. He looked like a rusty ghost -- hasn't eaten for five days . . ."

Next morning Ned watched as Heffer and the translator left the *Peleus* and were rowed to the fort. Later he saw four horsemen, two of whom were Spaniards, the sun glinting on their helmets, and one was certainly Heffer, who sat a horse better than Ned expected.

Watching the horsemen ride along the track stirring up a cloud of dust, Ned found himself looking at the fishing boats drawn up on the beach. They had pronounced sheers and high bows, and as he looked through the perspective glass he noticed that the nets were not still draped over the small shed he had seen the previous day. Not only that, he realized, there were many more boats now drawn up on the beach: they extended well beyond the shed. Another dozen? More, probably. Yet, apart from two or three men walking along the beach, there was no sign of fishermen. When did the extra boats arrive? They must have come during the night because he had not seen any fishing boats being rowed about during daylight.

Aurelia called to him to say the midday meal was ready, and after they had eaten, an hour after Heffer had gone to the fort, Ned decided he would go over to see Thomas. Aurelia said she was bored with staying on board alone and decided to go over to see Diana.

They found Thomas in a cheerful mood. "You don't know what a relief it is not to have Heffer's sheeplike face around the ship," he said. "He's a good sort but he tries my patience. Those teeth – I've never met a man before whose teeth bothered me so much. They're so big and yellow, and they protrude so far they keep drying. He says three words and then has to lick his teeth, otherwise his lips stick to them."

"Thomas!" Diana said sternly. "Stop being so nasty about the poor man. It's not his fault."

"No," Thomas agreed, with mock penitence, "it's not his fault that Nature made him look like a sheep and gave him a laugh like the braying of an ass. But it's not my fault, either!"

They talked of the view from the ship, the distant mountains fading into a faint blueness. "That's a well built fort," Thomas commented. "Nicely placed to cover the harbour entrance."

Ned picked up Thomas's perspective glass, adjusted it and looked at the fort. "Eight guns covering us this side, and eight more facing southwards." His eye caught the row of fishing boats. "Did you hear or see any fishing boats come in during the night?"

"No. Why do you ask?"

"There are now nearly twice as many drawn up on that beach as there were yesterday. I counted them yesterday out of curiosity.

77

Twenty-one. Now there are – " he began counting, "now there are thirty-seven."

"Well, most fishermen go out at night," Thomas said. "Perhaps they gave us a wide berth as we were strange ships."

"Perhaps," Ned said, "but it's odd that none of them fish during the day: they do at every other island . . ."

Thomas pulled out his watch. "Old Heffer's been gone a couple of hours. I wonder if he's seeing the governor or some functionary."

"You'll look silly if your 'old sheep' comes back having signed an agreement allowing trade," Diana said.

"I'd quite happily look silly," Thomas said evenly, "but let's wait and see . . ."

They had to wait another hour before they saw four horsemen approach the fort and then a party of soldiers escorting the two men down the jetty to the waiting boat.

When Heffer came back on board the *Peleus* he greeted the four people waiting for him with a stiff bow and said, by way of explanation, "I have to go back again tomorrow, at the same time."

"Did you see the governor?" Ned asked.

Heffer nodded. "Yes, and I gave him the message from Sir Harold. It was translated for him."

"How did he take it?"

Heffer thought for a moment. "Hard to tell. He's a fat little man whose face gives nothing away. He said he would consider the proposal and give me an answer tomorrow."

"He didn't say anything about having to ask Spain?"

"No. I asked him first about permitting a trade, and then told him we would otherwise force it."

"What did he do then – laugh?" Ned inquired.

"No, he gave no reaction. He's got to consider it, obviously, and he may have a legislative council to consult."

"Perhaps," Ned said doubtfully. "Anyway, no more news until noon tomorrow?"

"No," Heffer agreed. "I'm surprised he agreed to give an answer so quickly."

"So am I," Ned said. "That's why I don't think he has a legislative council to consult; it'd take a day or two to call them together."

"We'll see," Heffer said philosophically, and went below to change into cooler clothes.

Ned resumed his examination of the fishing boats and counted them again. "How far to that beach?" he asked Thomas.

"Something over half a mile. I'd say it's almost exactly half a mile to the fort."

"That's what I reckon," Ned said. "I wish I knew why those fishermen don't fish during the day."

"It's too hot for them," Thomas said. "Why row round in the heat of the sun when fishing at night is so much cooler."

'True, but where have all those extra boats come from?"

"I'm damned if I know," Thomas said, beginning to lose interest. "Perhaps they were already out when we arrived, and came in after dark."

"Why weren't the first lot of boats we saw out fishing as well, then?" Ned asked, still looking through the perspective glass.

"My dear Ned, I don't know and I must say my interest in Spanish fishing boats is very slight."

Ned put down the perspective glass. "Mine, too," he agreed. "Are we going to be offered something to drink? It's so hot."

79

Chapter Eight

Back on board the *Griffin,* Ned took out his perspective glass and inspected the fishing boats yet again. Yes, there were thirty-seven of them, and not a man on the beach now. They were lucky fishermen if not one out of thirty-seven boats needed some sort of repair. Then he realized that the oars were in the boats, lying along the thwarts.

The fishermen of Santo Domingo must be an honest crowd, he decided; everywhere else he had seen fishermen, they carried their oars home with them. In Santo Domingo they so trusted each other that they left oars on board . . .

He found he wished he had been present at the meeting between Heffer and the governor. Heffer was not the shrewdest of men, and unless the governor stood on his head, Heffer was unlikely to notice anything unusual.

Heffer had been taken to see the governor. Good, no problem there. He had then handed over a letter from Luce, which was written in English and which had to be translated. Did the translator write down the translation? Then the governor had told Heffer to come back at the same time tomorrow. Not nine o'clock in the morning, when it was still comparatively cool, and not at four in the afternoon, after siesta; no, at the same time, at noon, when the sun was right overhead and it was the hottest part of the day.

Ned put the perspective glass back in its drawer. There was something strange somewhere, but he could not put his finger on it.

"You look very unhappy," Aurelia said from the hammock on which she was sitting in the shade of the awning. "Worried, rather."

"Puzzled rather than worried," he said, and told Aurelia about the extra fishing boats and the oars left in them.

"Were there oars in the boats that were there yesterday?" she asked.

"I didn't notice," he admitted.

"*Chéri,* it seems to be an odd thing to be puzzling about," she said, laughing to take any edge off the remark.

"That's only half of it," Ned said, and went on to relate his curiosity about the time fixed for Heffer's meeting next day.

Aurelia thought about it. "You know, it could just be thoughtlessness. The governor is comfortable in his house and doesn't think about Heffer having to ride in from the fort in the heat of the sun. Why, don't you remember that you made old Loosely stop having legislative council meetings in the evenings because of the mosquitoes? I remember you were so cross because you found out that he didn't know the mosquitoes were worse at dawn and dusk."

Ned laughed at the memory. "Yes, it was small enough satisfaction that he thought mosquitoes just stung all day! They were certainly stinging him!"

"So you see," Aurelia said, "the governor here might be another Loosely, either not knowing or not thinking. Or even not caring."

"It could be," Ned said doubtfully, "but I don't like ignoring these nagging thoughts."

"You're just bored because you've nothing to do," Aurelia said. "You want to be giving orders and making things happen!"

Ned grimaced. "I think you're right," he finally admitted. "All this sitting and standing around doesn't suit me."

"It's your own fault," Aurelia said unsympathetically. "You told Sir Harold that you'd simply bring Heffer here, but wouldn't have anything to do with the negotiations. Now you're paying the price by being bored."

"It's not boredom that makes me puzzled about the boats and the time of Heffer's meeting tomorrow," Ned protested.

He sat down on a hammock opposite Aurelia. "You realize that we might find things changed when we get back to Port Royal?"

"In what way?"

"Well, now the brothels have been closed, some of the buccaneers will leave for Tortuga."

"But you and Thomas don't intend going there."

"No," he agreed, "because we have the houses built. But if all the buccaneers go, and the Spaniards in Cartagena do try an invasion . . ."

"*Chéri,* short of telling Sir Harold about our raid on Riohacha and making him reopen the brothels, what can we do about it?"

"Nothing, I suppose. But if the Dons do come and the buccaneers have left, we'll just have to get on board the *Griffin* and make a bolt for it. Go to Tortuga, or up to the Windward or Leeward Islands. Go back to Barbados, perhaps."

She shuddered at the mention of Barbados. "When the Roundheads drove us out, and we left that wretch of a husband of mine behind, I was so excited at being free that I swore I'd never go to Barbados again. Then when my husband was killed and I was truly free, I knew nothing could ever make me go. So if we have to escape, then not to Barbados! Antigua is too arid and I don't like the people there. But there are other islands, and we'll find somewhere."

Ned laughed and said: "Don't get too sad: the Spanish haven't come yet! They might only be planning a plate convoy."

"That would be exciting. We'd be pirates, according to Sir Harold, but it would be exciting to try and capture some plate ships. Would they be big galleons?"

"They might be, but I expect they'd be smaller. Galleons draw too much water to get into Riohacha and Santa Marta, yet the governor of Colombia was worrying about foreign ships seeing any of the vessels from Spain. Galleons would stay in Cartagena and sail from there to Havana and then out into the Atlantic."

"Would our ships stand a chance against frigates?"

"Not in size, but we'd outnumber them – perhaps as much as three to one."

Aurelia pulled her hair back clear of her forehead. "Which do you think it'll be – a plate convoy or an attempt to invade Jamaica?"

Ned pulled a face. "If the Spanish captured Jamaica and the buccaneers were dispersed, the Dons wouldn't have to worry about plate convoys: they could sail them at their leisure. They might meet trouble the other side of the Atlantic with French privateers, but they'd be content to risk that."

Soon Ned and Aurelia sat quietly and dozed in their hammocks. There was just enough breeze to flap the awning and keep them cool. When Ned woke from time to time – usually when a pelican splashed into the water nearby, or a couple of terns quarrelled with each other, squawking as they flew in tight circles – he found himself picturing the untidy row of boats pulled up on the beach. He was now almost certain that if the oars had been in the boats yesterday, he would have noticed them: oars in boats drawn up on the beach was something most seamen would notice. No oars yesterday; oars in every boat today. Why?

It was late afternoon, just at the time the mosquitoes would be coming out on shore, and he was thankful that the ship was anchored far enough out to be clear of them. Then he connected the boats and the noon meeting arranged for Heffer. He sat up suddenly, startling Aurelia, picked up the perspective glass and looked again at the boats. Still not a man in sight; no one repairing a broken thole pin or painting over a scratch on the elaborate designs on the sides. It was all too quiet.

He made up his mind: he would risk making a fool of himself. "I'm just going over to see Thomas: I shan't be ten minutes."

He shouted for Lobb to find some men to row him over to the *Peleus*. Once on board he walked Thomas aft, where they could not be overheard, and told him his suspicions.

Thomas listened to him carefully, and then shrugged his shoulders. "I'm sure it's simply a coincidence," Thomas said. "I'll do as you suggest, but I think you are too suspicious of the Dons."

"No one's ever grown old from trusting them," Ned said quietly.

"That's true. Anyway, I'll do what you suggest. Shall we tell old Heffer?"

"No, don't bother him: he'll only start braying, and you and Diana can do without that."

Thomas took his perspective glass out of its locker and looked at the boats. "You're right about the oars, and there's certainly not a soul on the beach. But the oars may just be a custom of the port: maybe people here don't steal as much as they do in Jamaica."

"Perhaps," Ned agreed, "but I'm pretty certain the oars weren't in the boats yesterday."

"You're not absolutely sure, though. Don't forget you were more interested in what the garrison was doing, and old Heffer galloping off on the horse."

"That's true," Ned agreed, and added: "Pity there's no moon tonight. Still, unless the wind gets up it'll be quiet enough."

Ned and Aurelia stood side by side in the darkness, looking over the *Griffin*'s bulwarks towards the shore. Round them men sat or sprawled on the deck, muskets or pistols beside them, and cutlasses at their waists. The *Griffin*'s guns were loaded and run out. Several pieces of slowmatch glowed in the darkness, hidden below the level of the bulwark, ready to be twisted round a linstock and used to fire the guns.

"It must be midnight by now," Aurelia said.

Ned had been listening to the sounds from the shore. There was the occasional sharp cry of a night heron; in the distance the pack of yapping dogs so familiar in any Caribbee town. The occasional subdued splashing of fish trying to elude an enemy made Ned listen carefully, and then relax when he was sure. The water gurgled alongside the *Griffin* as she swung gently to her anchor.

Lobb padded along the deck and stopped beside Ned. "Just the usual noises so far," he muttered.

"Yes, birds, dogs and fishes."

"I'm not sure whether or not we should be disappointed!" Lobb admitted.

"Plenty of the night left," Ned said.

"Yes, and the men aren't losing much sleep. Most of them are asleep already. They seem to find the deck as soft as their hammocks."

After another quarter of an hour Ned said to Aurelia: "Why don't you go down and have a sleep? You'll soon wake if anything happens."

Aurelia stifled a yawn. "I think I will. How about you?"

"I'm not sleepy," Ned said, thinking about the *Peleus*, where Thomas and Diana were probably having a similar conversation, and the ship's deck would be crowded with sleepy men, the slowmatches burning with the same slightly acrid smell.

After Aurelia had gone below, Ned found himself staring up at the stars as they shone between the clouds. The Southern Cross was bright on the horizon, almost vertical. Orion's Belt above, the Pole Star low on the northern horizon . . . So different from England, where the Southern Cross was never seen and the Pole Star was much higher. Yet his memory of things in England was now becoming appreciably fainter: he could remember the places where he spent his childhood, but Canterbury, London, Oxford, places he had only visited before coming out to the Caribbee – they were blurred in his mind.

He could remember the family home in Ilex, on the edge of Romney Marsh, in Kent; he could remember the estate at Godmersham, at the foothills of the North Downs, he could – was that a creak? Of oars against thole pins?

He stared out towards the beach, trying to penetrate the darkness. If only there was a moon!

He did not hear the noise again, and none of the five lookouts reported anything, so he must have imagined it. That night heron squawking – its cry was getting fainter, so it must be flying inland. Did something alarm it?

He found himself thinking about the house they had just built in Jamaica. Did Aurelia really like it, now it was finished? Well, she had said that when she was in the house she wished she was in the *Griffin,* and when she was in the *Griffin* she longed for the house, and since that was how he felt these days perhaps they would never find peace. What they were looking for was always round the corner.

Why was this? When he lived on the estate in Barbados, he had been content – no, he hadn't, he contradicted himself. Always he had dreamed about Aurelia, living on the neighbouring estate with that brute of a husband. Then, when he had to escape from the estate because the Roundheads were coming, he had persuaded Aurelia to come with him, and since then they had lived this curious gipsy life in the *Griffin* – until, just a few months ago, they had built the house. So now, with the brutal husband long since dead, the house built, and Aurelia agreeing they could be married as soon as there was a proper church built at Port Royal, everything had at last seemed at peace. Until the new governor arrived.

It might have been possible for the Privy Council to have made a worse choice than Sir Harold Luce, but Ned doubted it. Apart from being a prejudiced fool who would never admit he did not know anything, the man was obviously a convert: he had spent his life under Cromwell as a fervent Roundhead, and by means Ned could not fathom, he had managed to get into favour once the King was restored. Anyway, Luce's reputation, and a hint of his activities, had already reached the Spanish, so there was no certainty that Jamaica would remain a safe place where people could live happily.

Another squawking heron, and the dogs suddenly stopped barking – Ned turned his head, his ears straining for more sounds. The dogs started barking again, and a couple of fish jumped near the ship.

Time was passing: the Southern Cross had turned slightly and Orion's Belt had crossed a little more of the sky. Had he been thinking of this and that for half an hour? More, perhaps.

He froze: that was definitely oars creaking against thole pins, and as he leaned on the bulwarks, turning his head and trying to hear the noise again and be sure of its direction, one of the lookouts padded up and whispered: "Boats – we can hear the oars!"

"Rouse the men," Ned said. "Make sure they don't make a noise. Could you distinguish the direction?"

"No, just that it was towards the fort."

The man hurried off, his bare feet flapping against the planking. He bent over one sleeping man after another and shook them awake.

Ned found Lobb standing beside him. "Looks as though they're coming," the mate said.

"Yes, to us or the *Peleus,* or both?"

"Both, I reckon," Lobb said. "If they're using all those boats on the beach, there's a couple of score out there."

Ned listened, turning his head slowly. Yes, there were many boats and the men in them were rowing slowly, careful that the blades of their oars did not splash. The oars were probably wrapped with cloth for quietness but nothing could stop the thole pins creaking in their sockets.

Yes, boats seemed to be spread out from there, on the bow,

86

round to the quarter. There was just enough light from the stars for the men in the boats to be able to make out the bulk of the *Griffin*, but the boats were small and low against the dark background of the sea, impossible to see from the ship.

His eye caught sight of a tiny red glow to one side: one of his seamen was twisting a slowmatch round a linstock. The guns were already depressed as much as possible: they could not be fired at anything nearer than sixty yards, and he was sure the boats were already closer than that.

There would be about twenty boats heading for the *Griffin*, each with up to twenty men in them. Twenty? Well, including oarsmen. The creaking was getting nearer, and he thought he could now hear the rippling of the water at the stem of the boats.

"Ready with muskets and pistols," he hissed to the men behind and beside him. No shooting from the *Peleus*, so the Dons had not reached Thomas yet.

Then in the starlight he saw a black crescent approaching across the surface of the sea like a wind shadow: a score of boats perhaps thirty yards away, all converging on the *Griffin*, moving stealthily.

He could now see the blades of the oars shining in the starlight as they were lifted clear of the water. Twenty-five yards . . . twenty. Don't let them get too close, he told himself.

"Ready . . ." he called to his men. "Aim . . . fire!"

The crackling of muskets and pistols ran along the side of the ship, the flashes from the muzzles blinding him. Then more gunshots as men fired second muskets and pistols. In a brief lull he heard cries from the boats: some of the shots had found targets.

But the boats were still coming: fifteen yards, ten, and now they were curving round to come alongside: in a few moments it would be sword and pike, the *Griffin*'s deck suddenly turned into a slaughterhouse.

"Don't forget the roundshot," he yelled and at that moment heard the bow of one of the Spanish boats thud into the *Griffin*'s side below him. He snatched a roundshot from the rack, looked over the side down into a boat crowded with men, and hurled the roundshot on to them, hoping to stove in a plank.

Now the men were scrambling about in the boat, looking for hand and footholds on the *Griffin*'s hull and he straddled the bulwark, bending down to slash at the first Spaniard to start scrambling up.

The man fell back into the boat, upsetting a couple of men who were poised to jump upwards. Ned heard the clash of sword against steel beside him and saw in the faint light that Lobb had just cut at a man below him and his sword had glanced off a helmet.

This was work for a pike, Ned realized, and dropped his cutlass to snatch up a pike from the rack along the inside of the bulwarks. He twisted the seven-foot ash stave and leaned over the side to stab down at the nearest Spaniard. None of them had managed to get out of the boat; several were still tangled up with the body of the man he had first struck.

Again he stabbed with the pike and felt the point glance off a breastplate. So at least some of the Spaniards were wearing armour: well, if they fell in the water they would never be able to swim with that weight bearing them down.

He stabbed again and felt the point of the pike going into flesh: this time he had aimed below the breastplate. He wrenched the pike up again and plunged it down to the right. As a man screamed he twisted the point, pulled back and stabbed downwards yet again.

At the same time he realized there were now men fighting on the *Griffin*'s decks: further aft some Spaniards must have overwhelmed his men and got on board. What to do now – leave this boatload and fight those already on board, or prevent these men from getting on board? If left they would be on board in moments, so he continued stabbing down with the pike.

But a couple of men in the stern of the boat managed to get a grip on the *Griffin*'s chainplates and were almost up to the bulwarks. Ned moved aft a few feet – conscious that Lobb was not there – and stabbed at the first man who curled back like a shaving of wood and fell into the sea. In the meantime the second man swung upwards on to the bulwark and was poised there for a moment before jumping down on to the deck when Ned lunged again with the pike. It stuck into the man's thigh and with a cry he toppled over the side, taking the pike with him.

Ned, now defenceless, moved back to find his cutlass, kicked it and hurriedly snatched it up. He glanced aft for a moment and was startled by how many Spaniards were now on board the ship.

This single combat, hand-to-hand fighting was losing them the battle: they were being overwhelmed by sheer numbers. He glanced over the side and saw the *Griffin*'s hull was now crowded with boats, like puppies nuzzling a mother: the Spaniards had obviously all boarded on one side, instead of attacking the *Griffin* on both sides.

Ned suddenly made up his mind and, running aft, bellowed: "Griffins – to me! Griffins, Griffins!"

Most of the men heard him above the shouting and clashing of metal and ran aft to join him.

He could see the Spaniards left standing on the foredeck, no doubt puzzled to find that their enemy had apparently fled aft. That would give him a valuable minute or two to form his men up.

"Now, Griffins, keep together, and let's drive these devils over the side!"

He waved his sword: "Right, follow me into the middle of 'em!"

With that he ran down the deck shouting at the top of his voice. The Spaniards seemed to hesitate, more because of the shouting than because they could see anything, and as he ran Ned saw flashes from the *Peleus*: Thomas was fighting off his crowd of Spaniards.

Ned ran at the nearest Spaniard, saw a flash of metal and parried a slashing sword. Before the man had time to recover Ned flicked the tip of his cutlass upwards and caught the man's throat so that he gave a sickening gurgle before collapsing on to the deck.

There was a repeated shout of "Come on, Griffins!" from over on his right and Ned recognized Lobb's voice. Slowly the Griffins drove back the Spaniards, who seemed bewildered. Ned guessed it was all the shouting and yelling in English so he joined in, screaming, "Griffins!", a shout taken up by the rest of the men.

Then it went black.

Ned started recovering as men's feet trampled over him. His head was spinning and seemed remote from his body; he could not get his eyes to focus on the stars overhead. He felt his head: no blood. He must have been hit with the flat of a sword or the haft of a pike.

He scrambled to his knees, found he could balance himself and that his sword was still beside him. He stood up, paused a few moments getting his balance, and then joined in the whirling mass of men.

It sounded as though every other man was bellowing "Griffin!", and although still dazed it seemed to Ned that there were fewer Spaniards. He saw several men scrambling over the bulwarks and it took a few moments to realize they were leaving the ship, not boarding.

Ned no longer went for a single man; instead he hacked and thrust wherever he saw a man he could be sure was a Spaniard, and out of the corner of his eye he saw more men scrambling over the bulwarks.

He stumbled over a body and from the bang on his shin realized that the man had been wearing a helmet. The sharp pain seemed to bring him out of the partial daze and he began shouting "Griffin!" again, one of a couple of dozen or more voices which made up a strident chorus.

The Spaniards were shouting at each other but Ned could not make out what they were saying. The words were urgent, and suddenly the crowd of men round him was halved, those remaining still shouting "Griffin!" The Spaniards were climbing over the bulwarks and jumping down into their boats.

Then Ned recognized Lobb's shape in the darkness, and rather sheepishly stopped shouting. "I reckon that's the end of that," Lobb said.

Ned realized that the boats had to get back to the shore and would pass through the arcs of fire of the big guns. "Get those linstocks ready," he told Lobb. "We'll give 'em a farewell broadside as they go!"

With that he ran to the bulwarks, looked down at the boats, most of which had left the ship's side, and tried to follow their progress in the darkness. Just then, the clouds seemed thinner and the starlight brighter, and he could see that several boats were already twenty yards away, the men in them rowing hurriedly for the shore.

He heard Lobb shouting orders for linstocks and watched as the last of the boats left the *Griffin*. They were less bunched up than when they came but as Ned knelt down and sighted along a gun, he saw that a broadside from the *Griffin*'s guns, which were loaded with roundshot, should sink several of the boats and drown any men wearing armour.

He could see the boats while standing up, but they were still too near to be hit by the guns: the barrels could not be depressed enough, and if fired too soon the shot would pass over them.

"The men are ready with linstocks," Lobb was panting: he had obviously been running along the deck warning the men to get to the guns.

Ned stood back and looked both ways. Yes, he could just make out the guns' crews standing ready, the linstocks dull red glow-worms waiting to be pressed down on the priming powder.

Ned knelt beside the gun captain whose gun he had been using for sighting. "Can you see 'em?"

"Another ten yards," the man said, "when it'll be right into the middle of 'em!"

"Call out the distance," Ned said, shouting to the rest of the gunners, "Stand by!"

"Eight yards . . . five yards . . . couple of yards . . . – now!" the gun captain said excitedly.

"Fire!" Ned bellowed.

The *Griffin*'s side seemed to erupt flame and noise: the flash of the muzzles blinded Ned, and as he stood with his eyes shut he heard the thunder of the broadside echo across the city and bounce back from the mountains, the noise combining with the rumble of the recoiling guns.

Then he heard the screaming: from a quarter of the way to the fort stricken men were screaming: some of the screams were of pain, others ended in ominous gurgles as drowning men sank.

Already the gunners were sponging out the guns and beginning to reload.

Ned managed to spot Lobb and said: "Hurry, I want ten men in each of our boats, with oarsmen: let's get over to the *Peleus*: they might not have driven out the Dons."

The boats were hauled round, men tumbled into them, and they started rowing for the *Peleus*. "Hope Sir Thomas doesn't mistake us for more Dons," Lobb said.

"I'm glad you thought of that," Ned said, calling to the men to start shouting "Griffin" when he gave the word.

As they approached the *Peleus,* Ned saw boats leaving the side of the ship. "The Dons are bolting!" Ned said jubilantly. "They won't need any help from us, but we'll go alongside, just in case."

As the Spanish boats left the larboard side, so the *Griffin*'s two boats came alongside to starboard and Thomas, attracted by the shouting, appeared briefly to yell: "That you, Ned? We're all right. Can't stop, we're going to give 'em a broadside once they get far enough away!"

"We'll go back to the *Griffin*," Ned told Lobb. "They don't need us here, and we have some bodies to dispose of."

Aurelia was standing at the bulwark when Ned's boat came alongside. "We're getting the wounded below," she said. "But the bodies – fourteen Spaniards and six of our own dead . . ."

Ned climbed on board. "That broadside into the boats – it was a massacre."

"I was so frightened," Aurelia said. "That's the first time we've ever had to fight on board our own ship."

She hurried forward with the lantern, calling anxiously to some men to be careful how they carried one of the wounded below.

Once he had made sure that all the wounded had been treated – Aurelia acted as the ship's surgeon, saying that she wished she had Mrs Judd to help her – Ned decided to go over to the *Peleus*. The six wounded Spaniards were in no condition to cause any trouble, but Ned left a seaman to watch them.

The *Peleus* was in the same condition as the *Griffin*, but Thomas reported fewer casualties: eight Spaniards and five of the *Peleus* men dead, and nine on each side wounded.

"God knows how many we killed when we loosed that broadside into the boats," Thomas said. "We heard them screaming as they drowned. I reckon we must have hit a third of them."

Ned could just distinguish Heffer standing with Thomas and said: "Well, General, how do you like fighting on board a ship?"

"Can't see what you're doing," the general complained. "Still, we got rid of them!"

"The general fought like a fiend," Thomas said. "He was using a pike like an agitated grandmother poking a fire. Jab, twist and jab again! Makes a change from sitting in that little office of yours, doesn't it!"

"What happens now?" Heffer asked.

"We get ready to sail so that we're clear of here by dawn," Ned said, "out of range of those guns in the fort."

"But . . . but I am seeing the governor at noon!"

"Oh yes, I forgot," Ned said, thinking Heffer was making a weak joke.

"Yes, so I shall need a boat to take me over to the jetty."

Suddenly appalled, Ned said: "You mean you are serious?"

"Of course. I told you, the governor said to come back at the same time."

"But what do you think this boat attack was all about?"

"Just fishermen seeing what they could loot, I suppose."

"Fishermen in helmets and breastplates? They were Spanish soldiers. That, my dear Heffer, was the governor's reply to you."

"My dear Yorke . . ." Heffer protested.

"Don't be absurd," Ned snapped. "He told you to come back at noon because he wanted both ships to stay at anchor tonight. He arranged for the extra fishing boats to be dragged up on the beach, ready. And he sent all those soldiers to capture the ships. If we hadn't been ready for 'em, they'd have succeeded."

Thomas sniffed. "We've got you to thank for that, Ned: it was your sharp eyes that spotted the extra fishing boats, and you guessed why the governor was shilly-shallying about until noon. If we hadn't been waiting with pistols and muskets loaded, they'd have been all over us; we'd have had our throats cut in our hammocks."

Heffer said nothing, and Thomas asked in his booming voice: "Well, General, what have you got to say now?"

"Well, they certainly were wearing armour," Heffer admitted lamely, "so I suppose they must have been soldiers. But why did the governor . . ."

"Why didn't he say 'No trade!' to your face yesterday? It's not the Spanish way. And in any case you'd said you'd try to force a trade. That probably alarmed the governor – he misunderstood you: he thought you meant you'd try to force a trade with these two ships, so he reckoned that if he captured them he'd be safe!"

Heffer sighed. "I don't know what Sir Harold Luce is going to say about all this."

"There's not much he can say," Ned said shortly. "We told him the Dons would never agree to trading, so your report shouldn't be a mortal shock to him."

He turned to Thomas: "Are you ready to sail?"

"We've just got to hoist in both boats."

"Then we might as well get under way. As soon as they can distinguish us, the guns of the fort will be opening fire. I'd like to stay until daylight to see how many of those fishing boats reached the beach, but the sooner we get General Heffer and his party back to Port Royal, the sooner Sir Harold will hear the glad tidings."

 # Chapter
Nine

Heffer insisted that Ned and Thomas came with him when he went on shore in Port Royal to report to Sir Harold Luce. "I want you to tell him about the Spanish attack," he said. "You can explain it better than I."

"You mean, he won't believe you?" Thomas growled.

"It's not that," Heffer said uncomfortably. "He makes me so nervous that I can't explain things clearly. He doesn't seem to have that effect on you."

"No," Thomas agreed, "he doesn't make me nervous. He usually puts me into a vile temper."

"Well, try and be patient this time," Heffer said, licking his teeth. "The man has a very difficult job."

Thomas sniffed again. "He has a difficult job and he makes the worst of it."

As Ned and Thomas followed Heffer along the jetty after landing from their boats, Ned said: "None of our ships has left yet."

"No," said Thomas. "They've got the women from the brothels on board, I'll be bound. I never thought of that as a way round old Loosely closing the brothels. Keeps the ships here, and the men don't have to row ashore!"

"It won't work for long, though," Ned said. "The men will start quarrelling over the women."

"If the women have any sense, they'll change ships every week or so. A new batch of customers!"

"You're right," Ned agreed. "If they aren't doing that, I'll suggest it to the captains."

Luce was waiting in his office when Heffer, Ned and Thomas walked in, and while they were still standing demanded anxiously: "Well, what happened?"

"I can never think on my feet," Thomas growled. "Do you mind if we use these chairs?"

"Please do, please do," Luce said hastily. "Make yourselves comfortable."

When the three men sat down, Luce asked Heffer sharply: "Well, do we have a trade?"

Heffer shook his head. "The Spanish governor didn't say, but – "

"Didn't say?" repeated Luce, his voice rising excitedly. "What do you mean, 'Didn't say'? You went all that way and failed to ask him?"

"No, well, he didn't say in words, but it was what he did."

"You gave him my letter?"

"Yes, and we wrote the translation on the back."

"And you told him that if he wouldn't agree to a trade we'd force it? You told him that?"

By now Luce's voice was high-pitched, almost a yell.

"I did exactly as you instructed," Heffer said defensively, "but the Spaniard didn't give a definite answer."

"But – but you should have forced him to make one," Luce said, almost stuttering with rage.

Heffer held up both hands helplessly, as though about to pray.

"Don't just sit there!" Luce screamed. "The damned man must have given *some* indication!"

Ned judged that by now Luce had frightened Heffer into something approaching incoherence and said: "Yes, he gave some indication. In fact he gave an answer. He tried to kill us all and capture both ships."

Luce sat bolt upright in this chair as though someone had just stuck a pin in him. He thought a moment and then said crossly: "You must have provoked him." He turned to Heffer: "What did you say, you oaf? I knew I should never have given you such a delicate task."

Before Heffer could attempt to answer, Ned said: "Instead of

96

just nibbling away like this, why don't you let one of us explain what happened?"

"Very well, very well," Luce said impatiently. "You tell me."

Making it clear that he had not gone to see the governor and was relying on what Heffer had told him, Ned described the ships arriving in Santo Domingo flying flags of truce, and how Heffer had been taken off to see the governor. Ned mentioned casually that a large number of fishing boats had been drawn up on the beach, but Luce was not interested, motioning for him to hurry.

"So Heffer came back to say that the governor wanted to see him again next day at the same time, noon."

"Of course, of course," Luce said. "He wanted time to think."

"To me," Ned said, "it seemed that if he needed time it would be six months to send a despatch to Spain, not twenty-four hours. Anyway, during the night a score or more fishing boats were brought round to the beach – "

"For God's sake don't go on about those fishing boats," Luce exploded. "This was a diplomatic mission, not a fishing expedition."

Ned stared at Luce without speaking, and the governor calmed down. "Well, all right, I suppose you have a reason for mentioning the fishing boats."

"I have," Ned said dryly, and told Luce about the night attack on the *Griffin* and *Peleus* by the Spanish soldiers.

"They weren't soldiers!" Luce snorted. "They were just fishermen wanting to rob you!"

"We threw over the side twenty-two dead Spanish soldiers, most of them wearing helmets and breastplates. Spanish fishermen," Ned added sarcastically, "do not wear armour. We also lost eleven of our own men, dead. Thirty-three dead men does not sound like fishermen on the loose."

Luce was perspiring heavily now, and his small eyes flickered from one to the other of the three men.

"I still say you must have provoked the governor," Luce said to Heffer. "It was your manner, or something you said."

Ned tapped the tabletop. "Your Excellency," he said, "I told you before we sailed that the Spaniards would never agree to trade. I have more experience than you of the way they do business. I don't find it at all surprising that they attacked our

97

ships. But," he said, with a sudden angry outburst, "I find it surprising that *you* attack us. We carried out your instructions to the letter. It was because I did not trust the Spaniards that we kept watch that night and saved our throats from being cut and your own envoy taken or killed. Listening to you talking, I can only say that your ignorance of the Spanish mind frightens me: I'm appalled that you should be the governor of this island."

By now Luce was white-faced; his yellowed moustache and the way his face had shrunk before Ned's anger made him look even more like a ferret, but one that had been out in the rain.

"Don't you dare talk to me like that, you damned pirate," Luce spluttered.

"Pirate?" Ned repeated quietly.

"Yes, *pirate*. While you've been away some of your men have been making piratical attacks on ships off the Caymans."

"None of my ships sailed."

"They must have done. A coasting vessel came in from the Caymans yesterday evening complaining that she had been attacked by pirates as she was going to Grand Cayman for turtle."

"If some of our ships had attacked her," Ned said grimly, "she wouldn't have escaped."

"Your men were responsible," Luce declared. "Four of them. The master of the ship that was attacked is absolutely certain."

"Attacked by four ships?" Ned repeated.

"Yes, four."

"And he escaped from them and came to report it all to you?"

"Yes, he signed a regular protest. I have it here.'

"Did he name the ships?"

"No, of course he didn't: nor did he name the captains – I hardly expected him to go on board and ask them."

"You surprise me," Ned murmured. "Anyway, have you any more questions about the Santo Domingo affair?"

Luce shook his head. "No, though I can hardly say the affair was handled in a judicial manner."

Ned stared at him and the small eyes dropped. "You all did your best, I am sure," he added patronizingly.

"You are too kind," Ned said standing up. "If you'll excuse me I'll go and investigate the piracy which you allege."

As they walked along the jetty on the way back to their boats,

98

Thomas said crossly: "If any ship gets attacked within a couple of hundred miles of here, our people are going to be blamed."

"Of course. I expect old Loosely is waiting for them all to leave, now that he's closed the brothels."

Thomas laughed to himself. "He'd have a fit if he knew how many of his former soldiers have joined us, now the Army is disbanded."

He stopped for a moment and asked: "What do you make of this piracy business?"

Ned shrugged his shoulders. "We'll check with Leclerc or Saxby, but I'm sure none of our ships sailed while we were away at Santo Domingo. That means there are four ships out there acting as pirates and getting us blamed. We'd better find them and teach 'em a lesson. I wonder where they've come from?"

"The nearest of the three Cayman islands is only just over a hundred miles from Cuba," Thomas said. "The biggest is under two hundred miles away."

"And that one is about the same distance from Port Royal," Ned said. "It's impossible for any of our ships to have left after we sailed to Santo Domingo and have got back before us."

"Yes, old Loosely could never have worked that out for himself."

"He doesn't want to believe it," Ned said. "Blaming us is the easy way out."

"What do you intend doing?"

"Let's go and talk to Leclerc first."

The voluble Frenchman was emphatic: no ship at all had sailed from Port Royal while they were away, except the *Convertine* frigate. Three coasting vessels had come in and anchored, and of course the fishing boats had come and gone as usual.

Leclerc had then asked Ned about the hostages. "Are they being well guarded on board the *Dolphyn* and *Argonauta,* and Secco's ship?"

"I presume so," Ned said. "I can't see any of Gottlieb's or Coles's men being slack – not after what they went through at Riohacha."

After leaving Leclerc, Ned and Thomas went over to the *Phoenix,* where they were met by Saxby and Mrs Judd.

"I hope you've come to tell us we're getting under way again,"

Mrs Judd declared. "I can't do with this man," she pointed an accusing finger at Saxby. "He just fidgeted the whole time you were away. 'I wonder how Mr Yorke is . . . I wonder what Sir Thomas is doing . . . They ought to be back by now.' I tell you, it was like having a small boy on my hands."

Mrs Judd never spoke in a normal manner; she usually declaimed. She was used to getting her own way where Saxby and the crew of the *Phoenix* were concerned, and she usually forgot to adjust her voice and manner when talking to anyone else.

"Well, Martha, a short voyage out to the Caymans."

"The Caymans? What, are we going after turtle?"

The question was relevant because the three islands were famous for their turtles and very little else: there were no safe anchorages at any of the three islands. All of them, but particularly the largest, Grand Cayman, were infamous for the great swarms of mosquitoes that came out at dawn and dusk, and against which the smoke of tobacco leaves seemed powerless.

"Not turtles," Ned said, "but there are some pirates round there, apparently."

"Oh, pirates," Martha said, and apparently lost interest in the subject. "We'll have time to catch a few turtles?"

Ned grinned as Saxby looked apologetic. "Yes, Martha, we'll probably have time for that. It depends on what pirates we find."

The three ships sailed from Port Royal before nightfall, the *Griffin* leading, followed by the *Peleus* and the *Phoenix*. A brisk east wind scattered white crests across the sea; very soon after dusk a new moon showed up almost shyly on the western horizon, the whole of its orb faintly visible.

Aurelia was cheerful and as they finished their supper commented to Ned: "So thanks to Sir Harold we are at sea again!"

"Thanks to four ships acting as pirates," Ned corrected her.

"Pouf, pirates! Last week *we* were pirates when we went to Riohacha. It's an easy word to use."

Ned agreed, but added: "When Jamaica's ships are attacked, though, we have to do something about it."

"Oh, yes, of course, but I rather like being called a 'corsair': it is a nice word. Even better than buccaneer."

"I think I'd sooner be a buccaneer," Ned said. "There's

something rather comforting about having a sheet of paper signed by the governor. I miss not having a commission in my drawer."

The ship was pitching as the following wind filled her sails and sent her surging ahead of the waves, and the mainyard creaked and squeaked. The big mainsail occasionally lost the wind and filled again with a bang which shook the ship.

"When do we reach the Caymans?" Aurelia asked.

"They're very scattered. The biggest is Grand Cayman, but Little Cayman and Cayman Brac are seventy-five miles or so away to the north-east of it."

"So you may have trouble finding your 'corsairs'?"

"Yes, unless they are anchored at one or other of the islands."

"Where was our ship attacked?"

"Off Grand Cayman."

"What was she doing there?"

"Going in for turtles, I think. No other reason for visiting the Caymans. Just a few people live there – fisherfolk and turtlers."

"What would corsairs go there for?"

"They can get fresh water from a natural cistern at Gun Bluff, on Grand Cayman. Fresh water is hard to find on the other two islands. Turtles – the Dons like to get them for their shells."

"Apart from fresh water, there doesn't seem much to attract corsairs there!"

"If they're desperate, they might seize a few local turtle boats. Or capture something like the one that got away and started all this fuss."

"These corsairs must be buffoons if they let a coasting vessel escape them," Aurelia said. "If it was going to the Caymans for turtles, it can't be very big."

"That's what puzzles me. Firstly, why pirates bother with such a ship, and secondly, having bothered, failed to capture it."

Chapter Ten

For all the next day the big black frigate birds dived and curved over the three ships, swooping on swarms of flying fish that suddenly appeared, skimmed the tops of the waves for a few hundred yards and then vanished into the water with as little fuss as they made when they took off.

Aurelia stood on deck with Ned, looking aft at the *Griffin*'s wake. "Although they never attack anything but fish, I think those frigate birds look evil. Much worse than sea eagles."

"That's because they're black and so big. But what flyers! They have more grace than any other sea bird."

"Look at them diving after those flying fish!" Aurelia exclaimed.

"Yes, they must have phenomenal eyesight. And they can turn so fast."

At noon Ned took a sight and worked out the ship's latitude and sighed contentedly: the *Griffin* was exactly in the latitude of Grand Cayman, and from his estimate of the distance they had run since leaving Jamaica they should just sight the island at dusk. So they would have to lie-to for the night: none of the coasts of Grand Cayman were clear of reefs, which seemed to stretch across every bay, like coral nets to catch the unwary seaman.

Ned looked again at the chart of Grand Cayman. It did not give much detail, but the first part they would sight, at the eastern end of the island, would be the cliffs at Gorling Bluff. There were trees drawn round the Bluff, and whoever drew the chart had sketched in a reef surrounding the whole eastern end of the island like a barrier. There were three breaks in the barrier, one of which went through to Gun Bluff, and its natural cistern of spring water.

The biggest village was at the other end of the island, and had about the only sheltered anchorage – sheltered, that is, from the prevailing east wind: it was open to the northers of the winter. So, Ned considered, the four pirates would be at Gun Bluff watering, or at the other end of the island at anchor, or they would have quit the island altogether, in which case the chances of them being at Little Cayman or Cayman Brac were slight: they were tiny islands, uninhabited except for turtles and goats, and wild birds. Unless someone had been marooned there, or a ship wrecked . . .

How long would it take four ships to get fresh water from the cistern? A couple of days, he estimated. So they would no longer be at Gun Bluff. He rolled up the chart: this was a hopeless business; the ships could be anywhere.

For hour after hour the *Griffin,* followed by the other two ships, plunged westwards into the sun, which gradually drew lower and lower in the sky. Finally, at six o'clock when Ned was searching the horizon just below the sunset, he grunted and said to Aurelia: "There we are – the island is dead ahead."

"How far?"

"Ten or fifteen miles: just a smudge on the horizon."

"So we'll get there just as the moon appears."

"Yes, and as the moon gets up we heave-to for the night."

At dusk, the *Griffin* was about eight miles from the eastern end of the island and Ned turned her into the wind and dropped the sails. There was no point in heaving-to, he decided; easier to furl the sails and, with the sea not vicious, lie a'hull until daylight. The rolling would be uncomfortable, but they had pitched all the way from Jamaica, and the change of motion was not unpleasant.

It seemed everything in the ship creaked. The deck beams creaked, and in turn the deck planking creaked, and the cupboards and lockers creaked in sympathy. The great thick mast groaned aloft but creaked where it came through the deck. The rattle of blocks hitting the mast aloft was echoed by the mast and Ned cursed it.

The noises did not seem to bother Aurelia, but Ned had never been able to stand repetitive noises unless they were regular. The constant hiss of the ship running before the wind and surging forward over a wave did not bother him; but the occasional clatter of a block or the irregular banging of an unfastened door always roused him.

He had stood on deck and watched first the *Peleus* and then the *Phoenix* round up, drop their sails and lie a'hull. The dusk was reducing everything to a uniform greyness; it was the time of day he hated because quite innocent clouds turned dark and menacing; the seas seemed to grow bigger; it was easy, he admitted to himself, to imagine a storm was coming, or even a hurricane, although experience insisted that there was no swell, which was always the outrider of bad weather. No, it was just dusk; he hated it, and that was that.

Mind you, dawn could be just as bad: cold and hungry and sleepy, one could see dawn approach when the waves started taking shape: instead of a black mass surrounding the ship, one could begin to distinguish crests, and they soon became grey and menacing, and the clouds when they made an appearance were nearly always hard grey and menacing. Proper daylight took an age, and in the meantime the ship, as it became possible to see her, was not friendly: the line of bulwarks, seams of the deck planking, coamings – all seemed harsh and remote. But there was no colour: dawn was varying shades of grey.

For good measure, the devil take landfalls made at dusk: the chart noted that there were currents off this end of the island, and he had been careful to have the three ships lying in a position where if the wind freshened from the east during the night, it would not carry them on to the reef.

All this because of old Loosely, Ned thought to himself. If the damned man had not called him a pirate, he would still be in Port Royal harbour, comfortably at anchor . . .

All through the night, Lobb, Ned and the boatswain took it in turn to stand a watch, keeping an eye on the end of the island and the other two ships. There was a current but the wind died down, so the ships hardly changed their position.

At dawn next day it was possible to see the whole coast, and Ned could be fairly certain which was the gap in the reef that led to Gun Bluff. There was no ship anchored there; as he searched along the coast with his perspective glass he could not even see an open boat belonging to a fisherman or turtler. The waves thundered monotonously on the reef. "If they break with this sea, imagine what they do when it's rough," he commented to Lobb.

"Think of a hurricane," Lobb said lugubriously.

Ned shuddered. "I don't want to think of anywhere in a hurricane. Port Royal, maybe. Or English Harbour, in Antigua. Maybe the anchorage in Grenada . . ."

Lobb tugged at his beard. "Glad they don't have hurricanes in Kent," he said in his broad Kentish accent.

Ned grunted. "All that rain, though, and the cold. I think I'd prefer one brisk hurricane to a winter of Kentish drizzle and chills."

"Me, too," Lobb agreed. "Kent seems a long way from here . . ."

Once it was completely daylight, Ned told Lobb to get the mainsail hoisted and the ship sailing along the south coast of the island to the village at the western end. He then went below for a wash.

Without waking Aurelia he poured some water into a basin and found some soapberries. He sliced a few into the basin and then rubbed his hands with them, to make suds, and then he washed his face. It was remarkable how a wash put new life into a man, though it was a pity that no one got any fresh soapberries: these were beginning to dry and were reluctant to lather.

And, he thought sourly, here is the second son of Henry Sydney Broughton Yorke, the sixth earl of Ilex, cursing soapberry . . . At least his brother George, who had succeeded to the title, had no such problems – or, to be exact, had no such problem when he woke up about four hours ago. Where would George be, he wondered: at the northern estate, between Godmersham and Molash? No, that was never George's favourite; he would be at the southern, over at Saltwood, surrounding the castle. Or perhaps even at Ilex itself, the small Sussex estate house. Why the devil should he be thinking of George at this moment? Oh yes, he could trace the train of thought – he was annoyed that he had not sent a letter to George in the *Convertine,* telling him what a hopeless duffer was Luce. By now George should be getting into a position of influence – though it was doubtful that the seventh earl of Ilex would ever be in a position to influence the choice of the governor of Jamaica. It was more important, perhaps, that George kept his ears open for any hint that the King was thinking of honouring his agreement with Spain about the future of Jamaica . . .

He wiped his face vigorously, combed his hair, and was thankful that the ship had way on: it was easier to stand in the cabin when she was pitching than when she was rolling.

By the time he went back on deck the *Griffin* was still pitching her way along the south coast of the island, closely followed by the *Peleus* and the *Phoenix*. He could just see the headland ahead marking the south-western corner of the island, and round which they would turn to stretch up the west coast to the island's largest – indeed only – village, apart from a few tiny settlements.

Fifteen minutes later Aurelia joined him, her face freshly washed, hair combed and wearing a yellow-coloured jerkin. Ned nodded to Lobb. "If you want to go below and get some sleep . . ."

Lobb shook his head. "No, I want to see what's waiting for us round the corner. If anything, I think the birds have flown."

Ned agreed with him. "It's nearly a week since they attacked that ship. They'll have watered and gone on to look elsewhere."

"Where's 'elsewhere'?" Aurelia asked.

"If they expect to find some ships to capture, the Jamaica coast. If they stay at the western end they haven't much to fear."

"Sir Harold will have a fit!" Aurelia commented.

"Well, he can't expect the former buccaneers to go out and chase them. He's going to find out just how helpless he is without ships."

"Without you and your ships, *chéri.*"

"Yes, there'll be no more Santo Domingos; that was a mistake; I think it was one of those generous impulses on my part that will eventually prove costly."

"At least you have Heffer on your side."

"Heffer has as much influence on old Loosely as a puff of wind. Loosely listens to no one. He's too stupid to realize how little he knows."

Ned was bored with talking about Luce, and he looked back at the other two ships. "They look a fine sight," he said. "I can almost see Diana sitting on the bowsprit, instead of the ship having a figurehead."

Aurelia laughed. "What about Martha Judd for the *Phoenix*? What a sight that would be!"

"The sight would strike terror into the hearts of any Dons!"

Ned watched the coast and said to Lobb: "We can turn close under the headland. There's the usual reef but you'll see the sea breaking on it."

A few minutes later the yard was braced up as the *Griffin* turned to head northward, and as the ship swung Ned was ready with the perspective glass.

"By God, they're there!" he exclaimed. "Four of them, anchored off the village. Quick, Lobb, get those guns loaded. Have the men prepare muskets and pistols, as well; we may have to board 'em."

The four ships, almost certainly Spanish (since they were not from Jamaica), were not large: Ned estimated that each was half the size of the *Griffin*. Each would have a crew of thirty to forty men, and perhaps four guns. They were, he thought, just the right size for the job they had apparently set themselves: capturing small coasters and raiding small towns.

As Lobb gave orders to prepare the guns, Ned had men trimming the sails – the pirates were not expecting him, and the quicker he was alongside them the less time they had to get ready.

With the wind now broad on the beam, the *Griffin* sliced through the water, spray flinging up in sheets over the weather bow and the water trickling back along the deck in snaking lines.

The *Griffin*'s seamen were hurriedly ramming powder and shot into the muzzles of the guns, and other men were going round with their arms full of muskets and pistols, powder horns and bags of bullets. Ned pictured the same happening on board the *Peleus* and *Phoenix*; there would be the same level of excitement in all three ships.

With the sails trimmed he took up the perspective glass again. There was a row of black shapes on the beach that puzzled him, and after a few moments he was able to distinguish what they were: boats from the four ships.

He blinked as he counted them. The last few blurred and he started counting again. Six, seven, eight . . . Two boats to each ship: he realized that all the boats were up on the beach. He swung the glass to the ships. No, none had boats riding astern.

Then he could make out curious domed shapes beside the boats and, many hundred yards along the beach, some men, who seemed to be dragging some of the same curiously shaped objects.

Turtles! The crews of the four pirate ships – they were definitely Spanish from their sheers – were all on shore catching turtles: several of the turtles were turned over, lying upside-down and helpless beside the boats; the men were dragging more along the beach up to the boats, leaving tracks in the sand.

Two miles – the ships were no more than a couple of miles away, and the *Griffin* was making six knots, probably more. Ned estimated the distance of the men from their boats and their boats from the ships. It would be a close-run affair, but in any case the men would be returning to ships with guns unloaded and, most likely, muskets, pistols and cutlasses still stowed in arms chests.

As soon as Lobb rejoined him, Ned explained to him and Aurelia. "The biggest ship happens to be the nearest, so we'll tackle her. It's a race – can we get alongside before the crew get their boats launched and row back to their ships?"

"Burn or capture?" Lobb asked laconically.

"Capture to start with. If they're sound ships we'll take 'em back to Jamaica. We'll offer them cheap to Sir Harold, to start his own navy!"

Ned gave more orders for trimming sails: a few inches in on the jib and flying jib sheets seemed to bring an increase in speed; an easing of sheets and braces, letting the mainsail fill a little better, was a distinct help. Looking astern, Ned was sure they were gaining on both the *Peleus* and the *Phoenix,* but he knew excitement might be affecting his judgement.

He examined the beach again with the perspective glass and was surprised to see that only now were the Spaniards running along the beach towards the boats – they must have been slow to spot the three ships rounding the headland. Most of them still had a hundred yards to go to reach the boats; then they had to drag them into the water and row to the ships. And with any luck several of the boats would already be laden with live turtles, lying on their backs in the bottom but watching with those beady black eyes, ready to make a vicious snap at any foot or hand within range.

The *Griffin* was flying along now: spray spurted up to darken the lower part of the headsails; the yard creaked as it gave shape to the mainsail. Men were busy ramming home powder, shot and wads, and now Lobb was giving orders to half a dozen men who were coiling up ropes, to which grapnels had been secured. Sails trimmed, guns loaded, small arms issued, grapnels ready to be hurled on board the Spaniard . . . Ned ran through the list in his mind. There was nothing else: everything depended on how quickly those men could get back to their ships.

Turtles as allies: Ned chuckled to himself as he pictured agitated Spaniards hoisting up snapping turtles and tossing them over the side. Not tossing: each of those turtles would weigh at least a hundredweight, and they would be slippery: if the boat was afloat, then the sudden shifting of weight would make it roll, and the men would slip as they heaved . . .

He looked astern at the *Peleus*. Yes, there was no doubt that the *Griffin* had gained on her, and he could imagine Thomas cursing as his people trimmed sheets and tried to get a little more speed out of the ship. Judging from the way the *Peleus*'s forefoot was butting up the spray, the *Griffin* should look a fine sight – unless you happened to be one of the Spanish pirates, who must be wondering where the three ships had come from, and who they were. Had they heard that the buccaneers no longer went to sea?

How many men had the Spaniards left in each of the ships? Judging from the number on the beach capturing turtles, not many. It would make sense, anchored in what seemed a place utterly remote from the enemy and well sheltered from the wind, to send most of a ship's company on shore: there were plenty of turtles and they were heavy, so they needed plenty of men to catch them and turn them over on their backs, and plenty of men to carry them to the boats.

And the men would not be armed because they were only after turtles. Kept on their backs live, the Spaniards would have fresh turtle meat when they needed it, and he knew turtles lasted well and could go for days – probably weeks – without food. So the men on shore would not be carrying cutlasses or pistols to kill the turtles; they needed both hands free to carry them.

A mile to go: the breeze was if anything stiffer; the *Griffin* seemed to respond as she ran along the coast towards the ships which were lying head to wind, their bows pointing towards the beach. It was going to be a mad rush – the *Griffin* would have to steer for the ship which would be lying at right angles across her bow and then, at the last moment, luff up: a sharp turn to starboard which would put her alongside the Spanish ship. Furl mainsail, drop headsails, hook on with the grapnels – and secure the ship before the boats arrived from the beach . . .

He called over Lobb and briefly explained his plan. It was in any case obvious: in this situation there was little choice. "How many of us to board her?" Lobb asked.

Ned thought for a moment. The only risk – unlikely – was that the men in the boats were shrewd enough to board the *Griffin* from the other side. "Take half the men: you'd better choose 'em now, so they'll be ready."

Most of the Spaniards had reached their boats now and, yes, through the perspective glass he could see them manhandling live turtles out of the boats! One after another the domed creatures were toppled over the sides and left to lie on the sand. Thanks, Ned muttered to himself; you've all given me a few precious minutes.

Now the men were hauling the first of the boats back into the water: they had simply dragged them up the sand, instead of dropping a kedge as they ran in, so they had to drag them back into deep enough water to float: not just float, but float with a couple of dozen or more men on board. Yes, the first boat was afloat now and the men were scrambling in over the coamings. The first ones in grabbed oars and used them to pole the boat into deeper water.

Now a second boat was being dragged down the beach, and the men in the first settled down to row. They were rowing unevenly and excitedly; oar blades were sending up spurts of water as in the rush the men did not dip them deep enough.

Half a mile: now without using the perspective glass he could make out details of the first ship. She was painted green with red decoration on the transom. There were five ports for guns on this side, so she carried ten. Headsails had just been dropped to the foot of their stays, with no attempt to put a lashing round them. The mainsail was furled on the yard, but clumsily, just secured with a few gaskets tied loosely.

Ned suddenly realized that Aurelia was standing beside him. "Why don't you go below?" he suggested. "There might be some fire from that ship."

Aurelia shook her head and laughed: "What, and miss a race like this! You'll win: less than half a mile, and they'll never get out in time."

Ned was not so sure: the Spaniards were rowing together now; the first boat was spurting along with every sweep of the oars, and the boat seemed to gain speed as the distance grew shorter.

Five hundred yards . . . he could make out the guns along the Spanish ship's side and pick out all the rigging. And yes, there were three or four men looking over the ship's side at the *Griffin*. Four. No one else joined them. Four men left on board. And to which ship would that first boat go? Ned felt a moment's sympathy for the four men: they could see that the men who had been on shore were racing back to the ships, but they could also see that the chances were against anyone arriving in time to rescue them.

In fact, Ned thought, they know better than anyone who is going to win this race because they have a better view of the boats and the *Griffin*; the boats approaching from the bow, the *Griffin* from the beam. For a moment Ned felt sympathy for them: they must be feeling very lonely.

Four hundred yards, and the *Griffin* was dipping as she went over the crests and into the troughs. The sea was much calmer in the lee of the land. Ned turned and shouted at the men with the grapnels: "Now you men, a quick throw and then make fast the other end: heave in if necessary because we've got to hold that ship alongside us!"

He glanced ahead and then called to the men at the guns: "Don't fire unless I give the order: we'll carry her by boarding and there's no need to do any unnecessary damage if we're going to capture her."

And they were the only orders he needed to shout. "Stand by me, Lobb," he said. "Things are going to happen fast and I want you to repeat my orders."

Three hundred yards, and the four men watched the *Griffin* thundering towards them. Ned was reminded of a rabbit paralysed by the eyes of a stoat, unable to move yet knowing it was in mortal peril.

The first boat had about three hundred yards to go, but it seemed to Ned she was making for the second ship, which would be the one that the *Peleus* tackled. Yes, the second boat was the one making for the first ship, and she had five hundred yards to go, perhaps a little less.

Aurelia was holding his arm, through excitement not nervousness. "We're winning!" she exclaimed. She let his arm go, hurried to the ship's side and came back with a cutlass for Ned. "You're not going to board her with your bare hands, are you?"

"Four men – hardly seems fair, does it?"

"With four men nobody gets killed; with forty, there'd be a slaughter," she commented briefly.

Two hundred yards, and Ned tried to judge how much the Spanish ship was swinging in the wind: he had to judge where she would be when the *Griffin* finished her turn: if she had swung even ten yards more than Ned estimated there would be a ten-yard gap between the two ships, and by the time she had swung back the *Griffin* might have drifted away. There was no windward or leeward side: the wind was blowing equally down both sides of the ship, with just an occasional irregular puff to make her swing.

A hundred yards . . . in a matter of moments the distance would be measured in dozens of feet . . . Ned knew he was clenching his fists in an effort to concentrate, and his grip on the hilt of the cutlass was almost painful.

Fifty yards . . . forty . . . thirty . . . "Hard a'starboard!" he snapped at Lobb and shouted to the men: "Cast off those headsail sheets . . . brace the yard sharp up."

In a matter of moments the *Griffin* turned sharply to come alongside the ship. The headsails started flapping wildly and the mainsail lost its shape: for a few moments there was only the flogging of canvas, then with a crash the *Griffin* slammed alongside and Ned bellowed: "Over with those grapnels!"

The two ships began to draw apart for a few moments, then the grapnels sailed across the gap to hold the two ships together. Ned jumped on to the *Griffin*'s bulwarks to leap across to the Spanish ship, and even as he poised to regain his balance he registered that the four men had vanished.

A few moments later the Spanish ship's decks were swarming with Griffins and Ned looked forward: the second boat was still fifty yards away and – yes, it was being rowed more slowly: whoever was in charge of it was probably trying to make up his mind what to do.

Then he heard the flogging of canvas and the hiss of a bow wave, and the *Peleus* passed across their stern, heading for the second ship. Thomas, waving a cutlass, shouted something cheerful that Ned could not distinguish.

Ned then remembered seeing the name of the Spanish ship: he had seen but not registered the name painted on the transom in the last few moments as the *Griffin* swung alongside, and the name was one of those long Spanish ones, *Santa Levirata y Aninimas*.

He suddenly realized that the men were simply standing round: there was no fighting, and coming towards him were four Spaniards, treading nervously as four Griffins followed them with cutlasses prodding their backs.

Lobb was leading the procession, and as he reached Ned, he said: "We found these men hiding down in the after cabin. Are we taking prisoners?"

"Keep them for the time being." He glanced over the bow again and saw that the boat coming from the beach had now stopped; the men were resting on their oars. "We can question these chaps and see where the ships came from."

"Lucky we didn't spit 'em," Lobb commented. "They were singing such a mournful song we felt sorry for them."

Ned heard a heavy thud over to larboard and glanced up to see that the *Peleus* had just gone alongside the second ship, whose boat was still fifty yards short.

At that moment the *Phoenix* sailed past on her way to tackle the third ship, and Ned just caught sight of Saxby standing aft with Martha Judd next to him. The *Peleus* was alongside her target and Ned was sure the ship was already captured: there was no crackle of muskets and pistols; he could not see men scrambling about the decks of either ship.

Ned looked ahead and saw that all the boats had stopped rowing and at least two had turned and were heading back to the beach. Which, he realized, meant that they were abandoning the fourth ship.

He inspected her with the perspective glass. She was very small and armed with only two guns. Her crew would be perhaps twenty-five men. Should he leave Lobb and his boarding party with the prize and go round to take the fourth ship? At the moment there were more than a hundred Spaniards stranded –

either in the boats or on shore. If they were left without means of escaping, they would terrorize the villagers living here, and they would have to wait for the next Spanish ship to arrive to rescue them.

So . . . why not leave the little fourth ship for them to escape in, to return whence they came? If they could not all sail in her at once – and she was probably too small – she could always make two trips.

All he had to do was wait for Thomas and Saxby to complete their tasks. In fact he could go over and see Thomas now and give him his instructions.

"Hoist out a boat," he told Lobb. "I'm going over to the *Peleus,* and then I'll probably go on to the *Phoenix*. In the meantime, make sure that our prize is ready to get under way – I shall want you to take her back to Port Royal."

Thomas was jubilant. Ned went on board the *Peleus* to find him grinning broadly and hear him say delightedly: "Well, Ned, a pirate captured and not a shot fired nor a cutlass used in anger."

"We did the same," Ned said. "I imagine – " he gestured towards the *Phoenix* " – that Martha Judd has captured that one all by herself!"

"Thomas wanted me to go below," Diana said crossly. "What did Aurelia do?" she asked.

"Well," Ned said lamely, "I wanted her to go below but she refused."

"There you are!" Diana said triumphantly to Thomas. "And Martha Judd was on deck because I saw her when the *Phoenix* went by."

"I'd like to meet the man that could make Martha Judd go below," Thomas muttered, "but Ned did say he wanted Aurelia to go below."

"You men," Diana grumbled. "Frightened of ships that don't fire a single shot in their own defence."

Ned had no time for Diana's grumbles and said briskly: "Thomas, we'll leave that last little ship for the Dons to escape in: she isn't worth bothering with, and I don't like the idea of marooning them here: they'll start harrying the villagers."

Thomas nodded. "Prisoners are just a damned nuisance," he declared. "There were half a dozen on board this ship – shall I send them over to the little one?"

"Yes. I've some too, but I want to question them. Perhaps take them back to Port Royal."

"Don't bother," Thomas advised. "Question them and leave them here."

"Very well. You call in on Saxby while you ferry the prisoners across. Tell him to put a prize crew on board the ship he captured and be ready to sail for Port Royal the moment he sees the *Griffin* get under way."

The moment he was back on board the *Griffin* Ned shouted across to Lobb to send over the prisoners, who seemed convinced they were about to be hanged. Ned pointed to the most intelligent one and asked in Spanish: "What were you?"

"The cook," the man muttered. "Butcher, too. I was just waiting for the first turtle."

"When did your ship arrive here in this island?"

The man counted on his fingers. "Eight days ago."

"Have you captured any ships?"

The man shook his head. "We chased one on the second day, but she got away from us. English, she was."

"Where have you come from?"

The man seemed puzzled by the question. "Why, from Cuba, of course."

"What port?"

"Santiago. That's where most of our families live."

"Who leads you all?"

The man thought a moment, scratching his head. "Well, the captain of this ship, I suppose. The rest of them do what he says."

"Where is he now?"

The cook gestured towards the shore. "He went off with the rest of them to catch turtle – and see if he could get some lobsters from the villagers."

"Do you think you are going to be executed?"

"Yes," the man quavered, "me with a wife and seven children."

"Seven is too many," Ned said with mock seriousness. "Four might have been all right, but seven!"

"It's not my fault," the man stammered, beginning to perspire heavily.

"You must have an obliging neighbour, then," Ned said ironically, and signalled to Lobb. "Take these men to the *Peleus*.

Sir Thomas will take them to the fourth ship, which we are going to leave behind."

"Yes, she's very small," Lobb commented. "Leave her or burn her – she'd be worth nothing in Port Royal."

Ned said: "I'm only concerned that I don't leave this gang of pirates to harass the villagers: they've little enough as it is. Now, once we've got rid of these four, have you got all you need to take the prize to Port Royal?"

"Yes, while you were away in the *Peleus* I had a look at the stores and water. There's a couple of weeks' supply on board."

"Right," Ned said, "get this quartet over to the *Peleus*; the sooner the prisoners are on board the little ship, the sooner we can get under way."

Chapter
Eleven

The *Griffin* led the convoy of six ships back into Port Royal, and as she tacked her way up the anchorage, the others tacked in her wake, like obedient ducklings following their mother across the village pond.

As soon as they were anchored, Ned had a boat hoisted out and was rowed over to the *Peleus,* where Thomas agreed that they should visit the governor immediately. It might interrupt his siesta, Ned commented, but they had all lost sleep because of the man.

Sir Harold was seated in his office when they were shown in by his secretary, William Hamilton, who tried to give the impression that both Ned and Thomas were being extended a considerable honour in being allowed an audience with the governor.

Sir Harold looked up and said simply: "Well?"

Ned looked significantly at Hamilton, and when Sir Harold did not react said quietly: "It's not our concern if the governor conducts his affairs in the market place, but it is not our habit."

"Leave us," Luce told a red-faced Hamilton, who flounced out like a woman whose honour had been impugned.

"Well?" Luce repeated.

"The last time we were here," Ned said, "you called me a pirate."

"Yes, I did," Luce said. "Some of your ships had attacked one of our ships off Grand Cayman."

"Your Excellency," Ned said quietly, "on several occasions you have said things which were later proved wrong. Has anything happened to make you change your mind?"

"Indeed not!" Luce retorted. "Pirate I said, and pirate I meant."

"Sir Thomas and I, and another ship, have just been to Grand Cayman."

"How interesting – did you find any ship to attack?" Luce sneered.

"Yes, four. We captured them all but left one behind."

"You captured four? You have the infernal impudence to come up here and tell me you have just captured four of our ships?"

"I said we captured four ships," Ned said coldly. "I did not speak the word 'our'."

"Whose were they then?" Luce asked truculently.

"Spanish."

"Spanish?" Luce yelped. "That's just as bad! That's piracy!"

"If you call me a pirate again," Ned said quietly, "I shall challenge you, and to me you don't look as if your swordplay matches your tongue."

"Don't you dare to threaten me with a challenge!" Luce exclaimed, his voice high-pitched and nervous. "After all, I *am* the governor."

"Not even the governor can insult whom he pleases without answering for it – at least, not if he's a gentleman. I presume, Sir Harold, that you rate yourself a gentleman?"

"What on earth has all this got to do with you capturing four Spanish ships off Grand Cayman?" Luce asked evasively.

"Everything, apparently: you've just called me a pirate again."

"But you are!"

"There you go again," Ned said. "Making conclusions without knowing the facts."

"But you've just told me the facts," Luce said.

"You weren't listening. I said we captured four ships, and that they were Spanish."

"There you are!" Luce exclaimed. "Piracy!"

Ned sighed. "Really, you are too pathetic to challenge, even if you are the governor. Just listen. We captured four ships. They were Spanish. Now before you start jumping about any more, let me assure you they were pirates. Spanish pirates. They were raiding Grand Cayman – the defence of which is your responsibility – and had come from Cuba."

"But how do you know they were pirates?"

"I questioned some of the crew."

"I shall question them," Luce announced. "Then I can be sure."

"You'll have to go to Grand Cayman, then," Ned said. "We left all the prisoners there. If you go to the door and look across the anchorage, you'll see three of the pirate ships anchored close to the *Griffin, Phoenix* and *Peleus*. We brought the ships back because we thought," Ned added ironically, "that you might like to buy them, and start the Jamaica Navy."

"You don't expect me to believe all that story, do you?" Luce demanded.

"No, I suppose not," Ned said. "However, the three ships are there, with their Spanish names painted across their transoms, and we shall be applying to the court to have them condemned as prizes."

"I shall oppose it," Luce said hotly.

"I don't think you will," Ned said icily, "because by then you'll have said in public that I am a pirate, and I shall have challenged you, and as I suggested just now, you don't look the sort of man who is very handy with a sword. But perhaps you would prefer pistols? Never mind," Ned said dismissively, "our seconds can sort out all that when the time comes."

"I'm not duelling with you!" Luce said, almost tearfully.

"But you'll have no choice," Ned said. "You just said you would oppose the condemnation of the prizes in the prize court, and to do that you have to call me a pirate. If you call me a pirate, I shall challenge you. It's all very simple really."

Luce was perspiring so heavily now that the ends of his moustaches were hanging down. He put his hands flat on the table in front of him and started speaking in a placating voice.

"Perhaps I was a little hasty," he said. "All you need do is prove these ships belonged to pirates."

Ned cursed himself for leaving the four Spanish prisoners behind, but decided he was not going to have his word doubted by a man like Luce.

"I will prove it to the court," Ned said. "It is none of your business. What *is* your business is the fact that if Spanish pirates

119

from Cuba decide to raid the Caymans, it won't be long before you have them raiding Jamaica. And it's not necessary for me to remind you that you can't stop them. Don't rely on the former buccaneers," Ned said heavily. "I shall warn them that if they take any action against the Spanish, they'll be called pirates by the governor of Jamaica . . ."

"You leave me defenceless!" wailed Luce.

"You're defenceless anyway and it's your own fault," Ned said unsympathetically. "You disbanded the Army; you took away the buccaneers' commissions. Apart from taking your sword and dropping it down a well, how can you make yourself more defenceless?"

For the next week Ned, Thomas and Saxby lazed: they had their men changing some ropes – usually turning them end for end – and setting up the rigging. Decks were swabbed down each morning, a habit which set some men grumbling that it was like being in the Navy, but Ned was anxious that the planking should not dry out in the heat of the sun, making the wood shrink so that the first heavy rain, or voyage that brought seas over the deck, made water seep through the seams, dripping below on to clothes and bedding, making life a damp misery.

Every couple of days Ned went over to visit Sanchez, the governor of Colombia, while Thomas, to satisfy a quirkish sense of humour, visited the bishop. Ned failed to get any more information from Sanchez, who grumbled at being held a hostage.

"My people will pay a ransom," he protested to Ned on the third visit. "How much are you asking?"

Ned held up his hands expressively. "We haven't decided on a price yet. When you tell us what we want to know, we'll settle the price."

"What else can I tell you?"

"What those ships from Spain are going to do."

"But I don't know."

"Most unfortunate," Ned said, shaking his head. "Your memory is not like wine, it doesn't seem to improve with keeping."

"I want to get home to my wife."

"No doubt you do," Ned said, "but it all takes time. Keep thinking hard; you may remember something."

On the ninth day Lobb called down to Ned, who was in the saloon talking to Aurelia, that a canoe was coming out with Sir Harold Luce's secretary.

Ned thought wearily of other secretaries and messengers who had in the past come out with messages, and they all had one thing in common: they were covered with fish scales because the only boats they could use were the fishermen's canoes, and as these were unstable craft the messenger usually arrived pale-faced with nervousness as well as reeking of fish.

"Very well, keep him on deck: I'll come up as soon as you pass the word."

Hamilton, as smelly and nervous as Ned expected, brought a letter from Luce and waited for the answer. Would Ned and Sir Thomas call on the governor at their earliest convenience?

Ned thought of their last meeting and would have refused, but he knew he would receive no sympathy from Aurelia; she felt sorry for the wretched Luce and regarded Ned and Thomas as bullies.

"Tell Sir Harold we will wait on him within an hour," Ned said. "And next time pick a cleaner canoe: you are shedding fish scales all over my deck."

The embarrassed William Hamilton looked round him. On the deck, which was still damp from the latest swabbing, were many fish scales on which the sun glinted.

Ned collected Thomas on his way to the jetty. "Luce is a cool fellow," Thomas muttered. "Last time we saw him he was calling you a pirate and you were threatening to call him out; now it's 'at your earliest convenience'."

"He's in some sort of trouble," Ned said. "Nothing like trouble to make him change his tune."

"What trouble, though?"

"Nothing minor, I hope," Ned growled.

Sir Harold, who had been sitting at the table, jumped to his feet when Hamilton announced them. He came round the table, hand extended.

"My dear Mr Yorke, how very kind of you to spare the time. And you, Sir Thomas. I do apologize for bothering you. Please be seated."

With that he returned to his chair and pulled the ends of his moustaches, a nervous gesture which Ned had often seen before. He was slightly disconcerted because neither Ned nor Thomas had said a word and obviously he was not sure how to begin.

"You see," he finally mumbled, "we have a problem."

" 'We'?" Thomas asked uncompromisingly.

"Well, no, of course not," Luce said ingratiatingly, "the problem is entirely mine. By 'we', I meant Jamaica as a whole."

"Did you, by Jove," commented Thomas. "Well, it doesn't concern us, then, because we don't regard ourselves as part of Jamaica these days."

"Oh, but you must," Luce exclaimed. "A most important part of Jamaica. Stalwarts, that's how I regard you."

"What's the problem?" Ned asked coldly.

"Well, it's a problem you touched on when you were last here," Luce said. "You mentioned that after visiting the Caymans, we might find Spanish pirate ships attacking Jamaica."

"And now they are?" asked Ned.

"Well, I've no actual proof that they are Spanish," Luce said, "but five villages on the north coast have been pillaged and burned down and eight people killed by men who landed from ships."

"It can't be mice, then," Thomas commented acidly. "What makes you think it's Spaniards?"

"The man who rode in to warn me heard them speaking Spanish."

Ned felt exasperated: he had guessed it would happen, hence his warning to Luce. Now it had happened, and there was nothing to stop the Dons going on round the island, putting every coastal village to the torch. The Army disbanded and only a small militia which had not yet been organized . . .

Ned stared at Luce, was again reminded of a ferret in a trap, and said: "Only the five villages so far?"

"By the grace of God!"

"There'll be more," Ned commented. "Think how many villages are built on the coast."

"What can we *do*?" Luce wailed.

"Damned if I know," Ned said. "You can make us an offer for those three ships. You'll find enough seamen in the taverns. Send 'em off after the pirates."

"What good will that do? Seamen picked up out of the taverns won't know how to deal with pirates."

"No, they probably won't," Ned agreed. "My goodness, you *are* in a fix, aren't you?" With that he stood up. "Well, Your Excellency, thank you for telling us about it."

"Don't go!" exclaimed Luce, agitatedly. "Please sit down again. I need your advice."

Ned sat down with a show of reluctance. "I've given you the only advice I can think of: buy those three ships from us – we won't wait for the court to condemn them as prizes – and fit 'em out. I can't think of anything else, can you, Thomas?"

"No. Very sound advice, I reckon. The ships have plenty of provisions and more than enough water. We'd consider any reasonable offer, wouldn't we Ned?"

"Of course! I was just waiting to hear from Sir Harold."

The governor waved his hands helplessly. "What hope have three ships of finding these pirates?"

"We found four with only three ships," Ned reminded him.

"But where would they start looking?" Luce asked, a note of desperation in his voice.

"Why, wherever you tell them!" Ned said, apparently surprised at the question.

"But I don't know where to tell them: I've no idea what the coast of the island looks like. I've only the map."

"And a damned poor map that is," Thomas growled. "The coast where we built our houses is quite different from what the map says."

"You forget," Luce said woefully, "that I haven't been governor very long."

"I assure you," Ned said sarcastically, "that thought is never far from our minds."

"But you –" Luce paused, and then seemed to pluck up courage. "Can't you sail with your ships?"

"What, thirty ships to chase a few pirates?" Ned asked incredulously. "Anyway, chasing pirates away is not going to end the problem. They'll be back. Burn down villages at one end of the island, suddenly swoop down on the other, then the moment you relax swoop on the middle. Oh dear," Ned said, sympathy now in his voice, "you have a problem, Your Excellency."

Luce swallowed hard and said, the words tumbling out: "What would you do if you were me?"

Ned looked at Thomas, who nodded.

"If I was the governor," Ned said carefully, "I wouldn't waste my time with two or three pirate ships. I'd teach the Spanish such a lesson that they'd leave us alone."

"But what sort of lesson, pray?"

"These raiders come from Cuba, probably Santiago. Pick a town not far from Santiago and burn it down. Ransom a few of the leading citizens – the Dons will soon take the hint and leave Jamaica alone."

"But we can't go attacking a Spanish town like that," protested Luce. "That would be an act of war."

Ned thought of Riohacha, and heard the petard exploding against the doors of the fort. "Burning five villages . . . trying to capture that ship of ours off the Caymans . . . in effect capturing Grand Cayman . . . Seems to me the Spanish have declared war on us already."

"The choice is yours," Thomas said, fingering his beard. "Either let the Dons make war on us, and smile at 'em, or hit back. They couldn't blame you in London for hitting back."

"Oh yes they could," Luce said feelingly. "The King, the Catholic Church, the Pope and the King of Spain – they're all mixed up in this."

Ned thought of a possible Spanish attack on Jamaica, the attack about which the governor of Colombia was so reticent. "It'll be another three or four months before a frigate comes out from England with despatches – the *Convertine* has only just sailed. Another three months for her to return to London . . . that's seven months before London hears what you've done. In seven months anything can happen. Why, within seven months the Spaniards may have attacked us from the Main, or the King might have handed over the island to the Dons . . . Seven months is a long time."

"Where would you attack in Cuba?" Luce asked cautiously.

Ned shrugged his shoulders. "Santiago is too big for the purpose. Santa Lucia would be just about right. Thirty miles east of Santiago, a sheltered bay, and from all accounts a prosperous town."

"Do you think raiding Santa Lucia will deliver the message to the Spanish?" Luce asked.

"I'm certain of it, providing the attack is successful."

"Who would lead it?"

Ned shrugged his shoulders again. "You'll have to find someone. Why not General Heffer?"

"But he knows nothing about ships."

Ned could not resist his next remark. "You'll have only three ships, so it won't be an enormous expedition."

"Three ships?" Luce repeated. "But I thought you'd take all your ships!"

Ned pretended to look puzzled. "All my ships? But the Brethren of the Coast no longer exist. You took away their commissions, and said if they took any action against the Spanish, they'd be pirates."

"But this is an emergency!"

"For you, not for us," Ned said. "I'm afraid you must leave all those ships out of your calculations: they will not obey any orders you may give."

"Won't you lead them?" Luce asked pathetically. "It's our only chance."

"Lead a fleet of pirates?" Ned pretended he was shocked at the idea. "No, no, really, you ask the impossible."

"But Heffer and three ships won't do any good: Heffer and the dregs of Port Royal's taverns . . . It would be a waste of time sending them," Luce lamented.

"You *have* got a problem," Ned said sympathetically.

"Please, won't you reconsider? The buccaneers raiding Santa Lucia means it's bound to be a success. Heffer's not the man to lead three ships to go anywhere."

Ned pretended to consider for a minute or two and then shook his head. "No, I couldn't think of it," he said. "I would be acting as a pirate myself, and I value my good name. Nor would my men – my former men, I mean – want to be regarded as pirates."

Luce obviously wished he had never used the word pirate. "Well," he said, assuming the nearest he could get to a judicial manner, "men defending Jamaica would hardly be called pirates, you know. After all, the defence of this island concerns every man and woman that lives here."

"Ah yes, defending the island is one thing," Ned said, unable to resist giving the knife another twist, "but by raiding Santa Lucia they wouldn't be defending Jamaica, they'd be attacking Cuba."

Luce looked cornered once again and tugged at his moustaches. "Couldn't you persuade your men that they are acting with the governor's blessing?"

"With respect, they don't give a damn for the governor's blessing. They remember the governor took their commissions away from them – and shut down the brothels."

Luce flushed when Ned reminded him. His tiny eyes flickered back and forth from Thomas to Ned, as though trying to intercept any secret messages that might be passing between them.

Thomas caught Luce's eye and said lugubriously: "Mr Yorke's put his finger on the problems. Commissions and brothels. You took away both. You took away their livelihood and their pleasure. Don't forget they come from all sorts of countries – Spain, France, Holland . . . they don't really care what country owns Jamaica: to them it's merely an island with a convenient anchorage. Or, rather, an anchorage that *was* convenient, until the brothels were closed down and a number of taverns shut."

Luce stared at the table top, as if expecting a solution to appear out of the grain of the wood.

"Supposing I leave the same number of taverns . . ."

Thomas roared with laughter and slapped the table. "Yes, and offer each ship a cask of wine, eh?"

"I don't see what's so funny about my proposal," Luce said sheepishly.

Thomas turned on him, eyes glittering. "Your Excellency, your problem is that Spanish raiders are burning villages here in Jamaica. It's a problem that's not going to be solved by you reopening a few taverns."

"What am I supposed to do, then?" Luce sounded trapped.

"Do you really want to know?" Ned asked. "I'll give you our terms, but I warn you, we don't debate 'em."

"All right," Luce agreed, "let me have your terms – the terms for attacking Santa Lucia."

"First of all," Ned said firmly, "you allow Port Royal to be a base for the buccaneers. That means as many brothels and taverns as are needed for the men."

"Oh bless my soul," Luce mumbled while Ned paused for breath. "I don't know what my wife will say."

"Just think what your wife would say if Spanish pirates sailed into Port Royal and burned her house around her ears."

Luce nodded mournfully: for a moment, Ned thought, the ferret was replaced with a cadaverous bloodhound. "Just the brothels and the taverns?" Luce asked hopefully.

"Oh no," Ned said grimly. "Brothels, taverns and commissions for every one of the ships."

"But I can't do that," Luce wailed. "What would the Privy Council say?"

Ned stared at him. "What would the Privy Council say if the Spanish attacked and captured Jamaica? It wouldn't concern you, of course, since the Dons would have slit your gizzard."

Luce thought for several moments, swallowed hard and then nodded reluctantly. "All right, then, I'll issue commissions for three months."

Ned shook his head wearily. "You've misunderstood me. Port Royal is to be an open port for the buccaneers, and the commissions issued without any time limit."

"But supposing the Privy Council later order me to withdraw the commissions?"

"We'll deal with that when it happens," Ned said. "That would be a year ahead."

"When can you sail for Santa Lucia?"

"When can you issue the commissions and tell the people that the brothels are open again?"

"I still have the original commissions which I withdrew: they can be issued again. The brothels," Luce said, turning red, "are a different question: I understand most of the women have disappeared . . ."

Ned laughed. "That's no problem; I know where they are. Just give permission for the brothels to be opened again."

Luce nodded and rang the small silver bell on the table in front of him. There was a knock on the door and Hamilton came into the room. "All those commissions that were withdrawn from the buccaneers," Luce told him. "I want them."

"Very well, sir," answered a startled Hamilton. "They're in the next room."

"I don't care where they are, get them!" Luce snarled and Hamilton scuttled out.

Luce was obviously deep in thought and he said to Ned: "This raid on Santa Lucia – there'll be no looting, will there?"

"If there's to be no looting, there'll be no raid," Ned said abruptly. "You call it loot; my men call it purchase, compensation for the danger."

"I suppose so," Luce agreed helplessly. "I was thinking of the Spanish ambassador in London complaining to the King . . ."

"Think of the King being told that he has lost Jamaica to the Dons," Ned said unsympathetically. "You are looking at this through the wrong end of the perspective glass."

"I suppose so – ah, here are the commissions," he exclaimed as Hamilton came into the room with his arms full of rolled parchment. "Put them on the table."

Luce made a grandiloquent gesture to Ned, as if to say: "They're all yours."

"Are they all there?" Ned asked.

"Count them," Luce ordered Hamilton.

When Hamilton gave the total, Ned said to Luce: "Now some string to put round them!"

Chapter
Twelve

The buccaneer captains made an excited group as they gathered on board the *Griffin*. With the exception of Thomas, none of them knew the reason for the summons. They were a motley crowd but one or two of them dressed carefully, with neatly trimmed beards. Ned saw Edward Brace, the owner and captain of the *Mercury*, red-haired, tall, thin and angular, run his silver-backed turtleshell comb through a carefully trimmed beard, while near him was Jean-Pierre Leclerc, the French owner of the *Perdrix*, unshaven, his face greasy, his clothes looking as though they had been slept in for a month.

Charles Coles, owner of the *Argonauta*, was talking to Gottlieb, of the *Dolphyn*, and neither man showed any sign of their recent captivity. The blond-haired and blue-eyed Coles had the same hearty manner, and Ned could hear his Yorkshire accent as he talked with Gottlieb. The Dutchman, with widely spaced eyes, and hair so fair it was almost white and made his eyebrows nearly invisible, was grunting in reply to Coles's remarks. Secco, the swarthy and black-haired Spaniard, was talking to Saxby and another Frenchman, Rideau, listened.

Many men and many nationalities but, Ned thought, no real loyalties except to the Brotherhood. They were all refugees from some kind of persecution: the Frenchmen were mostly Huguenots who had fled from the Catholics; the Spaniards had left Spain because of some complex reason Ned had never fully understood. The Englishmen were all men who had quit the country under

Cromwell: not necessarily Royalists, but men who could not stand the grim don't-laugh regime – Roundhead haircuts, long prayers for all meals – imposed by the Puritans. All of them, Ned realized, were men who had to be free; who gave their loyalty to the Brethren but who were free men acting freely when they did it.

The last few weeks of idleness had not done some of them much good. The Riohacha raid had been a welcome interruption, but several of the men showed signs that they had been at the rumbullion too frequently, and that having the trollops from Port Royal's brothels on board was leaving them as dry as sucked oranges.

Ned stood by the aftermost gun on the starboard side and in front of him was a small table, looking incongruous on the *Griffin*'s deck. Finally he jumped up on to the breech of a gun and shouted for attention.

"Welcome on board," he said. "It's a long time since we had a meeting like this. Well, you're all wondering what it's all about. First, I have some news for you. The governor has given permission for the brothels to be reopened again, and the taverns that were closed can now reopen their doors."

The captains cheered in a variety of tongues and Ned grinned.

The captains watched curiously as both Aurelia and Diana came up from below, their arms laden with rolled up parchments, and put them on the table. The captains were standing too far away to recognize what they were and Ned pointed dramatically to them.

"There are your commissions," he announced. "Once again you are buccaneers. In a few minutes you can come up and collect your own commission, providing you agree with what I have to say next.

"As some of you know, Spaniards from Santiago chased one of our turtlers and raided Grand Cayman. Three of those ships are now anchored over there," he said significantly, pointing to the prizes.

"Now, the night before last, it seems more Dons actually attacked this island, burning down five villages on the north coast. You know as well as I do that that's only the beginning: in a few weeks we'll have a swarm of them coming over from Cuba and putting the torch to every village and town within reach of the sea.

"So now we get to the newly opened brothels and these commissions which the governor is very kindly returning to us. But of course there is a price to pay: we have to teach these Dons a lesson, and that means we'll raid one of their towns in Cuba, take what purchase we can lay our hands on, and set the rest ablaze.

"The governor asked me this morning if the buccaneers would be prepared to carry out this little task for him, and I, on your behalf, said I was sure you would – in return for the brothels, taverns and commissions.

"I'm going to keep the name of the town I've chosen secret until we sail, but I want to know which of you are coming and which want to stay behind. So those who are staying, walk over to the companionway."

Not a man moved, and Ned grinned. "I thought as much. Now the ladies will give you your commissions!"

Ned was startled by the cheering: the men yelled and hallooed, some even dancing a jig as they made their way over to the table. There Diana and Aurelia unrolled parchments, called out the names written on them, and passed them over. The men were obviously delighted at getting their commissions back and several playfully hit each other on the head, using the rolled parchments as clubs.

As soon as the commissions had all been handed out, the two women went below again and returned with baskets full of mugs and tankards. A seaman carried up a keg of rumbullion and put it on the table.

"Right," Ned called, "now you have your commissions and you know what we are going to do, let's drink to our success."

Saxby stationed himself at the tap of the keg and started filling tankards and mugs as the women handed them to him. Ned jumped down from the gun and Thomas came over to join him, fingering his beard and grinning.

"Just like old times, eh Ned?"

"Yes, they seem glad to be off again."

"The Riohacha affair whetted their appetites. Reminded them of what they've been missing. That was too tame for them, though; no purchase, not many flames!"

"We'll make up for it," Ned said. "They don't seem to care where they are going!"

"No, but just look at them clutching their commissions! They really do value those bits of parchment."

"I thought they did," Ned said. "That's why I was determined to get them from old Loosely. As far as I'm concerned I don't really care whether I sail as a pirate or as a buccaneer, no matter what I might tell Loosely," Ned went on, "but as far as these fellows are concerned it adds something — what is it, I wonder? Respectability?"

"Makes it all seem legal," Thomas rumbled. "Like being married: the ceremony doesn't really change anything, but it puts a seal on it."

Ned laughed lightly. "You should know, as an old married man."

"That bloody woman," Thomas swore. "Why couldn't I have met Diana first?"

"She'd have been about six years old then," Ned pointed out. "Rather too young for you to appreciate."

"She's old for her years," Thomas said with a grin. "Anyway, at least when I met her she wasn't married to anyone else."

"Aurelia was, when I met her," Ned pointed out.

"Ah, but he very conveniently got himself murdered."

Ned shrugged his shoulders. "We still haven't married."

"That's your fault," Thomas said unsympathetically. "Aurelia wants to be married in a proper church. You'll have to build one; you can't expect her to put up with that wooden shack. We'll call it 'St Ned's and All Saints'."

Ned walked over to Coles and Gottlieb, who had been joined by Secco and were talking away to each other. "Are your prisoners still happy and fit?"

"The governor is fit but not happy," Coles said.

"The bishop is happier now I give him better wine," Secco said. "They must live well, these churchmen."

Ned pretended to look shocked. "I'm sorry to hear you had been giving him poor wine."

Secco gave a rumbling laugh. "I went to the trouble of getting him Spanish wine. That was the trouble: he prefers French!"

Once the little fleet was clear of Morant Point at the eastern end of Jamaica, Ned tacked the *Griffin* to lead them to the north-

north- east to begin the voyage of about 150 miles to Santa Lucia.

The navigation was not too difficult: as the *Griffin* steadied on the new course, Cuba was dead ahead, the Windward Passage on the starboard bow and Hispaniola on the starboard beam. The buccaneer fleet, in the *Griffin's* wake, looked a brave sight, each ship butting into the seas knocked up by a brisk east wind. The *Peleus* followed directly astern, then the *Phoenix*. Behind them the rest of the buccaneers kept in no sort of formation, looking like a flock of sheep straying over a meadow.

At least the buccaneers now knew their target. Boats from the *Griffin* and *Peleus* had called on each ship just before they sailed and given them the name Santa Lucia. There was not much chance that the word could get to the Spaniards even if the buccaneers had been told the destination the day before, but Ned preferred to take no risks.

The only risk, he thought as he stood aft in the *Griffin,* staring at the ship's wake, was in guessing the strength of the west-going current between Jamaica and Cuba. Allowing it too little speed and they would get down to the west of Santa Lucia; allowing too much and they would arrive too far to the east.

"When do you expect to arrive?" Aurelia asked.

"With this wind we're making about five knots. Say thirty hours to reach the Cuba coast. Tomorrow night. I'm hoping we'll sight the land before it's dark, so that we have some idea where we are."

"And the raid on Santa Lucia? Have you planned it yet?"

"No, not yet," Ned admitted. "It's a town at the head of a shallow bay, and they're not expecting us. We don't need a complicated plan."

"Just storm ashore, shouting and screaming?"

"Or creep ashore, as we did at Riohacha. It depends – if the wind goes south there'll be too much surf to land anyway. That's why I'm leaving the planning to the last moment; we're at the mercy of the wind."

"We've picked a fine day for the crossing," Aurelia said, gesturing towards the sun and the cottonball clouds. "The flying fish like it, too."

Ned watched as a couple of dozen appeared out of the sea on the starboard bow, skimmed along a few feet above the waves and, after a hundred yards, disappeared into the sea without a splash.

Overhead four or five menacing black frigate birds wheeled in lazy arcs, waiting to swoop on the flying fish, often coming down to within a foot of the waves without appearing to move a muscle of their wings.

Ned moved back under the small awning stretched across a corner of the afterdeck, and Aurelia followed him.

"There's real heat in the sun," he commented. "You're as brown as – well, as brown as a piece of mahogany."

"I thought you liked me tanned."

"I do, but don't get burned: the sun is glaring up from the sea."

By next afternoon Ned could see the great mass of mountains forming the Sierra Maestra distant on the larboard beam; with the perspective glass he could just pick out Pico Turquino, the highest in the range and about in the middle of the coast.

The wind had been freshening for several hours, and Ned reckoned they were making a good seven knots. Even the smallest of the buccaneers was managing to keep up, and Ned hoped the increase in speed would mean that they would sight the coast around Santa Lucia while it was still light.

The difficulty was that no one knew exactly what Santa Lucia looked like. Or, Ned corrected himself, he had forgotten to ask people like Secco, who might have been there. The only thing he knew for certain was that the bay was clear of obstructions: the chart told him that there was no reef across the entrance, though the scale was too small to show isolated rocks.

He sat in the hot saloon working out his plan. The moon rose just before midnight, so that fixed the time of the attack: they would start in with the boats a few minutes after the moon lifted over the horizon, and by the time they reached the shore the moon should be high enough to help them land at the right place on the beach and then find their way about the town.

Lots of noise, or a silent approach? Well, the buccaneers wanted their share of the purchase this time, so it needed to be a silent approach: a lot of noise would raise the alarm too soon and give the wiser inhabitants time to hide their valuables – drop them down a well, for instance.

So, a silent approach. Silent, anyway, until they started the real attack on the town: then noise was inevitable. Hostages? Yes – the mayor, treasurer, a few leading citizens if they could be identified. What an irony that the governor of Colombia, the bishop and the mayor of Riohacha, still on board the buccaneer ships, were coming on this raid! But there had been no question of leaving them on shore at Port Royal. Had one of the buccaneer ships been unable to sail they could have looked after the hostages; but no one was staying behind this time.

Very well, the ships could wait off Santa Lucia, out of sight, until after dark, which was about seven. Then a careful approach, and they could anchor off ready to send all the men in just after moonrise. After that – Ned shrugged his shoulders: every man for himself.

There remained only to tell each one: that could be done later, because the wind would begin to drop about six o'clock, when the *Griffin* could go up to a ship and hail. Or, rather, as soon as the ships saw what she was doing they would sail past close.

Having decided on the broad outlines of the plan, Ned studied the chart. The scale was small, so there was not much detail, but the bay was a semicircle with cliffs on the left and flat land on the right. The town seemed to be built on a flat area exactly in the centre of the half moon of the bay, and it would be reasonable to expect sandy beaches: there the fishermen would draw up their boats, because a town like Santa Lucia lived beside and off the sea.

Time passed quickly, and soon Ned went on deck to inspect the land ahead. Twenty miles? About that. Yes, there were the hills, and the land flattened away to the eastward. They were making six knots but the wind was taking off: not enough to becalm them, but it might mean arriving late.

By six o'clock Ned was close enough to be sure: the cliffs were shadowed by the setting sun, emphasizing their position, and the land on the opposite side of the bay was flat. The bay itself was not obvious, but the shadows off the cliffs gave enough hint of the inward curve for Ned to be certain.

He called Lobb over and told him to work the ship over towards the *Peleus*, and then the *Phoenix*. It took only a few minutes to pass the details to the two ships and tell them to help give them to the other ships, which promptly started passing close when they saw what was happening. Ned, his voice hoarse, handed over to Lobb, who finally had to give up, and the bosun shouted the orders to the last three ships. Then the *Griffin* returned to her position at the head of the little fleet and steered for Santa Lucia.

Just as it got dark Ned had one final inspection with the perspective glass. Yes, there were the cliffs, curving inwards to form the western side of the bay, and there was the flat land doing the same on the eastern side. The town was just a small, grey blob, but had they been any closer it would have been possible for a sharp-eyed lookout with a glass to have seen the ships.

Aurelia looked at him with raised eyebrows. "You're certain of it?"

"It matches the chart," Ned replied. "Anyway, there's a town there, and it'll still do even if it's not Santa Lucia!"

"It would be nice to be sure!"

"I was sure until you came along and put doubts in my mind," Ned said. "You're supposed to reassure me; tell me what a wonderful navigator I am."

"I'll do all that tomorrow," Aurelia said, laughing.

By now Lobb had hoisted the small grindstone up on deck, and men were sharpening their cutlasses, the blades making a sharp, scratching noise. As soon as they had finished the cutlasses, they started on the pikes, holding them carefully so the ends were pointed.

With all the pikes sharpened and put back in their rack round the mainmast, Lobb gave out muskets and pistols. The men selected lead shot from the leather bags, rolling them along the deck to make sure they were spherical. Then, using the powder horns and careful to protect the powder from the wind, they loaded and primed all the guns.

So far the work had been done in the order of importance. In fact the men had little time for muskets or pistols; once fired, they were useless, except as clubs. Cutlasses were the most important and received the most care; men wanted a knife edge on the blade. Next in importance came the pikes, cast-iron heads fitted on the end of seven-foot ash staves, the heads designed for stabbing. The one thing a man did not want was his victim hanging lifeless on the end of the pike, collapsing over it as if it was a trident and making it hard to withdraw.

Some of the men had long knives, elaborate daggers which they

136

wore in rough sheaths at their waists. These were given an edge on the grindstone, but their owners treated them with delicacy, anxious not to overheat the metal on the stone, and particular how much water was poured on to the spinning wheel.

The men normally went barefoot in the ship and they now brought out the boots they would wear when they went on shore. Most were simply strips of leather which covered the foot and were then stitched so that they stayed in place. Once fitted, a boot stayed on until the owner had no more need for it, when the stitching was cut and the leather strip put away until wanted again.

The men started sewing on their boots as it became dark. As usual in the Tropics the light went quickly: no sooner had the sun slipped below the horizon than the darkness spread in from the east. With the last of the light Ned inspected the coast ahead yet again. Cliffs in shadow on the left, land flat on the right, a town in the middle: if it was not Santa Lucia it was its double and anyway would serve the purpose.

The stars which had come out even as the sun went down now brightened; the clouds and sea turned grey; distances became hard to judge. The buccaneer ships seemed to get closer to each other; the *Peleus* and *Phoenix* were almost within hailing distance.

The next few hours are the dangerous ones, Ned thought; every man is getting excited, and it is the time when ships collide in the dark. It is a strange thing that on an ordinary night passage thirty ships can sail along in company and there will be no danger of collision. But those same ships heading for a town they are going to raid may well collide with each other, as though excitement affected judgement.

There was a candle in the binnacle now, lighting up the compass, and the quartermaster was watching it like a hawk. With the *Griffin* heading directly for the distant town, Ned had read off the bearing and now with a small allowance for the current, the *Griffin* was sailing a direct course, with the rest of the ships following.

Now time was dragging for Ned. He went below to have his supper with Aurelia, and then came back on deck. There was just the creak of the yard, the occasional flap of the mainsail, and the hissing of the bow wave with an odd thump as an extra large wave hit the side of the ship.

An hour before midnight he thought he could just distinguish the cliffs on the side of the bay: a dark sliver on an even darker horizon. Ned looked, turned his head and looked back again. The sliver was still there, in the same place. Lobb was the next to see it, and then Aurelia. A comparison with the course they were steering put it beyond doubt: Santa Lucia – if that was the name of the place – was dead ahead, about six miles . . .

It was curious how in the darkness the ship seemed to slide through the water: almost as if the ship remained stationary and the water was drawn past it. Ned paced up and down the deck, constantly looking over the bow, and when the bay appeared beyond any doubt he was surprised at the speed the *Griffin* must have been making.

There were the cliffs, now very close on the larboard bow, and he stood on a gun to get a better view over the bow. Close astern the *Peleus* and the *Phoenix* kept station; astern of them, just a group of black blobs, the rest of the buccaneers followed. Followed the *Griffin,* Ned reflected: if he sailed on to a reef, the chances were that the whole fleet would follow, unless it was a very small reef.

Ned shook his head impatiently: he had led the buccaneers into various strange places at night without any problems, so why was he getting nervous about Santa Lucia? If he was honest with himself, he admitted, he was no more nervous now than he usually was: it was about this time that he wanted to turn the *Griffin* away and call the whole thing off. Leadership, he thought ruefully, is not a question of not being nervous; it just means that you learn not to show it.

Thank goodness the cliffs were on the west side of the bay; if they were on the east side they would blanket the wind which, instead, blew gently across the flat land on the eastern side. Santa Lucia was perfectly placed to be raided from seaward – providing there were no isolated rocks scattered about the bay.

He watched as Lobb brought the ship another point to starboard, so that she headed directly for the town, and Ned estimated they were well into the bay: the first of the cliffs were now on the larboard quarter; he thought he could distinguish the seaward end of the flat land on the starboard beam. He tried to estimate the distance to the town. It was difficult in the darkness, although some clouds shifted for a few moments, allowing starlight to show a thin line where waves were breaking on the beach in front of the town. A mile? Less.

"They're ready with the anchor?" he asked Lobb.

"Ready, sir," Lobb answered patiently.

Ned looked astern again. The *Griffin*'s two boats were towing astern, having been hoisted out half an hour ago, and they were throwing up a glow of phosphorescence. Yes, and he could just make out the *Peleus*'s bow wave in the darkness. He had noticed in the past how the water was often phosphorescent in patches. What on earth caused it? On a night like this it seemed eerie.

"We'll go in under headsails," Ned told Lobb, who gave orders to clew up the mainsail. Three quarters of a mile to the beach, perhaps less. And there was the smell of the land: a mixture of rotting cabbage and herbs, with a hint of damp earth . . . He heard the occasional squawk of some land bird and then the bark of a disconsolate dog. No shouts of alarm, no challenges, no pealing bells raising the alarm. The town slept.

In a way it was unfair, Ned mused: Santa Lucia was an innocent town, chosen by chance. But then the five villages set ablaze by the Spaniards on Jamaica had been innocent, too; their inhabitants had been fisherfolk and people farming the land nearby, people caught up in a Spanish decision to attack the island. They were innocent people in the Jamaica villages; they were innocent people in Santa Lucia. It was always the innocent who suffered – but then who was not innocent? In Cuba, perhaps everyone except the Viceroy . . .

There was a grating noise under the keel and the *Griffin* came to a stop. Even before Ned had time to register that they had gone aground the *Peleus* was passing on one side and the *Phoenix* on the other, showing that the ship was hung up on an isolated rock, not a reef, so that the rest of the ships could pass her on either side. But how many more isolated rocks were there, waiting hidden below the water ready to strand or hole an unsuspecting ship?

"I think we ran on it to starboard," Ned told Lobb. "We'll heel her to larboard and see if she comes off. Hoist up one of the boats by the yardarm, and run the guns over to the other side."

But it all takes time, he cursed: time in which the rest of the buccaneer fleet will have anchored and sent their men ashore. Hurriedly men cast off the breechings and train tackles of the guns on the starboard side and began to haul them over to larboard, the trucks rumbling on the deck. More men pulled one of the boats round while others scrambled up the rigging and out along the yard, reeving a tackle to hoist the boat.

"Will that be enough weight?" Lobb asked anxiously. "This wind isn't strong enough to help heel us much."

"As soon as we get the boat hoisted up we'll set the mainsail and brace the yard sharp up," Ned said. "If that doesn't heel us enough, then we'll have to start the water and pump it over the side to lighten the ship."

But who was going to lead the raid on the port? Ned thought whether or not to take the remaining boat and hurry for the shore, but he realized that with the distance involved and the delay he would arrive after most of the boats had landed and that it would then be hopeless trying to take command of more than a thousand excited men. But for running up on this damnable rock the *Griffin* would now be at anchor and her boats would be the first to land on the beach, leaving him properly placed to lead.

So now it was up to Thomas, who was more than capable of taking charge. The *Peleus* had passed close enough for Thomas to see what had happened and he would have wasted no time in deciding what to do.

By now all the starboard side guns had been pushed and hauled over to larboard and the men who had rove the tackle were dangling the rope down to those in the boat, which was now directly under the end of the yard.

Ned went to the bulwark and watched the men feed the rope through the lifting eyebolts and, as soon as they stood back with the task completed, Ned called to the men at the tackle. "Hoist away . . ."

Should he have filled the boat with water? It was only a question of pulling the bung out and letting the boat flood, but a flooded boat might be too heavy, springing the yard or parting the tackle.

Slowly the boat jerked into the air, and once it was clear of the bulwarks Ned gave the order to set the mainsail and sheet it home.

With the guns on the larboard side, the boat added its weight at the end of the yard, levering the mast over to larboard. Now the mainsail caught the wind and, as the men hauled on the sheet and braces, helped heel the ship further to larboard.

140

What did you do during the attack on Santa Lucia? Well, actually I watched from the middle of the harbour because we ran aground . . . The last of the buccaneer ships had passed the stranded *Griffin*, heading for the beach, and not one of them had stranded.

Aurelia had noticed and she commented: "I think we hit the only rock in the whole harbour."

"At least it didn't hole us. Remind me to talk to the carpenter – he was quick to get below and sound the well. We're not taking a drop of water so we've that much to be thankful for."

As Ned and Lobb stood silent for a moment, watching the big mainsail belly in the wind, ghostly in the darkness, they felt the ship grunt, then grunt again as the keel slid across the rock. And then suddenly the *Griffin* was under way once more, sailing unrestrained.

Ned snapped at the helmsman and the *Griffin* turned towards the town. "We're finished with the mainsail," he told Lobb. "Back the headsails while we get the boat back in the water."

He turned to the larboard side. "You men with the guns – get them back to starboard and secure the breechings and train trackles; if we roll they'll go clean through the ship's side."

Once again the heavy wooden wheels on the gun carriages rumbled as the grunting men pulled and heaved them back into position, and then they crouched as they knotted the heavy rope through the eyebolts fitted to the ship's side.

The boat was lowered back into the water, the tackle was cast off and men with the painter began to haul it aft. Ned called them to leave it alongside: the moment the *Griffin* was properly anchored, he intended to get ashore.

The headsails were sheeted home and the *Griffin* once again stretched towards the town. It was hard to see the beach for anchored ships, and Ned cursed: he would not be able to anchor close in, and that meant he would be even later in landing. The devil take that rock!

Lobb gave the order to ease the helm as the *Griffin* slipped past one of the buccaneer ships, and quickly followed that with instructions to luff up to avoid another anchored just beyond.

"Don't go in any closer," Ned said. "We'll anchor here."

With most of the buccaneers now ashore, judging from the

boats Ned could see on the beach, there was no need to avoid shouting orders, and after a bellow from Lobb the headsails slid down the stays and the *Griffin* slowly turned head to wind.

Lobb ran to the ship's side to see when the way had come off her and gave another bellow, which was followed by the splash of the anchor and the sound of the cable coursing through the hawsehole.

Ned hitched at his cutlass and pushed at the two pistols stuck in his belt. He jumped up on to the bulwark above the boat and shouted to the nearest men to join him.

A couple of minutes later he was seated on a thwart while the men fitted the oars into the rowlocks. He heard Aurelia call something and answered with a reassuring hail. Now the men began rowing briskly, and at that moment Ned heard the tolling of a church bell: the Spaniards were raising the alarm. How far had the buccaneers got?

The boat's keel grated on the sand and Ned leapt out. There were many boats on the beach, like great fish tossed up by the sea. The sand was hard and Ned held up his cutlass as he ran towards the tolling bell and the yelling of the buccaneers who had already landed. The men who had been rowing followed him, by now shouting with excitement.

That damned bell! It would get everyone excited and he could just see the church tower above the roof tops. He ran along one street and then turned into another, seeing the white-painted church on the far side of a small *plaza,* which was already teeming with men.

Drawing his cutlass he flung open the church door and ran in. A few moments later he found the bellringer: a man in his nightshirt ringing with something approaching a frenzy. "Stop!" Ned ordered in Spanish but the man was oblivious, apparently hauling in panic. Ned slashed at the bellrope above the man's head and the bell rang once more at the man tugged and collapsed. The bellrope flicked back and forth for a few moments and Ned decided to leave the man – priest or sexton? – slumped where he was, still holding on to a few feet of bellrope.

By now he had been joined by several of the buccaneers, who ran to the altar looking for gold ornaments and candlesticks. Ned left the church and walked over to the nearest house, banging on the door with the hilt of his cutlass.

A woman asked what he wanted in a voice trembling with fear. "Where does the mayor live?" he demanded.

"On the other side of the *plaza* – a double gate beside the big tree!"

Ned turned and ran across the *plaza,* calling to the buccaneers.

The mayor refused to come to the door of his house and the buccaneers soon smashed it in. Ned led them into the house and eventually found their quarry hiding under a big table in what seemed to be the dining room.

He was a plump little man also dressed only in his nightshirt, although Ned could not distinguish his features in the darkness. "Take him down to the boat and hold him there," Ned told three of the buccaneers.

Back out in the *plaza* he saw the flicker of flames coming from buildings at the seaward end of the town. A few burning houses, he thought grimly, will help us see what we are doing.

As he made his way towards the flames he heard Thomas's booming voice.

"Search these big houses," he was shouting. "They don't eat their meals off pottery!"

He found Thomas in the next street, cutlass in one hand and pistol in the other.

"Ned! You got off that rock then! Must be the only one in the bay. Gave me quite a turn when I saw the *Griffin* stop: thought it might be a wide reef. Not much purchase in this place!"

"I found the mayor," Ned said. "He'll be worth a bit of ransom."

Thomas waved towards the burning buildings. "Do we burn the whole town?"

"No, but a few of these big houses should go: the owners are the influential people in this town."

"What about stoving in some of the fishing boats on the beach? I saw a dozen or more drawn up when I landed."

Ned thought a moment then shook his head. "No, leave them: the fishermen are poor folk and have no influence."

"We were lucky there weren't any out in the bay to raise the alarm," Thomas said, pausing to shout orders to a group of buccaneers.

Ned watched as buccaneers smashed down another door and

ran into the house, shouting threats. By now several of them had lanterns and burning torches, and he could see the glow at many other windows as the men searched for valuables.

But Santa Lucia's streets stayed empty except for the roaming bands of buccaneers and if there had been a watch in Santa Lucia its members stayed behind closed doors. He heard a triumphant shout as one buccaneer found something valuable, and suddenly he realized that his heart was not really in the raid. Yes, the raid was necessary to teach the Dons a lesson and warn them off Jamaica, but terrorizing people like this, robbing them and setting their homes ablaze round their ears . . . ?

Yet it was a weird contradiction: if the Spanish raided a town in Jamaica they would have no hesitation in putting houses to the torch; nor, more important, would they hesitate to murder the occupants. From what Sir Harold had said, eight people had been killed in the five villages. Ned felt a chill; this was no time to be faint-hearted, he told himself. To the Spaniards – to any Spaniards, be they young soldiers or old women – the people of Jamaica were heretics, doomed to the rack, hellfire, brimstone and eternal damnation.

By now Thomas's buccaneers had searched the houses and were busy setting fire to two of them. The fires started as little more than bonfires in the rooms, but the wood was bone dry and in moments flames were leaping up, crackling like splintering wood and roaring as random puffs of wind fanned them. Walls collapsed with a crash; roofs caved in, hurling more wood into the fires.

Was it worth looking for the town treasurer, and finding out who were the two or three most prosperous merchants? Ned decided not: they would demand a high ransom for the mayor to make up for it.

Ned called to his buccaneers and made for the other side of the *plaza*. There were several big houses there that needed searching. Already he could see some of Thomas's men staggering down to the boats, carrying and dragging items they had found.

His own men were soon battering down doors, shouting at the terrified occupants and disappearing into the houses, their lanterns lighting up the windows as they flung open the shutters. Ned suddenly realized that apart from the crackling of flames, the loudest noise was the hysterical barking of dogs, which were obviously racing through the town in excited packs. There was the yapping of small dogs mixed with the deep baying of hounds, and all clearly frightened by the flames.

By now it was clear that many of the buccaneers had found wine and spirits in the houses and were getting drunk, but Ned knew it was hopeless to try and keep the men sober. If there was drink, the men would find it, and anyone trying to stop them risked his life. Ned knew that it would be stupid to risk his authority by getting into drunken arguments with a group of besotted men. Do as much as possible while the men were sober, and then get them back to the boats when they were too drunk to carry on. Buccaneer raids had their own pattern.

By the time dawn started picking out the shape of the houses, the buccaneers had searched through the last of the big houses and staggered down to the boats with their loot. Ned checked that the mayor had been taken out to the *Griffin* and handed over to guards. They did not speak a word of Spanish, but Aurelia would have acted as interpreter should any explanations be necessary.

The next time Ned found Thomas – still in control of several hundred drunk and half-drunk buccaneers – he raised the question of the mayor.

"Shall we ransom him here or take him back to Jamaica?"

"Lot easier if we do it here," Thomas said. "Once it's daylight, we'll gather up some of the townsmen and tell them what we want for their mayor."

"We might have taken all their money," Ned said.

"Then we'll take him away while they look for more!"

By nine o'clock, a dozen of the most important of Santa Lucia's inhabitants were lined up in the *plaza,* with the burned-out row of houses over on the left. The whole *plaza* reeked of the burned buildings, and the twelve men stood in a group.

When Ned walked up to speak to them, he realized that all twelve thought they had been selected for execution. Certainly the *plaza* looked a grim enough place for a file of musketeers to line up to form a firing squad, he thought to himself.

He stood in front of the twelve men. "A few days ago," he said in Spanish, "a number of your ships appeared off the north coast of Jamaica and set fire to five villages. Five up to the time we left; there may have been many more since then. And they killed eight people.

"So now you know why we are here: we could have burned down the whole of Santa Lucia, but as you see we have burned only a score of houses. We could have taken all of you as hostages, but in fact we've taken only the mayor.

"We hope you will complain to the authorities in Havana, and explain to them that this raid is a reprisal for the raids on Jamaica. Now, we have to talk about the mayor. Obviously you respect him, or else he would not be your mayor. To get him back, you are going to have pay a ransom.

"Don't," he said sternly, holding up his hand to silence some of the men who were beginning to protest, "argue that you have no money. You have plenty, and it is still where you hid it. I shall return here at noon, and you will all be here, and you will have with you enough gold and coins to ransom your mayor.

"How much? Well, we will be generous. This is a small town and your mayor is a small man. So we will fix the price at forty thousand pieces of eight, or its equivalent in gold objects. If you do not pay, then your mayor will be hanged – " Ned gestured across the *plaza*, " – hanged from that cotton tree over there . . ."

With that Ned gave what he hoped was a bloodcurdling laugh and stalked out of the *plaza*, followed by Thomas. As they reached the boats Thomas said: "My Spanish wasn't good enough to follow everything you said, but that was a diabolical laugh; it even made *my* blood run cold!"

"Well, I don't want to have to hang the mayor from that tree, so let's hope those worthies produce the ransom. Our men will also see what they missed!"

"Yes, I guessed you have given them time and let them go so that they can get their valuables out of their hiding places."

"Yes – robbing houses is a waste if the people have time to hide things. That's why it's better to attack a big town where there's a treasury. Still, I told them why they've been raided, so Havana will hear all about it."

By the time that Ned was rowed out to the *Griffin* he was beginning to feel the effects of a night's lost sleep. Aurelia reported that the mayor had been put below in leg irons, with a couple of seamen guarding him.

"He was terrified when he was brought on board," she said. "He was trembling so much I had a hard time making him understand what was going on. He's convinced he's going to be killed. He has a wife, seven children, his mother and four aunts depending on him; that he told me when he had calmed down a bit. Every one of them will mourn him, he says, and every one of them will starve if he doesn't provide for them."

"Did you reassure him that he wasn't going to die?"

Aurelia shook her head. "No: I found I had nothing but contempt for him. Once he found out that a woman appeared to be in command of the ship, he began weeping, trying to get sympathy – for himself and all his family."

Ned described the raid on Santa Lucia, and how a dozen of the town's leading citizens had until noon to collect the mayor's ransom.

"I saw many houses burning," Aurelia said.

"It probably looked worse than it was: a score at the most. Just enough to teach them a lesson." He took out his watch and looked at it. "The dozen worthy burghers have to be in the *plaza* at noon to pay the ransom. Wringing their hands and saying they have no money . . ."

"So what do you do then?"

"Frighten them. Daylight might have given some of them a little more courage."

"How do you do that?"

"I'll take the mayor with me – is he still in his nightshirt?"

Aurelia nodded. "He made me too cross to try to find clothes for him. Anyway, I don't think we have anyone as fat as that on board."

# Chapter
Thirteen

At noon Ned led the *Griffin's* men into the *plaza*. Groups of buccaneers from other ships still roamed through the town, occasionally breaking into a house but more often just drinking spirits from bottles and casks. In one street several men had set up a cask and were refilling the mug of any man that passed. The town, Ned noted, smelled like a bonfire doused with water: burned houses reeked like piles of wet charcoal.

He arrived at the *plaza* with the mayor, who was still barefooted and in his nightshirt, unshaven and pale-faced, his eyes flicking round him, as if wary that a cutlass could jab at him from any direction.

The group of citizens were standing in the same place, waiting for him. Ned counted them. Only eleven men.

"Where's the twelfth man?" he demanded.

"He hasn't come back," one of the eleven said.

"I can see that," Ned said, and gestured to some of his men.

They went over to the cotton tree and, starting off by climbing on to each other's shoulders, they got up the tree and two of them scrambled out along a branch. Round the end of it, as far as they could reach out, they tied a block, reeved a rope through it, and dropped the two ends down to the men waiting on the ground below.

As the men aloft climbed down, so a man on the ground tied a noose in one end of the rope, while several of the others picked up the other end and walked a few feet with it, until the noose was shoulder high.

As soon as they had finished, Ned gestured towards them and said to the eleven: "You – " he pointed to the most prosperous-looking of them, " – go over to that tree and put your head in the noose." He took out his watch and examined it. "Yes, you – " he pointed to the youngest-looking of the men " – have ten minutes to find the missing man. If you fail, then the men holding that rope will walk away from the tree and your neighbour will be hauled up head-first to the bough."

While the young man hurried from the group the prosperous-looking man sighed and fainted. Ned gestured to the other men to attend him, and turned to the mayor.

"You'll end up in that noose if they don't pay your ransom. Say a few prayers that your neighbours value you."

In fewer than ten minutes the young man was back with the missing citizen, who was white-faced and trembling. He looked at his neighbour, who by now had been revived and was standing under the tree with the noose round his neck.

"What happened to you?" Ned asked politely.

"I – well, I was detained."

"Indeed? You nearly caused the death of your friend," Ned said, gesturing towards the tree. He took out his watch and examined it again. "Yes, another four minutes would have done it. It's not long, four minutes."

He waved as he saw Thomas come into the *plaza* at the head of a score of buccaneers, and while Thomas came over to join him Ned said to the group of Spaniards: "You have the ransom?"

Three of them spoke at once, and Ned held up his hand to silence them and pointed at one man to be the spokesman.

"No, we haven't been able to find the money," the man said, looking first at the tree and then down at the ground. "Not nearly that money."

"How unfortunate," Ned said softly. "Well, if you say you can't find it, that's an end of the matter. Since you will now all hang, we might as well start with that fellow who has the noose round his neck. He can be first and the mayor last. That makes you the thirteenth," Ned said to the mayor, who groaned piteously and started saying prayers in a low, trembling voice.

"You can't do that!" exclaimed the man chosen as spokesman. "That's murder!"

"Some of your people murdered eight villagers in Jamaica," Ned said. "I'll hang eight of you first and then we'll have a pause before we finish off the last five."

"But you've given us no time to find the money!"

"You had two hours or more."

"We need more time," the man grumbled.

Ned spoke in English to Thomas, translating what had been said so far. Thomas had no sympathy. "String that fellow up," he growled. "The sight of him kicking about at the end of a rope might change their minds."

Ned turned back to the men. "Well, my friend and I agree: no ransom means you don't value your mayor, so he will be hanged. But," Ned added ominously and speaking very slowly and distinctly, "he'll be hanged last. He'll have the pleasure of watching the twelve citizens who did not value him being hoisted up to the bough first."

The spokesman took a step forward, his arms held out appealingly. "What can we say?"

"You can say 'Goodbye'," Ned said helpfully. "But you are wasting time; we'll start with the fellow who already has his head in the noose."

"But please," the spokesman exclaimed, "give us more time!"

"Can you find the ransom if you have more time?" Ned asked.

"We can try!"

Ned stared at them. "I suspect you are just humbugging me, but I'll give you one more chance. I'll let you go, one at a time and with two of my men escorting you, and you'll come back with as much money and plate as you can find. When the last man is back we'll add it all up, and if it comes to the ransom, you all will go free, taking the mayor with you. If you are short – of even one piece of eight – you'll all hang. And, of course, forfeit the money and plate."

He eyed the spokesman. "You can be the first to go." He called over a couple of buccaneers and gave them their orders, and the three men trotted out of the *plaza*.

"This is a gigantic game of bluff," Thomas commented in English.

Ned shook his head vigorously. "Oh no, I'm not bluffing," he said. "The tackle is rigged, the block is turning freely, and we already have the first neck in the noose. Oh no, I'm not bluffing. Nor do I think our Spanish friends think I am."

"No, they're sure they're done for," Thomas said. "It's just that I've never seen you so bloodthirsty before."

"No, you haven't, but I'm going to put an end to the Spaniards murdering our people and burning their villages, and this is the only way to do it."

By now the sun was directly overhead and men cast hardly any shadow. Ned felt as if the sun was beating him. "I am going to wait under the shadow of that tree," he announced. "Come and join me. It'll be a famous tree in Santa Lucia's history if these people don't pay up. I wonder what they'll call it."

"Not a lot of choice," Thomas said cheerfully. "Noose, hangman, gibbet tree . . . that's about it."

Ned sat down on the ground and leaned back against the trunk of the tree. He gestured towards the man standing with his head in the noose. "There's a fellow who doesn't think I'm bluffing," he told Thomas.

"Nothing like feeling the noose round your neck for believing you're going to be hanged," Thomas said. "Especially if you have any imagination."

Ned felt his eyelids getting heavy. "I'm going to doze for a few minutes; wake me when the men come back."

Thomas nudged him a few minutes later. "Here they come," he said.

Ned walked back across the *plaza* to where the man stood between the two buccaneers. "You managed to find something?"

The man gestured to the small sack one of the buccaneers was carrying. "In there – all I have," he said in a strangled voice.

"Tip it out," Ned told the seamen, who shook out half a dozen gold plates, several mugs, a crucifix, and what must have been three or four hundred pieces of eight.

Ned pointed to another of the group. "Now you," he said in Spanish, adding in English instructions for the two seamen.

"This is going to take all night, sending 'em off one at a time," he said. "I'll send a couple more as well."

He gave orders in Spanish to the two men, and in English to the four buccaneers who were to escort them.

"Supposing they end up just a little short?" Thomas asked.

"We'll give them the benefit of it," Ned said. "Likewise if they end up with more than we're asking, we'll leave the balance with them. After all, we mustn't get the buccaneers a bad name!"

As the men were sent off three at a time, and came back with their buccaneer escorts, the pile of gold began to grow larger. Gold cutlery joined gold plates, some men produced three or four crucifixes, two of them had swords with gold hilts inlaid with precious stones, all of them had many gold coins.

Ned looked round for the *Griffin*'s bosun, who had brought a pair of scales. "You might as well start weighing up the plate," he said. "But keep a careful tally."

The Santa Lucia citizens who had already brought their valuables watched as the bosun held up the scales after putting gold in one pan and a weight in the other. Sometimes he added extra weights to make the scales balance; occasionally he exchanged a piece of plate for something heavier or lighter. Each time he finally spoke a weight, which was written down by a buccaneer crouching beside him.

Ned could hear the figures, and murmured to Thomas: "Unless these last two or three let us down, I think we'll have it."

"No hangings, eh?" Thomas commented.

"We could hang this poor fellow who has been waiting so patiently with his head in the noose," Ned said jokingly. "I'm sure by now he's made his peace with his Maker!"

"By all means hang a few of them," Thomas said, running his finger round the inside of his collar. "After all, they've kept us waiting long enough in this hot sun."

But the last three men did not bring enough: there was little plate and few coins. Ned watched it all being weighed and counted, and then shook his head sadly.

"I said the ransom was forty thousand pieces of eight, or the equivalent, and you have produced only thirty-eight thousand. That's much too short. By the way," he said, as though it was an afterthought, "do any of you want a priest?"

They all did, and they told Ned where to find him. Ned sent a couple of buccaneers off to fetch him, telling them not to worry about explanations; just bring the man, by force if necessary.

Ned turned to the men again. "As soon as the priest arrives, he had better attend to that one over there first," he said, indicating the man at the noose.

The mayor was whimpering something and a few moments passed before Ned realized what he was saying. He turned on the man. "We are two thousand pieces of eight short. Are you saying you can provide the difference?"

"I think so; I don't know how much the plate will weigh. It should be enough," he said, with something approaching eagerness.

Ned gave orders to three buccaneers and then said to the mayor: "Go with these men. Search your house well. You've seen the tree and you've seen the noose."

"Oh indeed, indeed," the mayor exclaimed and hobbled off, the sharp stones obviously agony because of his bare feet.

Ned translated to Thomas what had just passed. "First time I've ever heard of a man paying his own ransom," Thomas said. "Still, his gold is as good as anyone else's."

The mayor and the buccaneers came back fifteen minutes later, two of the buccaneers holding sacks, which they tipped out on the ground.

Ned realized that the mayor must be the wealthiest man in Santa Lucia, and Thomas murmured: "Our fellows didn't search his house very well."

One of the buccaneers emptying the sack looked up at Thomas. "Had it all well hidden, sir. Secret hole under the floor of one of the rooms in his house."

"Did you – "

"Yes, the floors in all the other rooms," the man said with a grin. "Come up easy, they did. 'Mazing how the sight of gold doubles your muscles!"

The bosun held up his scales and began weighing the various items. After his helper had written down the weights, the bosun counted up the coins.

Then he gave the total to Ned and the mayor sighed and collapsed when Ned translated it into Spanish.

"They faint easily, don't they?" Thomas said unsympathetically. "That's just about enough, isn't it?"

"It'll do," Ned said. "When the mayor has recovered – ah, he's opening his eyes – we'll tell them all, and let that fellow take his neck out of the noose."

Chapter Fourteen

Sir Harold Luce tugged at the end of his tobacco-stained moustaches as he looked at Ned and Thomas across the table. "Do sit down," he said politely, remembering their last visit. "Welcome back to Port Royal. Did you have a successful voyage?"

"Yes, we achieved what we set out to do," Ned said.

"Do tell me about it."

"We went to Santa Lucia, raided it, set fire to a score of houses and ransomed the mayor. And gave the leading citizens a warning for Havana."

Sir Harold's sharp black eyes started to shine. "Oh ho, you ransomed the mayor, eh? For a good price?"

"For more than he was worth," Ned said contemptuously.

"You will of course be paying the ransom into the Treasury," Luce said.

Ned paused for a few moments. Pay the ransom into the Treasury? Was the man making an elaborate joke or was he serious? Well, he had no sense of humour, so one had to assume he was serious.

"I don't have the ransom any more," Ned said casually. And that was quite true: the purchase had been divided up before the ships left Santa Lucia: so much for each ship, and the captains had taken away the shares to divide up among their men. Within a few hours, Ned reflected, the first of the purchase would be spent in Port Royal's taverns and brothels; just as soon as the men could get ashore with the spoils in their pockets. Kinnock, the pawnbroker, would be doing a flourishing business as the men sold plate, cutlery and other items which had been their share of the purchase. Kinnock, he thought, was probably one of the richest men in the island. Certainly the most mercenary; he thought only of money; the most beautiful gold jewellery meant nothing to him but a price in pieces of eight; nothing wrought in precious metals had beauty, only weight.

Luce was frowning now. "You don't have the ransom? What do you mean? Where is it?"

"Oh dear," Ned sighed, "the fact is you *still* don't understand how the buccaneers work. For a start a buccaneer is just like any other businessman. O'Leary has his chandlery, Kinnock his pawnshop. A buccaneer captain his ship.

"Instead of hiring men to work for him in his business, he tells men they can come and work for him without pay, but they get a share of the profits. The profits are the purchase won in a raid.

"No purchase means no profit for the captain and no shares for his men. But men must eat, a ship needs new rope and sails and paint, and the captain can expect a fair return on the money he has invested in his ship."

Luce said impatiently: "I can understand all that."

"Very well," Ned said. "An expedition to Santa Lucia costs money. Food for the men, cordage and canvas for the ship, powder, shot . . . The captains paid these costs when the expedition started because they were betting on there being purchase to reimburse them. Had there been no purchase, then they would have been unlucky; they would have lost money. But there was purchase – thanks mainly to the ransom – so the captains have got their outlay back and a profit, and the men have in effect been paid. So there is no question of paying ransom into the Treasury."

"Oh yes there is," Luce said stubbornly. "You and your men went on this expedition with commissions which I issued. If you sail with commissions issued by the governor of Jamaica, it stands to reason that you must pay for those commissions by paying some of the ransom. Not all of it," Luce said expansively, with a show of reasonableness. "The captains can deduct their expenses, and you can allow the men the same pay a day that a seaman in one of the coastal vessels gets."

He rubbed his hands together, as if washing them. "There, that seems a fair arrangement. Let me have a list of expenses and the total number of seamen, and we'll work out the total and deduct that from the ransom. How much did you receive?"

Ned felt himself getting angry. The anger was flooding him in surges, like a rising tide. Luce knew well enough how the buccaneers worked: he was just trying to cheat them.

"I've already told Your Excellency that the ransom has been distributed. Neither the captains nor the men would have sailed on any payment-by-the-day basis: they have no loyalty to Jamaica, remember."

"Well, they should have," Luce snapped. "Anyway, that's the end of the commissions."

"What do you mean by that?"

"They are cancelled," Luce said coldly. "If the Treasury isn't to get its share of the purchase, then there is no point in you having commissions."

"But you agreed they would be permanent when you gave them out – permanent unless you have orders from the Privy Council."

"I have changed my mind," Luce said, with more than a hint of a flounce in his voice.

"So you have no further use for the buccaneers?" Ned asked.

"I can see no further need for them," Luce said airily.

The tone of his voice sent cold shivers down Ned's back. "I suggest you think again," Ned said calmly.

"I've no need to; I've already made my decision," Luce said.

"You've made your decision based on Cuba," Ned said. "Thanks to our raid on Santa Lucia, you think there will be no more raids on Jamaica from Cuba. But you forget the Main. You forget that the biggest Spanish base is at Cartagena. Cuba is of no consequence compared with the Main."

"We have nothing to fear from the Main," Luce said, waving his hand dismissively. "It's no good you trying to frighten me with stories of the Main. They leave us alone!"

Ned closed his eyes for a full minute, thinking. Then he decided to tell Luce about Riohacha, and the hostages on board the *Dolphyn, Argonauta* and Secco's ship.

"You will remember that before we took General Heffer up to Santo Domingo the buccaneer fleet sailed for a few days?"

"Yes," Luce said with a yawn, "I remember you were away a short time."

"But you don't know why?"

"Of course I don't. You didn't tell me, and," he added loftily, "I am not interested in your comings and goings."

"Well, I tell you. Two of our ships had been seized by the Spanish at Riohacha, on the Main, and their people imprisoned in the fort there. We sailed to rescue them. We did. And we found that both captains had been tortured by the Spanish, who were particularly concerned to know for certain if you had disbanded the Army here and withdrawn the buccaneers' commissions."

Luce shrugged his shoulders. "There's nothing very secret about that. Everyone here knows about it."

"It's not secret here, but it sounds so ludicrous to the Spanish that they find it hard to believe: they can't credit that the governor of Jamaica can be so stupid: to them it is like committing suicide. So they tortured our men to find out how true it all was."

"Sheer waste of time," Luce said.

"Perhaps," Ned said. "But I was curious about why our two ships had been captured, so I started asking a few questions of my own. I discovered that the Spanish were afraid that the ships would find out about some ship movements that had been going on. The Spanish on the Main have just been reinforced by more ships from Spain."

"Just gossip, that's all that is. Gossip you picked up from the taverns."

"No, not gossip," Ned said. "The man who told me was the governor of the province."

"I don't believe you," Luce said flatly. "The governor of the province isn't going to gossip with any buccaneers who call."

"Perhaps you would like to question him yourself?" Ned asked innocently.

"Are you suggesting that I go to Riohacha or Barranquilla, or wherever the governor lives?" Luce asked sarcastically.

"Oh no, nothing like that, you could question him here in this room, if you like, along with the bishop of the province."

Luce looked at him wide-eyed. "This is not a joking matter, Mr Yorke."

"I am not joking. Both the governor and the bishop are on

board my ships. I took the precaution of picking them up when I was in Riohacha: they were both there on a visit."

Luce's sallow face was beginning to turn red. "Do you mean to say you have a *governor* out there in irons on board one of your stinking ships?"

"We can put him in irons if you like," Ned said amiably, enjoying Luce's outrage, "but I think he would prefer to be at large. And his ship smells as sweet as does this house."

"Go and bring him over here at once!" Luce demanded.

Ned shook his head. "Oh no, I can't do that. I take back my offer of letting you question him in this room: you can go out to the ship if you want to talk to him."

"But the courtesies!" Luce snapped. "I must show him the courtesies due to a fellow governor. You wouldn't understand, but – "

"He's our hostage," Ned interrupted. "There'll be no courtesies – particularly since we found our captains chained up and unconscious in his prison."

"I insist!" Luce said hotly. "Fetch him here at once!"

Ned put his hands flat on the table with a slow deliberation. Then he stared at Luce, holding his eyes until the man looked down at the table.

"You tell me that our commissions are cancelled," Ned said, his voice quiet but each word spoken with chilly distinctness. "Yet you still think you can give us orders. Let me tell you, Your Excellency, the Spanish governor I have on board one of my ships means even less to me than you do, because he was responsible for torturing my captains. I'd cut his throat and toss his body over the side without a qualm. Not a qualm," he repeated, "and strip his body first for any rings or gems to pay for his keep."

"Don't you dare harm a hair of his head," Luce yelled. "Bring him over here at once! I insist!"

Ned looked at him coldly. "I tell you what. We'll cut the throats of the governor, the bishop and the mayor of Riohacha – I forgot to tell you we have him too – and leave them on the end of the jetty. Then we'll all be satisfied. You can play host – or gravedigger – to all three."

Luce looked at Ned's eyes and knew he was serious: this was no idle threat. "Why did you take them as hostages, then?"

158

"A precaution," Ned said. "The ships that have come from Spain will be used for one of two things – the governor says he does not know which. Either they'll be used to land Spanish troops here in Jamaica, or they'll carry plate back to Spain.

"If they try to invade Jamaica, hostages might be useful. Especially," Ned said brutally, "because the present governor of Jamaica is – capricious."

"Don't you call me capricious!" Luce exclaimed hotly. "I insist you show me respect."

"But I have shown you respect," Ned said. "I've considered you capricious – at least capricious – for a long time, but I have always been respectful: you must admit that."

Luce was silent for some time, obviously thinking over what Ned had been saying. Finally he unexpectedly asked: "Which do you think it will be – a plate convoy or an attempt on this island?"

"An attempt on Jamaica," Ned said without hesitation. "That's what we have to guard against. If the Dons in fact send off a plate convoy instead, well and good; we'll have lost nothing by being alert."

"I disagree with you completely," Luce announced, as though he had been considering the matter for a week and was now announcing it to a full legislative council meeting. "Obviously they are planning a plate convoy. The silver from Potosi has been piling up, and none of it is reaching Spain, where the government needs it. Why would they be bothered with an island like this?"

"Mainly because the only ships that could capture the convoy are based here," Ned said evenly. "There's no point in sailing a convoy that you know will be captured. If the Viceroy has any sense, he'll secure Jamaica first, and then sail the convoy. Not just that convoy but as many as he likes, since he'd then have nothing to fear from Jamaica."

"Nonsense," said Luce, "you are just frightening yourself." He gave his moustaches another tug, as if to make them flare out. "Well, Yorke, there we are: I want those commissions back, and I want the governor."

The room seemed oppressively hot. "We'll deliver both – to the end of the jetty," Ned said ominously.

As soon as he realized what Ned had said, Luce went white; perspiration started to bead his forehead and upper lip. "You'd never harm that governor," he said, but he clearly did not believe his own words.

Ned laughed melodramatically, decided the laugh was effective, and sniffed. "He's just eating up food and drinking valuable water," Ned said. "He's just a nuisance to all of us. If what you say is true, the chances of using him as a hostage are remote. Why should we keep him?"

"But you – you can't just murder him like that!"

Ned decided to risk another melodramatic laugh. "Can't we?" he asked. "Governor, bishop and mayor – just carrion!"

"No, no," Luce said desperately. "Just bring them over here. I'll look after them. I don't mind the cost," he said eagerly. "It would be an honour."

"Exactly," Ned said. "That's why we'll keep 'em. We have the right attitude to Spanish governors and prelates!"

Chapter
Fifteen

Thomas poured more rumbullion from the green, onion-shaped bottle and took a sip from his mug. "There's no way that we are ever going to change old Loosely's attitude: he just sits in his little office, shuts his eyes, and thinks that no one can see him."

Ned said quietly. "Does it really matter what he does or thinks? The fact is that unless the buccaneers do something, there's nothing to stop the Spaniards taking Jamaica if they feel like it."

"It seems too damned unfair that the buccaneers have to repair the gaps left by the Privy Council or the governor," Thomas complained. "The Privy Council care so little about the island they won't even send out a frigate to help defend it, yet at the same time they think the buccaneers are naughty boys. And Loosely messes about with commissions as though he's playing cards."

"Yes, it's unfair," Ned said, "but we can't change it. Anyway, we ignored Loosely's demand for the ransom!"

"What on earth was that?" Diana asked.

Ned explained about the governor's initial demand.

"The man's mad!" Diana exclaimed. "He'll soon start issuing letters of marque and charging for them."

"Yes, the Port Royal buccaneering fee. But the only thing that would knock any sense into him would be a good fight. Seeing half a dozen Spanish ships anchoring off the Palisadoes and putting a thousand soldiers ashore, or something like that."

"It'd be too late for him to get frightened then," Aurelia pointed out. "They'd capture the whole island with a thousand men, wouldn't they?"

"With no buccaneers to interfere, they could probably do it with five hundred. Take Port Royal, anyway, and whoever has Port Royal controls the whole island."

"If only we knew what those extra Spanish ships were going to do," Aurelia said. "Come here or go to Spain with plate."

"If only we could be sure they were going to Spain with plate, we could get ready to capture them," Thomas said. "It seems such a waste of time sitting here in Port Royal in case they should attack."

"It's not knowing that's the trouble," Diana said. "We've got to find out somehow."

"That damned Spanish governor knows," Ned growled. "I'm sure of that. We should fetch him over from the *Argonauta* and persuade him to talk."

"How are you going to do that?" asked Diana.

"Tickle him – or burn the soles of his feet," Thomas said grimly. "If he doesn't know for certain, he can make a pretty shrewd guess."

The more Ned thought about it, the more he was certain that Thomas was right. Sanchez would be in the Viceroy's confidence: he would be one of the first to know that ships had arrived (almost certainly unexpectedly) from Spain, and be told what the Viceroy intended to do with them. So far Sanchez had protested that he did not know, but it was more likely that he not only knew but might well have been asked by the Viceroy for an opinion.

"Mind you," Thomas said, "by now I should think the word has got out in a place like Cartagena, so if we had someone there he could find out if it's a plate convoy or Jamaica."

"It means going over there and capturing a coasting vessel," Ned said.

"Secco would like to go," Thomas said. "Any excuse to kill off a few more of his countrymen."

"Very well," Ned said decisively, "let's do that. Ask Secco and question Sanchez again."

"I'll go on deck and tell Lobb to send boats for both of them," Thomas said, emptying his mug of rumbullion. "Anything to get the taste of old Loosely out of my mouth."

After he had left the saloon, Aurelia said: "I still think you are too hard on Sir Harold: he's very new to the job, and you must make allowances."

"But we *do* make allowances," Ned said. "You only hear us describing what *he* says; what you don't hear is Thomas and me explaining things. For instance, when he demanded the ransom this morning, I found myself explaining how the buccaneers operate: the costs, the sharing of the purchase and so on."

"There you are! All this time and he doesn't know how the buccaneers operate."

"We've told him a dozen times," Ned said patiently. "If it doesn't suit his latest mad idea, he conveniently forgets."

"You exaggerate!"

"No, I don't," Ned protested. "Why, this morning he said he did not need the buccaneers any more because there was no further threat to Jamaica. I had to point out that there was probably no more threat from Cuba, but what about the Main? Oh, don't bother about the Main, says he, they've never attacked us."

"What about Riohacha?" Diana asked.

"Yes, I then told him about Riohacha – and that we had the governor, bishop and mayor on board." He laughed to himself at the thought of it.

"What's so funny?" Aurelia inquired.

"The old fool's first thought was to have the Spanish governor brought over to him as an act of courtesy! Pay his respects to a fellow governor!"

"What did you say to that?"

"I said we'd cut his throat without batting an eyelid and dump his body on the end of the jetty."

"What effect did that have?"

"Oh, upset him no end. He probably thought it would offend the Dons – and we mustn't do that!"

"So what happens now? Are you going to hand Sanchez over to Sir Harold?"

"No, we're not," Ned said emphatically. "Luce was also talking wildly about cancelling commissions again. At that point I decided we were on our own: what Sir Harold does or doesn't do is no longer our concern. If we want to stay in Port Royal, then we defend it; if we want to go to Tortuga, we leave Jamaica to the Dons."

"I must admit he tries one's patience," Aurelia said. "But you must seem a couple of wild men to him!"

"If he stopped to think, we've served him well. Why, when he had orders to start or force a trade with the Spaniards, who took old Heffer up to Santo Domingo? Luce hasn't the wit to buy the three prizes we took at Grand Cayman so that he has some transport. Yet he has the money in the treasury – we know that since we put it there after the Portobelo raid. Damnation take it," Ned exclaimed explosively, "since we first came here we've supplied the guns they've got in the batteries, and we've supplied the money and plate they have in the treasury. What would this island do for currency if we'd never raided Portobelo and brought back all that coin?"

"All right, all right," Aurelia said, "I know all about that: I was there, too, remember?"

At that moment Thomas came back into the saloon. "The two boats have left. Tell me, Ned, how do you suggest we persuade this fellow Sanchez to talk?"

Ned grinned happily. "Your mention of burning the soles of his feet gave me an idea."

"Which bit of his anatomy are you going to singe?"

"His pride. Being Spanish that's his most sensitive possession. Just you wait and see."

Ned was thankful that the saloon table was large. Sanchez sat against the bulkhead on the starboard side, with Thomas next to him, then Diana and Secco at the end. Ned sat against the bulkhead on the larboard side opposite Sanchez, with Aurelia next to him.

There was an empty mug in front of Sanchez and Ned pointed to the onion bottle of rum. "This may take some time," he said casually, putting an ominous note in his voice. "Perhaps you'd like a drink?"

The Spaniard shook his head.

"Wine perhaps?"

Again the Spaniard shook his head, obviously deciding that whatever his fate he was going to meet it with a clear head.

"You are missing your family, I imagine," Ned said in Spanish.

"Of course. They won't even know what has happened to me."

"Oh come now, someone at Riohacha must have seen us taking you away and guessed what happened."

"I hope so. My dear wife, and my children . . ."

Ned had a picture of a woman ignored and bullied by her husband who probably had a grossly inflated idea of how a governor should behave. Like her, the children would be cowed. All of them might well be thankful that the lord and master of the house was absent . . .

"Yes," Ned said conversationally, "and of course you have to live with the thought that you'll never see them again."

"Never? I thought you were going to ransom me!"

Ned shook his head regretfully. "Not ransom, no. A hostage, yes, but they'll sacrifice you: they'll have no choice."

"They? Who are 'they'?" a bewildered Sanchez asked.

"Whoever leads the expedition. There'll be two of them, I presume; one commanding the soldiers, the other the ships."

Sanchez shrugged his shoulders and looked down at the empty mug. "I have no idea what you are talking about."

"The landing in Jamaica," Ned said, keeping the tone of his voice casual, as though referring to something they all knew about. "I was saying that if we kept you as a hostage and promised we would cut your throat if a Spanish soldier was landed, those in command would ignore us – which of course would lead to your throat being cut."

"But that is barbarism!" Sanchez exclaimed, going pale. "That would be the same as murdering me!"

"Yes, I can see that from your point of view it must seem so," Ned said. "As far as we are concerned, though, it is straightforward: if the commanders decide it is more important to invade Jamaica than save your life, well . . ." Ned drew his finger across his throat expressively.

Sanchez reached out for the rum bottle and poured a quantity into the mug. He sipped some of it, revealing a shaking hand, and was obviously trying to collect his thoughts. Finally he said: "How did you find out about the invasion plans?"

"You just told me," Ned said calmly. "At Riohacha you told us the ships could be used for a plate convoy to Spain. Now you've made it clear that the Viceroy plans an attempt on the island."

Sanchez swore violently and slammed his mug down on the table so hard that the rum left in the bottom jumped out and started spreading across the table.

Thomas asked: "What's happening, Ned? I couldn't follow all that."

Secco, laughing delightedly, explained in English: "Oh, so neatly done! Mr Yorke trapped him! Now we know what the devils plan to do!"

Ned explained to Thomas and Diana what had been said – Aurelia had already followed the dialogue.

"So that's what you meant about going for his pride!" Thomas exclaimed. "After you seemed to know all about it, he couldn't claim to know nothing."

"I don't think it even occurred to him," Ned admitted. "He just thought we knew – and I told him that as a hostage he'd probably get his throat cut. That's an unsettling prospect, I imagine."

"It could be," Thomas agreed with a grin. "Was that why he slammed down his mug?"

"No, that was when I told him of my bluff. He has the Spanish fatalism about death."

"What do we do?" Thomas asked. "Now we know they're going to try to invade, we need to know when."

"I don't think they've decided on a date," Ned said. "Don't forget that the *Dolphyn* and *Argonauta* were taken to make sure they didn't see any ships assembling. And this fellow – " Ned nodded towards Sanchez, " – gave no sign of knowing the date when I said that as a hostage he'd get his throat cut."

Secco coughed and Ned glanced across at him. "I'll find out," the Spanish captain said. "There'll be talk in Cartagena or Santa Marta, and the captain of some coasting vessel will have heard of it. I'll take one or two and question the masters."

Ned thought a few moments. "I don't like the idea of you going off alone."

"There mustn't be too many ships," Secco said. "A single ship cruising along the coast – that's one thing: no one gets frightened because he is probably smuggling. But two or three ships cruising together – why, everyone will stay in port, the buccaneers are out!"

This had already occurred to Ned, but the idea of Secco – a Spaniard who would die a horrible death if they ever caught him, because they would call him a traitor – alone on the coast seemed unfair on the man. But Secco wanted to sail alone; he could see that, ironically, there was danger in strength.

"Very well, but take no chances. No landing on the Main. Just question shipmasters. The date, within a week, that will be enough."

Secco grinned cheerfully and stood up, bowing to Diana and Aurelia. He shook hands with Thomas and Ned and left the cabin with a light-hearted wave of his hand.

Chapter Sixteen

For the next two weeks the deck of the *Griffin* was a mess of cordage, with men hammering wooden fids as they spliced new rigging. New shrouds had to be eye-spliced and then the splice wormed, parcelled and served to protect it, so that the splice was covered as though by a glove to keep rain water out.

Halyards were unrove and stretched out on deck so that the new ones would be the same length, allowing for stretch. Every man on board, it seemed to Ned, was either tucking in a splice, or worming a rope by laying a thin line in the space between the strands to make the rope round, then parcelling it by passing a thin line round and round tightly, as though the rope was a cotton reel, finishing up serving it by stitching on the glove of canvas.

Before it was hoisted aloft the standing rigging was painted with Stockholm tar, and the servings covered with pitch. It was a tedious, messy job, and Ned was soon tired of the thud as a shroud or halyard was dropped to the deck, and the way that the smell of hot pitch bit the back of the nose, quite apart from the special precautions against fire that attended the heating of the pitch.

Over on board the *Peleus* Thomas was also using the time to change some of his ship's rigging, and a few other of the buccaneer vessels, knowing that with the *Griffin* unrigged, nothing would be happening, used the time to replace rigging, coat their masts with linseed oil to preserve the wood, or put on a coat of paint.

"The ship smells like Mr O'Leary's shop," Aurelia commented wryly. "Linseed oil, new rope, pitch . . . all the things he has in his chandlery. And Stockholm tar: what a lovely clean smell!"

She pointed to a couple of dozen blocks hanging up on a line, where the wooden cheeks had been coated with linseed oil. "Those pulleys – like starlings on a clothes line."

"Blocks, not pulleys," Ned corrected her for what seemed the thousandth time.

"Blocks!" grumbled Aurelia. "Why a pulley on land becomes a block in a ship I don't understand. And sheets! You sleep in them and use the same word for the rope that trims the sails. You English. No logic. Mouse, mice, but not house, hice."

Ned grinned in agreement. "It is all part of a mystery made up by sailors to confuse land people," he said. He pointed to one of the ropes lying on the deck. "Why would that be an eye splice in the end: why not a round splice? And why is the wooden piece inserted in it called a thimble, which is the name of the thing with which you protect your fingertips when sewing?"

Aurelia smiled ruefully. "All right, I'll learn in time, but it's very muddling."

She pointed and exclaimed delightedly: "Ah, here come Diana and Thomas."

As soon as Diana had come on board she confessed: "We are refugees. Thomas just gets bad-tempered with the ship in such a mess, and there is so much rope all over the deck I feel we're trapped in a net."

"Some fish!" Thomas commented. "An eel, maybe." He turned to Ned, tugging at his beard and turning up the end. "We're taking a chance changing our rigging around now."

"I know, I feel completely unsettled with the ship helpless. But if we have to fight the Dons, I want to be sure of my shrouds and halyards! Anyway, we should get a day or two's warning from Secco."

"That's another thing," Thomas said miserably. "It's a bit late to say it now, but it's risky relying entirely on Secco. Supposing he's captured, or loses his mast in a squall . . ."

"He wanted to go alone," Ned pointed out, "and for a very good reason."

"I know, but I keep looking over the Palisadoes and seeing a

Spanish fleet approaching, and the *Peleus* with half her rigging down on deck."

Ned laughed in what he hoped was a reassuring manner. "There are enough of our ships with their rigging still standing to drive off the Dons!"

"You hope so. But we don't know how big those ships are that came from Spain. Supposing they're frigates, or even larger."

"Trouble," Ned said succinctly. "We'd be in trouble. But do you think Spain has a dozen frigates to spare? If she has, she'd have sent them long before now, because you can be sure the King of Spain wants silver and gold. He's always short of money, and he's unlucky that he's on one side of the Atlantic and his riches on the other."

"Yes, you may be right, he'd have sent them sooner," Thomas admitted. "In fact," he said brightening up, "he may have sent over a few merchant ships with a frigate or two to escort them. Frigates can't carry much plate."

"Nor troops, guns and horses," Ned added.

He moved out of the way as some seamen began coiling up a rope. "Phew, it's so hot here on deck. Let's go below and have some limejuice." He pointed at Thomas's stomach. "That's getting enormous. No rumbullion for you."

"You sound like Diana," Thomas grumbled. "She swears rumbullion is fattening; now she rations me to a glass of wine at a meal. I tell you, Ned, it's no fun getting fat . . . ."

They had been sitting in the saloon sipping juice and gossiping for more than an hour when there was a banging on the door, and at a word from Ned, Lobb came into the cabin, looking excited.

"One of the men up the mast says he's sighted Secco coming back. He's certain it's him."

"How long before we're rigged again?" Ned asked immediately.

"If we put some of the old rigging back, four hours," Lobb said. "We've almost finished anyway."

"Very well, just carry on; we'll wait and see what news Secco has for us."

It took half an hour for the Spaniard's ship to get in and anchor, and another fifteen minutes before Secco himself arrived alongside the *Griffin* in his boat.

Before that, Ned and Thomas had stood on deck, inspecting the Spanish ship with the perspective glass.

"No sign of damage," Ned said. "No scorching at the gunports. I don't think he's been in action."

Nor had he: the Spaniard climbed on board laughing and joking and with a deep bow for Aurelia and Diana.

"What would you do if the Spanish fleet had been chasing me?" he teased Ned. "All your rigging down on deck! Would you attack with rowing boats?"

"We had faith that you'd give us plenty of warning."

"Yes, I can do that. All the ships – nine merchant ships and a frigate – are waiting in Santa Marta."

"Santa Marta?" Ned repeated, startled. "Not Cartagena?"

"No. From what I heard they will be embarking horses and troops at Santa Marta. The delay is because although the troops are coming from Panama, the guns and horses are coming from Caracas, so Santa Marta is more or less halfway."

"From whom did you get this information – a ship?"

"I stopped three and had the same story. Then I went up to Santa Marta and had a look for myself. And then I came here."

"What did you see in Santa Marta?"

"The nine merchant ships. Five of them are quite big – bigger than anything we have. And the frigate is about the same size as the *Convertine*."

"The merchant ships – they are well armed?"

Secco nodded. "Unfortunately, yes. I think they had extra guns fitted for this voyage: I counted more gunports than I would have expected."

"And there is no question but they are coming to Jamaica?"

"None," Secco said firmly. "All three captains were sure of that: they knew the ships are just waiting for the troops, guns and horses. Some soldiers have already arrived in Santa Marta from Cartagena and Barranquilla. In fact one of the captains said there is trouble with the local people because the soldiers are behaving badly, drinking too much and insulting the women."

"How many troops do you reckon these merchant ships can carry – allowing for horses and guns?"

"The five big ships – say six hundred men each, a score of horses, their guns and powder and shot. The four smaller ones – well, three hundred men and fifteen or so horses and guns."

"Just over four thousand men," Ned said. "We needn't worry

too much about the horses and guns; they'd have to be unloaded into boats, and that would take time. But four thousand men – say five thousand, just in case you've underestimated and the frigate carries some. Five thousand Spanish troops against a hundred or so of old Loosely's militia, if he could ever get them together."

"It sounds as though the Dons mean business," Thomas said. "I was thinking – those merchant ships probably have more guns than any of our ships, and each one will have five or ten times as many soldiers as we have seamen . . ."

"Makes boarding us easy, doesn't it?" Ned said. "One thing's obvious . . ."

"It may be to you but it's not to me," Thomas grumbled.

"Well, we'd be silly to wait for the troops to embark, wouldn't we?"

Ned sat for a while thinking while Secco poured himself rumbullion into a silver mug, one of a dozen Ned had taken on some earlier raid. Bigger ships, four or five thousand men, horses and guns . . .

Well, if the ships are bigger than those owned by the buccaneers, it will be silly to try and fight them at sea. If each carries a number of troops, the Spanish will try to close and board, and the buccaneers will be heavily outnumbered.

Probably the most important thing at the moment, Ned thought sourly, was to keep the information from Sir Harold: the last thing they needed was the governor interfering with ideas or wasting their time cavilling about commissions. If it was a question of saving Jamaica, Ned decided, the devil take commissions and, for that matter, Sir Harold Luce as well. If Luce knew the size of the threat to the island, he would probably panic. That was if he believed it. More than likely he would cast doubt on Secco's news. Not just cast doubt but flatly contradict it.

Ned turned to the others. "First, we must keep all this from old Loosely."

"By God, yes!" Thomas exclaimed. "Can you imagine, the place would be awash with cancelled commissions, demands that we don't upset the Dons, and he'd want the Spanish governor and the bishop brought ashore to have their wigs powdered."

Ned held up another finger. "Second, there's no point in

waiting to meet the Dons off Port Royal: if they've any sense they'll try to board us and they have plenty of men.

"Third, and most important, if we destroy the ships they can't sail anyway.

"Fourth, if we are going to destroy the ships it has to be before the troops embark, and that means, ladies and gentlemen, attack them in Santa Marta, as soon as possible."

"You're right Ned!" Thomas exclaimed. "A sudden raid, sail in, sink or capture, sail out and home – and then tell old Loosely!"

Secco put down his mug with a bang. "And it can be done," he exclaimed. "When I think of what I saw in Santa Marta, there is room for us to get in to attack. There's only one fort and the gun platforms are probably rotten. A splendid plan," he said appreciatively.

Ned looked at Thomas. "Can you get your rigging up and be ready to sail by nightfall?"

"Just give me a couple of hours," Thomas said.

Aurelia stood up. "I'll go and tell Lobb," she said. "He said four hours for our rigging, but once he knows we're all waiting to sail he'll halve that."

"Tell him to send both boats round to call a meeting of captains on board here as soon as possible. Inside the hour. And the boats had better warn the captains that while they're over here their mates should be preparing for sea."

Secco said: "If you will give me pen and paper, I'll draw a rough chart of Santa Marta with the position of the ships. The captains can look at it."

Ned went to a drawer and took out a quill, pen, knife, ink, sand box and paper, putting them down on the table in front of the Spaniard. "Amuse yourself by making some copies," he said. "You've plenty of time before the captains arrive. Put in as many soundings as you can . . . remember what happened to me at Santa Lucia!"

Ned watched Secco as he frowned and slowly drew from memory the chart of Santa Marta, which was on a stretch of coast running south-west and about seventy-five miles westward of Riohacha, towards Cartagena. Inland of it were the peaks of the Sierra Nevada de Santa Marta, with the Pico de Santa Marta only a dozen miles away to the south-east.

173

Secco drew with his tongue protruding from the effort of concentrating. He held the pen like a man more used to wielding a sword than a quill, but the final chart contained all the information that a sailor needed.

As soon as he had drawn the first chart he glanced at Ned, as if asking for approval. Ned nodded appreciatively and Secco took up another sheet of paper and once again dipped the quill in the ink.

By the time the first of the captains arrived, Secco had drawn enough charts for each of them to have a copy and he put the cork back in the inkpot with a sigh. "I'm glad I do not have to use a quill very often," he said. "Just look at my fingers – more ink on them than on the paper!"

As soon as the captains had all arrived and assembled on the afterdeck – excited because they had all seen Secco return, and they knew where he had been – Ned as usual stood on the breech of the aftermost gun on the starboard side. He greeted the captains and then told them of Secco's voyage and what he had found.

He described his plans for the attack. Then he said: "You have all got some blocks of pitch on board, and one of my boats is already collecting all that O'Leary has in his shop. I want you to take it and put it on board the three prizes we brought back from Grand Cayman. That's the first thing. Then will you put half a case of powder on board each of them. That along with a demijohn of spirits. Not your best; if you've some rough stuff your men don't like, that will be fine. Make sure you spread these things among the three ships; we don't want it all on board one of them."

Several of the captains looked at each other and nodded knowingly: they could guess what Ned had in mind.

Ned then described Secco's patient work with the charts and he paused while Aurelia gave a copy to each of the captains.

"Most of you know Santa Marta already. That's how the Spanish ships are anchored – or were, when Secco saw them. Some may have moved, especially if they are getting ready to embark the guns and horses. No one likes embarking horses, so you can be sure they'll try and arrange as little boatwork as possible. But the dock is too shallow for some of the big ships to get alongside, so some boatwork is inevitable."

When Ned had finished explaining and asked if there were any questions, Leclerc and Brace asked about soundings close in to the shore, where the four smaller ships were anchored. Then Coles asked about the hostage he had on board.

"Getting very sad is Sanchez," Coles said. "Ever since he came over here he doesn't seem to think about much except getting his throat cut. Asked me if I had any orders about it."

"I hope you didn't reassure him too much," Ned said laughingly.

"No, I wasn't sure what it was all about so I just gave a diabolical laugh and walked away."

"We're keeping him, the bishop and the mayor in case we need hostages," Ned explained, "but as things are now – after the news we have from Secco – I doubt if we'll have any more use for them. So if the attack goes well and you get the chance, perhaps you can put the three of them ashore. Don't waste time or take any risks, but just bear it in mind."

"I think that Sanchez will be quite disappointed if I don't cut his throat on the beach," Coles commented. "Perhaps he doesn't fancy going back to his wife."

Ned held up his hand and called to the captains. "I haven't made it clear," he said, "that any of you are welcome to cut out the Spanish ships. Destroy or capture – whichever you like."

Chapter
Seventeen

Ned had the perspective glass to his eye, and Aurelia and Lobb were standing beside him. "There we are," he said cheerfully, "there are the white cliffs near Taganga, the only ones like that along this coast. There's the cathedral in Santa Marta – I can just make out the two domes. And behind the town, a dozen miles to the south-east, the Pico de Santa Marta. Pity the haze is hiding all the other peaks of the Sierra Nevada: we'd have been able to estimate our position a lot sooner, because you can see most of the Sierra Nevada for forty miles on a clear day."

"I seem to remember the town of Santa Marta itself is on a flat plain," Aurelia said.

"It is," Ned replied. "The mountains start rising inland. There, the haze is clearing to the eastward: seems strange seeing snow on those peaks and yet it's so hot down here."

Ned could imagine that every perspective glass in the flotilla was now being used. It was strange how the haze had hidden the land until a few moments ago, when it cleared between the flotilla and the shore as though someone had pulled aside a curtain.

He looked round at the rest of the ships. Astern in their usual position were the *Peleus* and the *Phoenix*; then came the rest of the flotilla in no particular order, except that the three ships taken at Grand Cayman were in the middle, as though the other captains were protecting them, like mother hens with their chicks.

They were being sailed well and Ned was thankful that, so far anyway, his idea of giving the commands to the bosuns of the

Griffin, *Peleus* and *Phoenix* had proved a good one. With the prospect of bitter fighting, he was loth to lose Lobb, and he knew that Thomas and Saxby would be equally unwilling to give up their mates.

Ned had spent twenty minutes with the bosuns, giving them copies of Secco's chart and explaining what was expected of them. They had six men each, and they would soon be preparing their ships. They knew about getting to windward in the anchorage, and none of them underestimated the risks they were facing.

It was a few minutes past noon and the sun, almost directly overhead, was like the open door of a furnace. The awning gave Ned and Aurelia some shade but the rays reflected up from the sea in dancing diamonds and the wind was hot; it sapped the energy when it should have refreshed.

When Ned looked again, the snow-covered peaks of the Sierra Nevada had vanished as more haze appeared. Just as well, Ned thought to himself; it was tantalizing, when one was almost gasping for breath and everything was so hot, be it wooden decks or metal fittings, to see snow. Up in those peaks, Ned guessed, men could freeze to death . . . Down here they were being almost boiled like lobsters.

The buccaneer flotilla was reaching along at about five knots. In two hours, perhaps two and a half, they would all be fighting for their lives. But this attack on Santa Marta had to be carried out in broad daylight: there was no moon, and trying to find nine ships (and the frigate) in complete darkness would be hopeless – and, with the alarm raised, there could be no second attempt the following night.

"That new rigging has stretched," Lobb commented, pointing aloft.

The new halyards did not matter: as they stretched it was just a question of swigging them up tighter, but the shrouds were different. The lanyards at the lower end had to be tightened up, but this could only be done satisfactorily when the ship was at anchor. Now, with the shrouds a little slack, the mast could work, and it did, creaking at the partners.

Ned watched for a minute or two. Yes, although the mast was working there was nothing to worry about. The mast was sound; in fact in the sunlight it still glistened from its recent coats of linseed oil.

Ned moved his feet carefully. The pitch in the deck seams was so hot that it was sticky; one had to be careful to stand on the planks and not on the seams. Damn the heat. Then he thought about beating down the English Channel at this time of the year; there would be a strong south-wester, it would be freezing cold with no chance of getting warm, and the decks would be swept with spray, soaking you with no chance of getting dry. Soaking wet and freezing, or half roasted and nearly panting for breath? Give me the heat, he decided; it lasts only a few hours each day before cooling down for the night, but for the poor miserable seaman fighting his way down Channel night merely made it colder and the cold felt worse. No sane man who had sailed in the Caribbee ever volunteered to sail in northern waters . . .

Now he could see the white cliffs and a hint of the cathedral without using the perspective glass, and the Pico de Santa Marta stood four-square like a signpost. In this wind a reach meant they could lay Santa Marta; unless there was a change in wind direction as they approached the land (not unknown, particularly in this weather) they should be able to sail straight into the Bahia Santa Marta without altering course.

"When we get back to Port Royal," Ned told Lobb, "you shall have a whole week to set up the rigging and change the old stuff you had to put back. You can worm, parcel and serve to your heart's content."

"Thank you, but personally I'm sick of rigging," Lobb said lightly. " 'Worm and parcel with the lay, turn and serve the other way'," he repeated parrot-fashion the rules for the work, a phrase dinned into a seaman from the time he first set foot in a ship as a boy.

"It's the stink of pitch and Stockholm tar that bothers me," Ned said. "And madame grumbles about it, too."

"You're lucky, it's about the only thing I *do* grumble about," Aurelia said. "Never a moan about the stink of the bilges or the smell of boucan . . . I am a treasure among women."

"And we all appreciate you," Ned said lightly. "You and Diana – and Martha Judd: but for you three we'd be savages, tearing at our food with bare hands and wearing only the hides of beeves."

"True," Aurelia said coolly. "You almost sound as though you mean it – about wearing hides, and tearing at food."

An hour later, using the perspective glass, Ned could make out the masts of the ships in the harbour, and he told Lobb to prepare the ship for action. The guns were loaded and run out, the grindstone hoisted on deck once again to give the men another chance of putting an edge on their cutlasses and a point on the boarding pikes.

Ned looked at the three Grand Cayman prizes and was pleased to see the men bustling around on deck. They would be removing all the hatch covers and throwing them over the side, and then using axes to cut holes in the decks and bulkheads, to ensure that a good draught blew through each ship. And then they would scatter the chunks of pitch and, at the last moment, leave heaps of gunpowder joined by slowmatch and with the demijohns of spirits near powder which would blow them up and ignite the spirit, spreading the flames.

Now he began to feel the apprehension that always came before an action. Had he forgotten something that could endanger the operation or cost men's lives? Would he be unlucky, as he was at Santa Lucia, and run aground at a critical moment? Would a raking broadside tear through the *Griffin* and kill Aurelia? Would a random roundshot tear off one of his limbs? Would the Cayman prizes be successful or would they cause more harm to the buccaneer flotilla? Would – and this was much more likely – would the expedition find that the Spanish troops were already on board the Spanish ships, ready and waiting with musket and pike?

"The largest is anchored up to windward: lay us alongside her," Ned told Lobb. The whole of the Bahia Santa Marta lay open in front of them; the nine ships were anchored right across their bow. So far not a shot had been fired; it was as though the Spanish had not noticed them approaching.

Suddenly a little wreath of smoke appeared at a gunport of the frigate, followed a moment later by several more. Ned heard the calico-tearing noise of shot passing overhead. Yes, the frigate quite sensibly was firing at the nearest ship, which happened to be the *Griffin*.

All the Spanish ships were heading into the wind, which meant

179

into the shore. The frigate, anchored by chance some distance from the other ships, was catching a different slant of wind so that she was almost broadside-on to the approaching buccaneers and could bring at least some of her guns to bear. But the approaching buccaneers could do nothing to fire back; they would be helpless with their guns unable to bear until they could get broadside-on, and that meant getting alongside.

Ned saw the three Cayman prizes now working their way up to windward, as he had instructed, so that they would get into a position where the Spanish ships were to leeward of them. The *Peleus,* following astern, was bearing away slightly, intending to tackle the second merchant ship to windward, and Saxby was obviously proposing to attack the third. The rest of the buccaneer flotilla was in no sort of formation; it was evident that each of the Spanish ships would be attacked by several buccaneers at once, which would be like a pack of dogs attacking a bull.

The men were standing by at the guns; linstocks were being waved like wands, pieces of slowmatch wound round them, the glowing ends fitting into the Y-shaped crutches at the end.

Beside the guns, cutlasses, pikes and muskets were lying ready for use. The *Griffin's* buccaneers had strips of coloured cloth tied round their foreheads to prevent perspiration running into their eyes. Most of them were bare from the waist up, stripped so that they could move freely. All were barefooted although several of them fidgeted, finding the deck hot to stand on.

Ned took one last look at the ship towards which the *Griffin* was heading and put the perspective glass back in the drawer. The soldiers were not on board – at least, they were not lining the bulwarks with muskets and pikes, nor was there any sign of troops on board the other eight ships.

More guns fired from the frigate: the wind must have swung her a little more so that extra guns could bear. There were three thuds as shot hit the *Griffin,* but there were no shouts or screams from wounded crew. Now they would be reloading the guns in the frigate and Ned hoped the Spaniards were so excited that they slowed themselves down.

The ship he was going to attack was painted a plum red and her masts were yellow. Yes, she had six gunports on this side, but the way she was heading not one of the guns could be brought to bear yet.

Forty yards to go; at the moment the *Griffin* was steering directly for the ship; at the last moment she would have to luff up, furling sails at the same time, and slam alongside her, guns firing.

And it was up to him to judge the exact moment when the *Griffin* luffed up. A few moments too early, and she would stop short of the ship and be blown away from her by the prevailing wind; a few moments too late and she would overshoot.

There is, Ned warned himself, no second chance.

Forty yards . . . thirty . . . twenty . . . ten . . . "Luff her!" he bellowed at Lobb. "Let fly the headsails sheets, furl the mainsail!"

Now the *Griffin* was alongside the Spanish ship, whose bulwarks were six feet higher than the *Griffin's*. Ned faced his gunners. "Fire when you bear!" he shouted and two of the guns spurted flame and smoke immediately, rumbling back in recoil.

"Grapnels over!" Ned yelled at the men standing between the guns.

More guns fired; then the *Griffin* was close alongside the Spaniard, her hull grinding against the other ship.

"Board her!" Ned commanded as he ran for the bulwark, cutlass in his hand. Men left the guns, snatching up cutlasses and pikes and leaping on to the bulwarks and then clawing their way up the side of the Spaniard.

Ned wriggled up a chain plate, swung himself on to the Spaniard's bulwark and dropped on to the deck.

There were thirty or forty Spaniards waiting there, some with boarding pikes poised and the others wielding cutlasses, but they stood away from the bulwarks as though the broadside from the guns had driven them back.

Ned waited until he sensed that a dozen or more buccaneers were behind him and then, yelling "Griffins!", ran towards the nearest group of Spaniards. One man lunged with a pike and Ned slammed it aside with his cutlass, turning the movement into a slashing blow so that the blade bit into the man's skull. As he fell Ned was just in time to parry a cutlass blow from another Spaniard and was saved from a lunging pike by a buccaneer who drove the haft downwards so that the point stuck in the deck. While the bewildered Spaniard tried to wrestle it free from the planking Ned slashed at him and the man screamed as he crumpled.

By now more buccaneers were pouring over the bulwarks, some with muskets. One fired so close to Ned that he was almost deafened and with his ears ringing he slashed his way into the same group of Spaniards.

A wild-eyed man with long, curly hair screamed as he slashed at Ned with a cutlass, but he was not holding the blade square and it slid away as Ned parried, swung the cutlass up and cut down with it. The blade bit into the man's shoulder and he reeled backwards and collapsed.

At that moment Ned felt an agonizing pain and out of the corner of his eye saw a pike: the point had caught his right arm. He wrenched himself away, punched the haft with his left hand and turned to slash at a man with a cutlass on his right.

But before the blade drove home the man fell and a yelling Lobb grinned at Ned, waving the pike with which he had spitted his victim.

Ned was conscious of gunfire on the starboard side of the ship: the rest of the buccaneers must be in action. Then suddenly he saw the smoke. Sailing down towards the anchored vessels, running before the wind, were three ships almost entirely enveloped in smoke: the Grand Cayman fireships!

He dared not spend much time looking at them – a moment's inattention had already seen him stabbed in the arm with a pike – but he could see flames beginning to lick at the hulls. They were being steered directly towards the smaller merchant ships anchored closer in, to windward of the others.

By now the Spanish ship's deck was a whirling mass of men shouting and screaming, slashing with cutlasses, jabbing with pikes, and one buccaneer was whirling a musket round his head, holding it by the barrel, and screaming defiance at the top of his voice as he launched himself at the nearest Spaniards like a spinning wheel.

Ned realized that the fight was moving several feet away from him: the Spaniards were retreating fast and most of the men he could see were buccaneers, easily distinguished by the rags round their foreheads.

The Spanish ship's deck was now littered with bodies; blood

streamed across it as though someone had been emptying it in buckets. Suddenly there was almost a silence, and Ned guessed the Spaniards had surrendered.

"Griffins!" Ned shouted, knowing the buccaneers were quite likely to kill the remaining Spaniards in their excitement, not understanding Spanish and not caring much anyway.

After several shouts the buccaneers stopped fighting and Ned saw that only six or seven Spaniards were left on their feet, and they had thrown down their cutlasses and pikes.

"Secure the prisoners!" he told Lobb.

Now Ned looked at the fireships. The first of them, shapeless from the flames enveloping it, was within a few yards of running into one of the anchored merchant ships. He could see a small boat pulling away from it – the bosun and his crew escaping. The second fireship, a few yards from another ship, was gradually turning broadside-on in the wind, but she would still hit the bow of her target. The third fireship, with no flames coming from it yet, was a good forty yards from its target and still towing the boat which the crew would use to escape. And the target, Ned suddenly realized, was the frigate: the Spaniards were firing at it, but even as they did flames leapt up from the hatches, the boat was dragged up close, and the crew jumped into it, casting off.

The fireship burst into flames as he watched and Ned realized that the roaring noise he could hear in the distance was the sound of the flames fanned by the wind. The fireship headed for the frigate as though drawn by a magnet and lodged across its bow just as the merchant ship caught by the first fireship began to blaze.

Well, Ned thought, fireships worked for Sir Francis Drake against the Spanish Armada off Calais, and they are certainly working for us here at Santa Marta . . .

Now to secure the ship they had just taken and go on to tackle the next. But one glance aft at the *Peleus* and the rest of the buccaneers showed him there was no hurry: each of the merchant ships had two or three buccaneer ships alongside: some had a ship on each side, with one more hanging on each quarter.

Only then did he realize that the fort had been firing; the gunners were probably shooting at the fireships, unable to fire at anyone else in case they hit their own ships.

By now the frigate was ablaze, looking as if she was holding the fireship in a warm embrace. The other two fireships had set their targets on fire, and Ned saw that the three boats, carrying the bosuns and the volunteer crews, were all rowing for the *Griffin*, the nearest ship.

They were all brave men: Ned had warned the bosuns of the risks they would have to run, steering their ships for the targets while starting the fires, and there would be only moments left for them to scramble into the boats and row to safety. But the bosuns had laughed; handling fireships took the monotony out of life. And the crews were cheerful enough. Come to think of it, there was probably less risk in handling fireships than boarding a Spanish ship and, within moments, finding yourself in a life-or-death fight with cutlass or pike.

Damn, his arm was beginning to hurt. He looked down and was startled to see his sleeve soggy with blood. Well, the hand, although stiffening up, still worked so it could only be a flesh wound. Aurelia would soon have it cleaned up when he got back on board the *Griffin*.

Right, now to check up on what's happening. Two merchant ships burning from the fireships and – he ducked as a great flash preceded the rumbling roar of the frigate exploding: the masts collapsed like falling trees and curved into the water, trailing yards and sails; great wooden deck beams and hull frames flew slowly into the air in wide arcs before splashing down into the sea. In a matter of moments what had been a ship was changed to a ring of boiling water in which a scattering of wreckage bobbed about. There was no sign of life; Ned had grabbed a perspective glass from a drawer, but could not see a man swimming or clinging to wreckage.

He then looked astern, inspecting the ships with the glass. Yes, the next nearest merchant ship, and the one beyond, attacked by the *Peleus* and *Phoenix*, had obviously surrendered: there was little or no movement on deck. There was still fighting on the next ship – which would be the sixth – but the seventh seemed to have surrendered. There was still a lot of movement on the deck of the eighth, but the ninth seemed quiet – yes, he could see men climbing back over the bulwarks into the buccaneer ships.

Ned turned to Lobb and said: "Send the prisoners and wounded on board the *Griffin*. Have the carpenter inspect this ship, and then you can select a prize crew. I'm going back on board the *Griffin*: I'd better get this tied up – " he held up his arm, " – and I want to talk to the fireship men. That was quite a bang when the frigate went up. Didn't take long for the flames to reach her magazine."

"My ears are still ringing," Lobb said ruefully. "By the way, the fort will soon be shooting at all of us."

"We can cut our cables if they get too close," Ned said. "But I doubt if those gunners get much practice."

Ned found it hard to climb back on board the *Griffin*: his arm was beginning to stiffen rapidly and it was hard to grip anything with his hand. As soon as Aurelia saw him she insisted that he came down to the saloon to be bandaged.

"What about the other wounded?" Ned protested.

"No one has come back wounded yet," she said. "You're the first."

It had long been the rule among the buccaneers that the wounded were treated in the order in which they presented themselves, so Ned went down to the saloon, where Aurelia had roughly-cut bandages and basins of water already set out on the table.

She slit the cloth of his sleeve, washed away the blood from the wound, and commented: "You were very lucky, Ned: another inch and it would have cut the muscle badly."

With that she began tying a bandage while Ned mumbled: "My fault anyway; I wasn't looking, and this Don came up where I didn't see him."

"The fireships," Aurelia said. "They did everything you wanted them to?"

"Yes. Have the bosuns come on board?"

"Yes, they're all here, as excited as small boys who've just raided an orchard. I had to laugh: the first thing our bosun asked me when he got on board was whether I heard the frigate blow up. I should think they heard it in Riohacha!"

"I hope you told him that."

"Oh, I did; I made a fuss of all of them."

Ned ripped off a bit more of his shirt and said: "I must be getting back on deck. You'll have plenty of wounded down in a few minutes – some will be Spanish."

He reached the deck to find Lobb supervising the transfer of the wounded, lowering them from the merchant ship's higher bulwark down to the *Griffin's* deck.

"How many?" Ned asked.

"Five of ours – none badly – and seven Spanish. We had two men killed; the Spanish lost eight."

Ned caught sight of the three bosuns and went over to congratulate them.

"Cor, you warned us they'd burn quick," the *Griffin's* bosun said. "That wood was dry! And that spirit sprayed all over the place – that helped the flames. But the frigate!"

"Who did that one?"

"I did," the bosun said proudly. "I reckoned she was the one ship that could cause us trouble – if she'd swung she could have raked you."

Ned shook him by the hand. "She made quite a bang. If we ever want someone to command a fireship in the future, I'll come to you!"

Just then he saw a boat approaching with Thomas in it.

Whetstone had a rough bandage tied round his head and his hair was bloodstained. The moment he came on board and saw the bandage round Ned's arm he bellowed: "Ah, they spitted you too, did they Ned?"

"What happened to you? Bumped your head on a deck beam?"

"I slipped while parrying a cutlass," Thomas admitted shamefacedly. "It just parted my hair. Diana was anxious to wash and bandage it but I wanted to get over here and see you. What do you reckon?"

Ned took up the perspective glass, examined the last two ships and when he was satisfied there was no more fighting, put the glass back.

"We've done the job," he said. "Two merchant ships burned to the waterline and the frigate blown up. Seven merchant ships captured. Did you have many casualties?"

"None dead, seven wounded. Eleven Dons killed and wounded."

"We were lucky," Ned said soberly. "If the Spaniards had embarked the soldiers, we'd have had a hard time."

"Unless the fireships frightened them, I don't think we could have done it," Thomas admitted. "Those damned bulwarks are so high – can you imagine a few hundred soldiers with muskets firing down on us . . ."

Thomas moved out of the way as some wounded men were carried down to the saloon. "Those bosuns did well with the fireships!"

"Yes, it was lucky they could get far enough to windward to run down on the Spaniards. And burning that frigate was a blessing – she could have caused us a lot of trouble: I must admit I underestimated her."

Thomas shrugged his shoulders and winced as the movement hurt his head. "Now what – select prize crews? They'll soon wake up in that fort and it may get hot for us."

"Yes. We'll use the three bosuns again – they deserve it. And our three mates. That's six. Secco's mate is a good man so he can take the seventh and we'll need ten seamen in each prize. Ten of mine, you can give up ten and so can Saxby. We'll need forty more. Well, whichever ships captured them can provide the men."

Thomas was looking pale, and Ned told him to sit down. He sat on the breech of a gun and admitted: "I feel a bit shaky. Must be this bump on the head."

Ned called to the three bosuns, who came running across the deck. "Now you've lost your ships you'd better take over your new commands."

The men grinned and Ned said: "Sort them out between you, but you'll command the fourth, fifth and sixth prizes and take them back to Port Royal. You'll be getting prize crews from the ships that captured them."

Then Ned called Lobb. "Take command of our prize. The three bosuns will be commanding three, and I want Secco's mate for the seventh. And whoever captured them can provide ten men for each ship. Go round and give the orders. We all sail back to Port Royal together, starting at dusk. That is, unless the fort starts troubling us, in which case we'll sail at once. Watch the *Griffin* and follow her movements."

Ned sat down beside Thomas. "I must admit I'm feeling a bit shaky, too. This arm hurts when it hangs down, and it hurts even worse trying to hold it up."

"You need a sling," Thomas said. "Here – " he held Ned's shoulder and ripped off the other sleeve, fashioning it into a sling, tying the knot round Ned's neck and carefully easing in his arm. "How's that?"

Ned nodded gratefully. "Feels much better. I might have thought of it myself."

"You've had other things to think about. By the way, did you see any survivors from the frigate?"

"Not a soul: I looked with a glass but there was nothing – just wreckage."

"I saw quite a few men escaping in boats from the two merchant ships that burned," Thomas said. "A dozen from each, perhaps more. Rowed for the beach as though the devil was after them."

Ned adjusted the sling on his arm. "How are you feeling now?"

"Just a headache. Feels as though someone is pounding it with a club." Thomas stood up shakily. "I'll think I'll be getting back on board," he said. "Diana told me this would happen. It's only a gash, too."

"It's not the pain," Ned said. "I think there must be some shock to the system, and it takes a while to arrive. Don't forget to get your prize under way!"

Chapter
Eighteen

The convoy of ships arrived at Port Royal, changing formation into a long line so that they could tack up the anchorage without risk of collision. The mates and bosuns handled the prizes as well as the other captains.

"I can just imagine how much Lobb is enjoying himself," Ned said to Aurelia. "Commanding a bigger ship than the *Griffin*!"

"How is he going to like coming back to us as just the mate?"

"I don't think he'll grumble. Sailing that ship with ten men and no mate is hard work. I doubt if he's had much sleep."

With that he gave the order to tack, and the *Griffin*, at the head of the long line of ships, turned in towards the Palisadoes.

"Will you go straight over and tell Sir Harold what's been going on?"

"No fear!" Ned answered crossly. "He'll probably start up again about that damned governor and the bishop!"

"Well, at least you can tell him that they – and the mayor of Riohacha – have all been put ashore in Santa Marta, and released politely without any ransom being paid."

"The buccaneers won't like that," Ned said. "The governor was worth fifty or sixty thousand pieces of eight, and the bishop even more, since the Church has plenty of money. That's more than a hundred thousand pieces of eight we've given up, assuming we threw in the mayor for nothing. All to stop that damned Loosely from nagging."

"Oh come on," Aurelia chided. "It suited you not to wait in Santa Marta, haggling over ransom."

"I agree, but we could have held on to them and sent over a flag of truce in a couple of weeks' time."

"Well, you've got seven good ships out of it, so the buccaneers will not be out of pocket."

"After he wanted to have the Santa Lucia ransom money, I wouldn't put it past old Loosely to try to get some of the prize money awarded by the court for these ships."

"Tow them out and sink them, then," Aurelia said sweetly. "Get cross with Sir Harold, not me!"

Ned shouted again and the *Griffin* came round on to the other tack. Then he glared at Aurelia.

"Do you really think I should go running over to old Loosely and tell him what a good boy I've been?"

"Yes," Aurelia said calmly. "It won't do any harm to show him what a narrow escape he's had. It's better you tell him everything than have him hear the story in bits and pieces."

"You don't realize how much I detest the man," Ned complained. "It's as much as Thomas and I can manage to be civil to him."

"I got the impression you are rarely civil to him," Aurelia said drily. "Anyway, I'm sure you don't detest him any more than he detests you."

"If only I could be sure of that," Ned growled.

It took seven tacks for the *Griffin* to get up to the usual anchorage off the governor's jetty, and as soon as he had the ship properly anchored and saw the *Peleus* astern, with a boat being hoisted out, Ned said: "I'm not going over to the governor unless Thomas agrees."

"You're behaving like a sulky boy," Aurelia said, and went below before Ned could think of a suitable reply.

Thomas was wearing the bandage round his head but at a rakish angle when he and Diana came on board the *Griffin*, but it was obvious to Ned that the wound had been more serious than Thomas had admitted.

Diana pointed to the sling. "And how is your arm?"

"It's started to heal properly, but aches like the devil without the sling." He looked across to Thomas. "How's the head?"

"Healing up slowly. The cut's in the roots of the hair, and it tugs every time I move my head."

Diana said: "He's just realized how often he shakes his head. It doesn't hurt when he nods."

"Now's the time to get him to agree to everything."

"You'd think so," Diana said, "but he's been like the proverbial bear with a sore head. I can't do anything right."

"Don't listen to her," Thomas growled. "All she can say is, 'What are you going to tell Sir Harold?' "

Ned groaned. "You've been getting it too? I've just had an hour of it from Aurelia – who'll be up on deck in a moment."

"What *are* we going to tell him?" Thomas asked.

"Well, he won't notice that we have seven prizes. I suppose we'd better tell him the whole story, but if he mentions the word 'pirate' then I shall walk out, and we can all move to Tortuga – emptying the brothels first."

Sir Harold was sitting at the table in his office when Hamilton showed them in. Luce was white-faced, his moustaches hung down, and as soon as he saw Ned and Thomas, he leapt to his feet, pointing a quivering finger.

"Where have you all been?" he demanded.

Ned startled, shrugged his shoulders, feeling his arm give a twinge, and said casually: "We went on a cruise."

"Cruise? You went cruising while Jamaica is in terrible danger? Have you no sense of responsibility?"

"Very little," Ned agreed amiably, "and never on odd days of the month. Why, what's the matter? You seem uncommonly disturbed."

"*Disturbed*!" Luce shouted. "By God, man, the Spanish are coming!"

"Well, I'm blessed," Ned said calmly. "Coming from where?"

"The Main of course: they've collected a big army, put it on board a couple of dozen ships they've collected – more in fact – and they are on their way to Jamaica! What do you think about that?"

"Most alarming," Ned agreed. "When are these ships due here?"

"Any moment!" Luce said excitedly. "You must sail and drive them off!"

"How do you know all this?"

"A fisherman who was doing some smuggling saw the ships in Santa Marta."

"And he reported to you?"

"Yes, he came straight back to Port Royal and told me what he'd seen. We estimate the ships could be here later today."

"One of the last things you said," Ned reminded him, "was that after Santa Lucia was raided we had nothing to fear: that the Spanish would never attack from the Main."

"I know I did, but I knew nothing about all these ships."

"Yes, you did, because we told you," Ned contradicted. "We told you that the Spanish governor we had taken as a hostage had told us about the ships."

"Ah yes, that governor," Luce said, his voice still high-pitched with excitement. "Perhaps we can use him as a hostage."

Ned shook his head. "No, I'm afraid you can't do that."

"Why not? These ships will be here any minute, and we've no army should they manage to land troops."

"The ships are already here," Ned said quietly. "They're in the anchorage already."

Luce rubbed his forehead, puzzled. "What on earth do you mean? They haven't even been sighted yet. I have lookouts on Fort Charles, and they haven't reported seeing anything."

"They reported the buccaneers returning?"

"Yes, of course: for a while we thought you were the Spaniards."

"We were," Ned said drily. "What was left of them, anyway."

"Oh stop talking in riddles," Luce said crossly. "The lookouts reported you returning, and here you are. Now we have to prepare to meet the Spanish ships. Don't be so obtuse, please. We are talking of the safety of the whole of Jamaica."

Ned sighed and arranged his arm more comfortably in the sling. "Your Excellency," he said heavily, "you try the patience of lesser men. When we warned you that there was danger from the Main, you sneered at us. That was the last time we saw you. Now, the next time we see you, you are pleading with us to sail and drive off a Spanish fleet coming from the Main.

"Yet," and Ned said the word as though he was slashing with

a knife, "when we tell you that the Spanish ships are already here, you won't listen, or you pretend not to understand."

"But I *don't* understand," Luce wailed.

"Your lookouts are not very good," Ned said. "If they had been keeping a good lookout they would have noticed that there were seven extra ships, and these seven are all larger than the rest of the buccaneer ships. Those seven, plus two burned to the waterline in Santa Marta and a frigate blown up, are the Spanish ships you're talking about."

"But where are all the soldiers?"

"Still in tents at Santa Marta, along with their horses and guns."

It was all too much for Luce: he tugged at his moustaches as though trying to wake himself up, and then rubbed his forehead briskly. "I don't understand," he admitted. "How are the Spanish ships here if the troops are still in Santa Marta?"

Ned lifted his right arm and rested it on the table. "You should listen carefully. We understood from the Spanish governor that ships had arrived from Spain, and neither Sir Thomas nor I assumed they had been sent over by some whim of the Spanish King. Eventually, we tricked the Spanish governor into admitting they intended to invade Jamaica – "

"That was Mr Yorke, and very cleverly done," Thomas interrupted.

" – and that the ships and troops would sail from Santa Marta. It seemed to us that if we were quick we could get to Santa Marta and destroy or capture the ships before the troops embarked: we knew that most of the troops would be coming from Panama, and the horses and guns from the Caracas area.

"And that's what happened. We used the Grand Cayman prizes as fireships, and burned two merchant ships and blew up the frigate. The rest, seven ships, we captured by boarding."

"Is that – your arm, and the bandage on Sir Thomas's head . . . ?"

"Yes, we were not nimble enough."

"Er, the Spanish governor . . . ?"

"We landed him and the bishop and mayor on the beach at Santa Marta," Ned said. "We had no further use for them and they were getting in the way, you understand."

"The ships you've captured – you'll be wanting them condemned as prizes in the court?"

Ned eyed him suspiciously. "Yes. Though why we should bother, I don't know. Spoils of war, that's what they are. There's not a single piece of eight in it for you," he added. "Not one."